Wishes and Wellingtons

ALSO BY JULIE BERRY

Lovely War

The Passion of Dolssa

All the Truth That's in Me

The Scandalous Sisterhood of Prickwillow Place

The Emperor's Ostrich

WISHES
AND
WELLINGTONS

JULIE BERRY

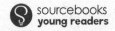

Published by Sourcebooks Young Readers, an imprint of Sourcebooks Kids
P.O. Box 4410, Naperville, Illinois 60567-4410
(630) 961-3900
sourcebookskids.com

Originally published as an Audible Exclusive audio production in 2018 by Audible, a division of Amazon.

Library of Congress Cataloging-in-Publication Data

Names: Berry, Julie, author.
Title: Wishes and Wellingtons / Julie Berry.
Description: Naperville, IL : Sourcebooks Young Readers, [2020] | Audience:
    Ages 8-11. | Audience: Grades 4-6. | Summary: Maeve Merritt, chafing
    against the rigid rules of her London boarding school, finds her life
    transformed by the genie she happens upon--and by those who want to
    steal him.
Identifiers: LCCN 2020005287 | (hardcover)
Subjects: CYAC: Genies--Fiction. | Boarding schools--Fiction. |
    Schools--Fiction. | Friendship--Fiction. | Orphans--Fiction. | London
    (England)--Fiction. | England--Fiction.
Classification: LCC PZ7.B461747 Wis 2020 | DDC [Fic]--dc23
LC record available at https://lccn.loc.gov/2020005287

This product conforms to all applicable CPSC and CPSIA standards.

Source of Production: Maple Press, York, Pennsylvania, United States
Date of Production: August 2020
Run Number: 5019289

Printed and bound in the United States of America.
MA 10 9 8 7 6 5 4 3 2 1

For my mother,
Shirley Keith Gardner,
the original spunky girl.

Wishes and Wellingtons

CHAPTER 1

I 've always been too prone to solve problems with my fists. It's the reason Mum and Dad sent me to Miss Salamanca's School for Upright Young Ladies, and the reason Miss Bickle, the needlework instructor, sent me this morning to Miss Salamanca's private office. Apparently, I needed reminders of how upright a young lady ought to be, and those reminders, ten to one, were about to be striped across my lower back.

I sat stiff as a poker in the straight-backed chair facing Old Salamanca's desk, feeling upright enough already. But judging from her hawk-eyed gaze, we clearly did not agree. The puffs on her dress sleeves seemed to swell with her indignation.

"Miss Merritt," Old Sally began, "at this very moment, young Miss Treazleton lies in the infirmary with a cold steak over one eye. What do you say to that?"

And what should I say? That I was deeply sorry? Not likely.

"I say, she's lucky it's steak and not liver."

Old Sally scowled even more.

"Steak's got a nice homey smell to it. Cools down a bruise in no time."

The headmistress brought her bony hand down on her blotter with a bang. "Young ladies at my school shall *not* brawl like alleyway hoodlums! Have you no regard for your family, your upbringing?"

I shrugged. Family? My mother shipped me off to this desert island after one too many brawls with the village boys. (Normally we got along, but they didn't like losing to me at cricket.) Right now, Mother and my older sisters were probably in a dither over dresses. Except for dear old Polly. She never wanted me sent away.

Old Sally sighed like the early Christian martyrs must have before heading into the amphitheaters for another day's toil with the lions. This again.

"Let's take another approach. *Why*, Miss Merritt, did you strike Miss Treazleton in the eye?"

The straight answer would have been that one never needs a reason to sock Theresa Treazleton in the eye. She walks into a room, she has it coming.

But Old Sally wanted facts. So I gave them to her.

"Because Miss Treazleton stabbed me with a needle." Not even darling, wealthy, adorable Theresa Treazleton and her chestnut ringlet curls could be pardoned for such a crime. "A four-gauge." The Mother of All Needles.

Old Sally sucked in her breath. It whistled around her buckteeth. "Where?"

I studied my fingernails, finding them suddenly to be objects of deep interest. "In needlework class."

"No, where on your *person*?"

I held myself more upright. "In my never-you-mind."

Old Sally rapped her fist on her blotter once more. "I will not be spoken to in that manner by a mere slip of a girl! Out with it, young lady. *Where* did she stab you with a needle?"

I had tried to spare her. She asked for it.

"In my arse."

The whistling around her teeth could have guided boats across the Channel in a fog.

"Maeve Merritt! *Where* did you acquire such language?"

If I'd been any more upright, I'd have poked holes in the ceiling.

"Never you mind."

CHAPTER 2

Foul language. That's how I came to be banished from two days of classes, with no excuses made for the missed work or failed examinations. I got dump duty. This, Miss Salamanca said, would spit-polish my tarnished character, or words to that effect. Something something, if I was determined to act like gutter trash and speak like gutter trash, I could jolly well spend some more time with the gutter trash and learn how well it suited me.

I didn't half mind it. Aside from the stink.

That's a lie. I hated it. But not as much as I hated sitting in Miss Guntherson's French class.

My old governesses used to try the punishment method to reform my character, too. Back before Mother farmed out my discipline to school. It didn't work. Those governesses never lasted long on the job. How I chewed through all the Miss Emmas and Miss Charlottes, back then... Perhaps my days at Miss Salamanca's were likewise numbered. They'd be numbered zero if I had my wish.

It was a cold, late afternoon in December, my second day of grubbing with the rubbish. The wind bit through my stockings and spiraled up my legs. The sun was no more than a pale hint behind thick clouds, soon to set. Half an hour more, and I'd be summoned in to wash and eat in the back kitchen, away from the starched pinafores and delicate noses of the other upright young ladies who weren't shamed by a punishment, at least at the moment.

I wore Wellingtons and canvas gloves as I sifted through the dustbins, the trash heaps, and the gutters, separating out the tin cans and the stuff that could be burned in the furnace from the fireplace ashes and stuff to be collected by the dustman. My face grew sooty and my lungs felt like an ash pail. My canvas gloves sopped with rotting apple-peel mush and cabbage soup. If I tried darting off through twisting streets and alleys and getting lost in London, I wouldn't be hard to find. "Sergeant, the runaway is a skinny girl, oh, about thirteen, wearing Wellies and a gray serge uniform. Smells like a compost heap."

I wondered, a time or two, what Mother and Dad would say if they knew they were paying tuition for me to paw through trash piles looking for tin and wool. Dad was always carping about money. He was a senior clerk, though not yet an officer, at St. Michael's Bank and Trust. And Mother, between her ladies' societies and hat shopping and fussing over my older sisters, Polydora, Deborah, and

Evangeline ("soon to be married, praise heaven") probably wouldn't worry too much about me garbage-grubbing. Provided, that is, that no one who knew us saw me doing it.

To be precise: Mother never fussed over Polydora. Polly's not the type of person one fusses over. It's probably why she's my favorite. She's got much too sound of a head on her shoulders for fuss and nonsense. Now, Deborah and Evangeline, on the other hand...

Mother had let my older sisters leave school at the age of twelve, firm in her belief that too much education spoils nice girls. Dad's checkbook fully supported Mother in this proposition. As for me, they said, an active mind like mine needed stimulation and discipline—as far from home as possible, where I couldn't outrage the neighbors and shame the family by sneaking out my bedroom window and wickedly fraternizing with *boys*. Playing marbles, hopscotch, hoops, and jacks, it seems—especially with boys from the wrong families—is a scandal and a sin. If so, I'll take a fiery afterlife. It beats playing dollies and tea parties with prissy girls like the sort Mother kept hoping I'd socialize with—the fluffy daughters of her feathery friends.

"Move it along sharpish." Mrs. Gruboil, the cook, and a general pestilence to all the downstairs help, poked her red nose out the window shutters to remind me she was watching. "That job'd best be done come supper." The shutters banged shut.

Misery. That's why parents send daughters away to schools full of wrath and bile. So they can blight their young lives with a heaping dose of misery. They deserved to have their money wasted.

A movement from across the back alley caught my eye. It was that scrawny ginger-haired boy from the orphanage, spying on me from over his back-garden gate. Mission Industrial School and Home for Working Boys. What a place.

I scowled at the boy and threatened to heave a rock. He ducked and disappeared. We'd never met formally—I didn't even know his name—but most of the orphan boys at the charitable home had heard of my throwing arm. I'd overheard one say it was too bad I couldn't play cricket. I might turn out to be passably good bowler, if girls could play. Little did they know!

But December wasn't cricket weather, and I had a foul job to finish. I moved on to the next rubbish pail and plunged my arm up to my wrist into the cloudy ash, and pulled out something flat and heavy. A sardine can, unopened. Of all things! How did *that* end up in the dustbin? Mrs. Gruboil, the cook, was mad about sardines. She often smelled fishy, in fact. I couldn't fathom her throwing a full can away.

I shook the sardine can and examined its lid. Underneath the grime, it was nicely decorated. Enameled, even. I'd seen collector tins like this in greengrocer shop windows. "Sultana's Exotic Sardines, packed in salted oil, imported exclusively by the Eastern Trading

Company, Liverpool." I hoisted up the hem of my petticoat and polished the can for a better look.

I could almost swear the tin wiggled in my hands.

"You sardines aren't still swimming in there, are you?" I said aloud. I polished the tin some more. It nearly slipped through my fingers.

"You see that, Miss Salamanca's School for Upright Young Ladies?" I cried, waving my tin of fish at the brick wall that faced the alley. "Work me to the bone, scrimp on my meals. Now I'm having tremors!"

Mrs. Gruboil banged the shutters in reply.

I sat down on the back step of the old school building. On an impulse, I turned to make sure there were no faces in the windows watching me sneak teatime sardines. I preferred them on buttered toast with mustard, but my fingers would do. Naturally, Mrs. Gruboil hadn't called me to tea when the other young ladies were served.

This was one of the fancy sardine tins that came with a key to open it. I'd never opened one before. Cook always did this sort of thing back home. But I'd watched her do it, so now I wrenched the key off and fitted the little flap inside the slit on the key. Then I cranked the key back.

A thick, sulfur-colored vapor poured out through the growing opening.

"*Faugh!*" I pinched my nose and waved away the putrid odor. "They're rotten!"

The vapor swirled around my head but wouldn't stop streaming out from the tin. I flung it on the pavement and fanned the air desperately with my scarf.

"Desist!" a voice roared from amid the sulfurous plumes. I stopped cold. Whoever it was, it sounded ferocious. But I couldn't see anyone. Just this pestilent cloud of mustard-yellow smoke. I took off my coat and flapped the air with it.

"I said, desist!" bellowed the voice. "Cease your flapping, you wretched female, or I'll feed you to sharks in tiny pieces."

I stuffed my arms back into my coat. Whoever this voice belonged to—undoubtedly, a murderer—a murderer in a *sardine can?*—it seemed better to face him warm than frozen stiff.

"Who are you calling 'wretched'?" I cried. "You're nothing but fish stink and bad manners."

"Manners?" came the voice again, cold as the sea and full of contempt. "Where I come from, a girl with manners like yours would be skinned and boned and eaten for supper."

The vapor spun and twisted upon itself like a storm. Bits of it broke off and drifted away, and the main body of smoke reached tendrils after them to try in vain to gather itself back. I'd never seen such a marvel. Certainly not in London. And London has its share of noxious vapors, to be sure.

"I was just about to eat *you* for tea: skin and bones and all," I replied. "And I would have, too, if you hadn't turned out to be festered."

Rage seethed around him. He blasted me with his fishy breath.

"Festered? A mere mortal calls me festered? Your kind is food for vultures and worms. I, Mermeros, consort with warriors and kings! Lords and princes beg favors at my feet."

"What feet?"

The mist was definitely assuming a human-like shape now. A head, and arms, of sorts, and a massive trunk, though the legs drifted off to little more than a tether binding the apparition to the sardine can.

I knew it! *I knew it.* I could jump, I could scream, I could dance a jig. And *I'd* found him, so he was mine, mine, mine! From a tin? Why not from a tin? These were modern times. They could put anything in tins these days.

A djinni! My very own djinni!

He was huge. Twice the size of most men. But I'd learned, growing up playing ball with village boys, never to let my smaller size get into my head.

He thrashed about, stretching and grimacing, pulling on his cheeks, and flinging his arms out every which way. It was as if he were made of clay and was now trying to reshape himself properly after being cooped up in a sardine tin. Oh, but he was a ferocious-looking devil! Deep green and gray skin, mottled and rippling, like waves on a stormy ocean. Bristling white eyebrows over bulging fish-green eyes, glaring poisonously. The most absurdly long-tailed mustaches, curling in outrageous white loops inches past his face. A huge-domed head, round and bald as a billiard ball.

He looked *mean*. Mean and old. Older than London, maybe, and London went all the way back to the Romans! But there was nothing weak about this old man. His massive green muscles rippled with power, though he had nothing but smoke where legs ought to be.

"Mermeros," I said. "That's a funny name. But I know what you are. You're a djinni!"

His nostrils flared. He folded his thick green arms. "Do I require baby females to tell me what I am? A djinni, eh? You know *nothing*." He sniffed the air and surveyed the alleyway. "Tell me," he demanded, "what place is this? What sovereignty? Name your king, and the number of your present year."

I laughed aloud. "You're a fine one to talk about knowing nothing."

He only glowered at me.

"This is London, capital city of the United Kingdom of Great Britain and Ireland, seat of the mighty British Empire," I told him, not without some pride.

"Britannia..." he echoed softly.

"Our king, if you must know, is *Queen* Victoria, thank you very much, and the year is eighteen ninety-six."

His eyes bulged. "Eighteen ninety-six? Is this, how do they call it, anno Domini?"

I nodded. "Time flies, eh?" Imagine, not knowing the year!

"That's three hundred years I've been dormant," he moaned. "Nobody's found... Wait. Did you say your empire is ruled by a *queen*?"

"God save her," I replied. "Ever since she was eighteen years old."

"A *woman*?" He pressed the heels of his green hands into his forehead. "A *young* woman. By heaven, it's no wonder girls are impudent nowadays. What kind of a world is this?"

One much more to my liking than whatever world he'd come from, that was plain!

But, back to business. If he thought he could put me off the scent of my prize, then he didn't know Maeve Merritt.

"Come," I said. "Admit it. You are a djinni. You are so a djinni. I've read about them. You must grant three wishes to whoever finds you. And I found you! So you belong to me. Those are the rules."

Mermeros darted close to me until his giant face was inches from mine. "Then make a wish, Girl Hatchling," he said softly. "Make one right now. The best you can think of."

He hovered right over me, watching me closely.

A wish right now? Why not? Why wait? Then again, shouldn't I think about it first?

"Go on," he said. "Ask me anything. You're not afraid, are you? You're not such a weak-brained girl hatchling that you can't even think of one tiny, pathetic wish?"

If Mermeros were a Luton boy from back home, or one of those orphan boys across the alley, he'd have an aching jaw right now, and I'd have an aching fist. But socking my djinni probably wasn't the best way to begin our friendship.

I stroked my chin and walked slowly around him, pretending to think of a wish but in reality studying my prize.

He wore a vest of shimmering fish scales, and an embroidered skirt pinned like a kilt around his waist. Over it, like a belt, he'd tied a yellow silk sash. A thick silver hoop dangled from one ear, and—I couldn't be certain, but I'd almost swear—an enormous shark's tooth on a leather lace dangled at his throat.

"You can't do it, can you?" He folded his great arms across his chest and smirked at me. "You lack the stomach to command me."

The teeth behind his full turquoise lips were sharply pointed, like a fish's.

"How do I even know it's worth the bother?" I said. "How do I know you actually have the power to grant wishes?"

He bared his sharp teeth, then snapped his fingers. Immediately beside him stood a sinewy tiger, half as long as the alleyway, and ready to pounce. Mermeros studied my face and frowned. He snapped again, and the tiger vanished. Now a cobra coiled beside him, its hooded head darting back and forth seductively. Fascinating! But Mermeros's eyes shot daggers of annoyance at my lack of fear. One more snap, and the cobra became a gigantic wild boar, its spiky back hair quivering, its red eyes burning.

I'd never been so close to a bloodthirsty monster, unless you counted my sister Evangeline before she'd had her breakfast tea.

"Brilliant," I said. "Can you conjure up a bear?"

Mermeros's green face turned a livid shade of purple. "Your wits are lacking, female. Strong men tremble at the sight of my menagerie."

"How about an octopus?"

Just then, Mrs. Gruboil rattled her shutters once more, then poked her nose out of the window. My heart stopped. If she or anyone at Miss Salamanca's School saw my green giant, they'd snatch him for themselves. He was mine, I'd dug in the trash all day and found him, and I was not about to let him slip through my grasp.

But Mrs. Gruboil never looked from left to right. A half-naked hovering green bald man out of the corner of her eye wasn't worth turning to investigate. That is the problem with adults. They won't bother to see what ought not to be there.

Mrs. Gruboil sniffed the air and scowled. "You've kicked up a stink, Miss Maeve. Hurry up, I said, and get those cans put away so you can wash!" She shut the window once more.

Mermeros looked affronted not to have been noticed, the peacock.

"You'd better get back into that sardine tin," I told him. "We can talk more later."

"I will *not*." He stretched his huge arms. They were banded with tattooed rings in darker shades of blue and green. "I have no wish for further conversation with *you*."

I crawled underneath him and snatched the sardine tin, then cranked the key backward to unfurl the tin covering. A sardine can, once opened, could never be shut again, but perhaps, I gambled, this one was different.

And right I was. It sealed shut, pulling Mermeros inside.

"Desist!" He billowed larger, looming over me so his fish-green eyes glared down into mine. His fists clenched, his muscles bulged with menace. "I warn you, female hatchling, not to incur my wrath. A thousand lifetimes are not enough to make Mermeros forget…"

But the cord of smoke was tugging him down into the tin, like the winding of a sailor's rope on a spool. His green body turned back into thick yellow fumes once more and was sucked into the sardine tin, which sealed itself shut with the key back in place on the bottom, good as new.

I slipped him into my pocket and ran inside.

CHAPTER
3

D on't look now, girls. Maeve the Knave has come back inside for her bread and water."

I stalked by Theresa Treazleton in a perfect imitation, if I do say so, of the way *she* usually pranced around. Nose held high. Wouldn't she pop her eyeballs from her sockets if she knew what I had in my pocket?

Supper was over, and the rest of the girls were assembled in the sitting room on the third floor of the school, in the common hall outside the dormitory rooms for the seventh form. I'd already bolted my meal standing next to the sink in Mrs. Gruboil's kitchen. A potato without butter, and a lukewarm chicken wing, just to remind me of my inferior punished status. I could smell from the dining hall the piping-hot chickens with potatoes, and gravy and hot apple crumble. But, no matter. My mind was too full of my astonishing discovery to dwell upon food. A djinni! Here, in London, and in 1896 of all things! Here we sat on the very verge of the twentieth century, and there I was, finding djinnis. It was just like in the book *One Thousand and One Nights*. How many times had I read Polly's gilt-edged copy and envied the boy Aladdin!

After washing up, I headed up the stairs and encountered Theresa holding court in the sitting room, thronged by her minions. Theresa's father ran a large shipping enterprise that made him rich as a lord, thereby guaranteeing his daughter would be the nastiest and most sought-after girl at any boarding school in Britain, except for the schools where daughters of *real* lords were sent.

Theresa's black eye had gone from being truly blackish-purple to just purple, with a tinge of yellow at the edges. She reminded me of the pansies on Miss Salamanca's office wallpaper.

"Maeve Merritt," Theresa purred. "You poor thing. Having to muck about in the refuse for two days! And all because you were never taught to behave as a young lady should."

She simpered at me. Her minions did the same.

"Kind of you to pity me, Theresa dear," I said. "I should pity you, Miss Purple-Face."

Theresa shot up out of her chair.

"You take that back!"

"Shan't."

Her fingers curled into a fist. "I ought to give *you* a black eye," she said.

I thrust out my chin so she'd have an easy shot at me.

"Go ahead. I'll hold still for you."

I knew she'd never dare. Theresa fumed till spittle shone on her lower lip. She looked at her fist as though it had already been injured on my skull, then released it. "You're ugly, anyway," she said. "Look at yourself. Filthy as a chimney sweep."

"Filthier," chimed in Honoria Brisbane, Theresa Treazleton's chief minion, with the pert little face of a weasel. "Chimney sweeps don't smell like barnyards."

"Have you sniffed a chimney sweep lately, Honoria?" I said. "The company you keep! Well, good night. I'm off to take my bath and get to bed. Don't strain your tongues gossiping."

I strolled out of the sitting room and down the corridor to my bedroom. I knew I'd been sassier with them than I ought to be, and I was only asking for retaliation, which would in all likelihood occur during my bath, but carrying an almighty djinni in my pocket made me bold. So what if Theresa and Honoria and the others stole all my stockings and petticoats? My djinni could conjure up clothes fit for a queen or, better yet, clothes fit for a boy heading off to exploring the jungle. Oh! Now *there* was an idea. I should wear trousers! What a scandal. But when I considered that three wishes were all I'd get from Mermeros, I decided I didn't want to waste one on useless clothing. So I stuffed a valise full of all my necessaries, just in case Theresa and

Honoria had evil plans, and brought it with me into the bathroom, which I could lock from within while I took my soak.

The bath did wonders, and I was feeling much better when I lugged my valise, sardine can and all, back to my bedroom and prepared to climb between my sheets. I wore a fresh, clean night-dress, and my skin had that lovely tight, clean, soapy feeling that meant I'd scrubbed off every speck of dust and rubbish from the trash heaps.

I pulled back the bedspread and gasped. There, tucked between the sheets, was a note scrawled in large letters. "I know about your green man," it said.

CHAPTER 4

I t's awfully chilly in here, Maeve," said a voice behind me. "What did you open the window for?"

I was too distracted by the note to pay attention to Alice at first. Alice Bromley shared my room with me at Miss Salamanca's school, and she was a brick, really, once I got to know her. When I first met her, I thought she'd be the pretty, silly sort who wouldn't dare muss her hands nor scuff her shoes. That was wrong of me. Alice is sensible, if a bit timid. True, she's much too anxious about rules. But she's as kind as Christmas, and loyal as anything. There's none of that silly goggling around after Theresa Treazleton that most of the girls did all day. She has no use for Theresa, nor for the school. She pines for home and her beloved grandparents. Can't blame her for that. Before this day's find, I would have said having Alice as a roommate was the only good thing to happen to me at this school.

"What's that you're reading?" Alice peered over my shoulder.

"What ghastly writing. And what's that saying about a green man?" She giggled. "Do you have a green man, Maeve?"

I let the note fall back on the bed. Alice wouldn't betray me, I thought. But would she believe me?

A chill breeze from the window blew over my wet hair and made me shiver. I crossed the room and closed the window. "I didn't open the window. It must be that the maid... Oh!"

Down below, across the alley, in the back garden of the charitable home, I saw the red-haired orphan boy by the light spilling from their kitchen windows. He was watching *my* window. He ducked out of sight behind the woodshed, but even in the dim light there was no mistaking his orange hair, sticking out from under his cap. I waited.

"What is it?" Alice joined me and peered outside. "I don't see anything."

The orphan boy poked his head out slowly, then darted back out of sight once he saw me watching.

So. *He* was the spy who threatened to upset my secret prize! We'd see about *that*.

"There's a boy down there!" Alice gave me a little shove. "Don't stand in front of the window in your nightdress, you goose!" She sank onto her bed and began unlacing her boots. "You're quite a mystery tonight. Did you think you saw a burglar?"

"No burglar," I said. "But it *was* that boy who climbed in here and left this note." I pulled the curtains firmly shut, then folded the incriminating slip of paper and stuffed it in my emergency valise. Young Master Redhead may have seen my green man once, but I'd make sure he never did again.

"Then he must be mad." Alice wrenched off a boot. "The poor orphans, driven to insanity through the despair of loneliness and grief..."

"Oh, pooh," I said. "You're a kind soul, but those 'poor orphans' are just as rascally as any other boys. Back home, the boys in the village and I used to..."

"Your life back home always sounds so wonderfully savage." Alice sighed and attacked the buttons on the high collar of her dress. "I wouldn't dare have half the adventures you do. What would Grandmother say?"

"Your grandmother can't say *anything* about what she doesn't know." I shoved my valise under my bed and slipped the precious sardine can into the pocket of my dressing gown, hanging near my bed. I'd have to come up with a better hiding place for it, but, for now, I wanted to keep it close.

"I miss Grandmother." Alice looked wistful, then she brightened. "Speaking of notes, you received a letter from home today." She pulled an envelope from her pinafore pocket and handed it to me.

It was from my eldest and best-beloved sister, Polydora. The only one of my three sisters whose brain wasn't positively pickled by too many fashion magazines. Tall, thin, with spectacles and without marriage prospects, Polly was the only one back home who wrote regularly. Mother—hah!—barely wrote at all. I slit the envelope open and scanned the first lines.

"Dearest Maeve," it read in Polly's smooth, regular handwriting. "How I laughed when I read your last note! But you mustn't be so glib about your teachers. It borders on disrespect, and it will interfere with your learning. Mother and Father send their love"—I wondered if they actually had, or if Polly was just being sweet as usual—"as do Deborah and Evangeline." Now I knew Polly was fibbing. "We're all eager for your Christmas visit." *Hmph.* Not all, I'd wager. Mother was probably breaking out in hives at the thought of me coming home. "All is hubbub here since Evangeline's engagement was announced, and there is a never-ending stream of tradesmen ringing our bell to show us silks and laces and stationery and candied almonds for the party. Mother is in her element, though Father worries constantly about the cost..."

I stuffed the letter in the pocket of my dressing gown, to save it for later. I always loved hearing from dear old Polly, but she *would* ramble on, and I had too much on my mind just now to be bothered with the cost of Evangeline's bridal veil. I'd be glad of a diversion during tomorrow's French class. I'd read the letter then.

I crawled under the covers and lay there thinking of my djinni and all the wishes I might choose. The diamond mines of Borneo! The silver mines of Peru! Not that I wanted wealth above other things, though I was no fool where money was concerned. With sacks of silver and diamonds and gold, they couldn't very well order me into itchy, gray serge dresses anymore, nor make me conjugate my French verbs so I could someday find an ideal husband. (Perhaps I was intended to marry a Frenchman?) My mother had sent me to Miss Salamanca's school to make a young lady out of me, so that in a few years' time—very few, judging from Evangeline—she could marry me off. It was the one and only respectable way to dispose of a daughter. Unlike the good old days, before dear old Henry VIII, when parents could farm daughters off to abbeys to become nuns.

I wanted a different life. Independence. Travel. Sports. And all those things cost money. But with a djinni in my pocket—literally— who could stop me? I could travel the world, like Miss Isabella Bird. I could buy a great country house, turn the back gardens into my own private cricket lawn, and invite the best players in the country to play. But they'd have to let me bowl. And wear my own cricket flannels and cap. Oh! I'd start a cricket team for girls and teach them how to play. A whole league! I'd spread girls' cricketing across the British Isles!

Maeve Merritt. Girl Traveler and Female Cricketing Champion of the World.

I lay there, heart thumping, imagining, and finally I decided I could wait no more to let Alice in on the secret. A secret this fantastically huge and stupendously amazing just couldn't be kept by one person alone, or she might explode. Besides, I would want to know, if I were in Alice's shoes. Wild horses wouldn't drag her secret out of me. Friends are friends.

I sat up underneath the covers.

Alice had loosened her butter-colored hair and was now braiding it for bed.

"Alice," I said. "Can you keep a secret?"

Her eyebrows rose. She hurried to my bed and sat by my feet. "Absolutely," she whispered. "Is it something about the orphan boy?"

I wrinkled my nose in disgust. "No! This is a mysterious and fantastical secret. You'll find it hard to believe. And you mustn't breathe it to a living soul."

Alice inched closer. "I swear it on my mother's grave," she said. "They can torture me with hot brands, but I'll never…"

"Fine, fine." Hot brands! Of all things! I pulled the sardine can from my dressing gown.

"*That's* your secret?" Alice's disappointment was plain. "A can of fish? I prefer kippers over sardines, myself."

"No, silly," I said. "This is no ordinary can of fish." I lowered my voice even further. "*There's a djinni inside.*"

Alice pursed her lips and gave me a long, slow look. "You're not joking with me again, are you, Maeve?" she said. "This isn't a prank?"

I shook my head. "On my honor, it isn't," I whispered. "I'd show you here, but then we'd be found out. I discovered him in the dustbin today, during my punishment. He conjured up a tiger and a cobra before my eyes, right out there in the alley! He came right out of this tin, sure as sugar."

"But I thought djinnis lived in lamps," Alice protested. "What's he doing in a sardine can? And how did such a sardine can come to be here, in London, in Miss Salamanca's School's dustbins?"

"I can hardly guess." I gestured for her to speak more softly. "But he's there. Right in there. And he's going to grant me three wishes. Think of it, Alice! Any three wishes my heart desires! I only wonder what to choose. I could travel to Florence, to Venice, to Jerusalem, and Constantinople. Or Cairo, and Giza—to see the pyramids! I could ride up the Congo, perhaps, and go on a safari…"

Alice finished her braids and drifted back to her own bed.

"A djinni, in London, today," she mused. "In a sardine tin." She lay down, then sat back bolt upright again. "And you say the orphan boy next door saw him?"

I nodded. "Why would he leave me a note, if he hadn't?"

"'*I saw your green man*,'" she repeated to herself. "'*Your green man*.'"

I could tell she was beginning to believe me, though it irritated me that she was more swayed by the orphan boy's note than what I told her with my own lips. I might have been somewhat prone to exaggeration here and there—merely for the sake of a good story—but I was a truthful person. Essentially. Except to people who didn't deserve the truth, like Theresa.

"Won't he try to break in here again, then, and steal your djinni?" Alice asked.

I slapped myself on the forehead. Good, sensible-thinking Alice! "'Course he will!" I said. "We need to get ready for him."

"How?"

I considered this. "Oh, if only I had my cricket bat," I said, "but that's hidden at home where Mother and Dad will never find it." My gaze fell upon the washbasin. "A jugful of water would be a decent weapon, for starters," I said. "I'll run to the washroom and fill it up."

I seized the pitcher from the washstand, pulled my dressing gown over my shoulders, and opened our bedroom door. In the dim hallway, I noticed two girls in their nightgowns, whispering to each other from their bedroom doorways. They were Theresa Treazleton and Honoria Brisbane. At the sight of me, both of them quickly shut their doors. I heard giggling from the passageway. The little minxes! Did they think I cared about their nasty secrets?

I charged along the corridor. Then, just as I passed their bedroom doors, my foot caught something. Down I went with a terrific crash, landing splayed out in the hallway. My forehead met the floor with a painful *crack*, and the hand I'd tried to catch myself with socked me in my own left eye. My pitcher shattered into a thousand fragments. And the sardine can in my pocket landed right underneath my hip bone, where I was sure I'd wear a hideous bruise for days to come.

Through my spinning senses I heard a sound. Muffled hysterical laughter, coming from the bedroom doors on either side. I craned my neck back and saw the length of twine wedged tightly between two bedroom doors.

A trap! They'd tripped me on purpose as punishment for sassing Theresa earlier. And there they were behind their doors, gloating.

My head spun with pain. One hand was peppered with small cuts from the shards of the broken pitcher. My hip throbbed, and if that wasn't a goose egg forming above my left eye socket, then I was a leprechaun.

In the dark hallway gloom, I saw red. I pushed myself up to my knees, pulled the sardine tin from my pocket, and fumbled for the key with my bloody fingers to open the lid.

The reek of sulfurous fumes filled the hall.

"Not you again," Mermeros moaned. "I prayed from my prison that a war chieftain would capture your tribe and discover me among the booty."

"No such luck," I said. "No war chieftains in this neighborhood."

"Why are you groveling on the ground like a worm? You dropped the weight of the pyramids on me."

Theresa Treazleton opened her bedroom door. She looked ghostly in the dim light, with her pale face and her long white night-gown, and her chestnut braids pulled far back behind her head.

"Maeve, dear!" Theresa began in a syrupy-sweet, lying voice of pretend concern. "Did you fall? How clumsy of...you..."

Her jaw dropped.

She saw him.

Would the djinni murder her for me?

My left eye was so swollen, I couldn't open it.

A giggling Honoria Brisbane opened her bedroom door. Her braids swung over her shoulders.

Not murder. Just revenge. This was worth a thousand wishes. So I'd better do it right. I didn't really want to injure them. Not seriously. I'm not a monster. I decided to attack their vanity. That would serve them.

Your green man.

Braids.

I confess, I wasn't really thinking straight. I had, after all, just hit my head.

"Dye their braids green," I whispered to Mermeros, "with a stain no human dye can undo."

"The girl hatchling is a mistress of ruthless cunning," Mermeros said with a sneer. He pressed his hands together and bowed in mock reverence. "Never in all the history of the world has a wish been so boldly spent."

There was a flash of light behind each of my tormentor's scalps, like halos around the darling angels, enough to show my one good eye that Mermeros had done it. He'd turned both girls' braids a pulsing, luminous poison green. Then he slithered back into his sardine can and sealed his own lid shut.

They looked ridiculous. The hair lying along their scalps hadn't changed. Honoria's blond head, and Theresa's chestnut one, were just the same. But their braids looked like poisonous snakes from the Amazon rain forest.

Honoria Brisbane's giggles died away. Whether it was the vague green form of a man in a cloud of noxious smoke, or the flash of light, or the sight of Theresa Treazleton's famous chestnut braids turned green, I can only guess, but she fainted dead away, landing on top of me like a sack of carrots in a grocer's crate. She squashed me flat on the floor once more by fainting just as any well-raised young English lady ought to do at a time like this. Miss Salamanca would have been proud to see it.

Approaching footfalls sounded in the stairwell.

Then Theresa Treazleton did something that would almost

have made me admire her, if it didn't make me wish I *had* gone straight for murder. From her sewing basket, she snatched a pair of scissors. Seizing Honoria's braids, she hacked them both off in two vicious, sawing strokes, leaving the short remainder of her brutally mangled—but naturally colored—hair.

"What are you doing?" I gasped.

She glanced in a mirror, then, twisting her arms behind her own head, she favored herself with the same treatment. She gathered up the fallen green braids and stuffed them underneath her bed pillow, then tossed the scissors down in the shards of smashed water jug, beside where I still knelt, stupefied with pain.

Miss Salamanca appeared around the corner. She placed her hands on her hips and surveyed the scene. I had to crane my neck to see her. Honoria Brisbane still lay in a heap, draped over my fallen body.

"Maeve Merritt," she said, with her disdainful, pinching nose showing off her lovely buckteeth. "Why am I not surprised? And *what* have you done to Miss Brisbane?"

Covered in blood and bruises, with Honoria Brisbane pinning me down, *I* was the guilty party? The bitter injustice would have stung more if I weren't so accustomed to it.

Theresa appeared beside me, her cheeks now streaked with convincing tears. "She attacked us with scissors, Miss Salamanca!" Theresa sobbed. "I *had* to throw my water jug at her in self-defense!"

Miss Salamanca's lips pressed together so tightly, she looked like a long-legged prune. I struggled to my feet, not caring what happened to Honoria. But my movements startled her into wakefulness.

"The green man..." she said faintly. "Dreadful!"

Old Sally's sharp ears missed nothing. "What's that she said?" she said. "'Green *man*,' did she say?" Her tone of voice suggested, not for the first time, that men were creatures for whom she could not comprehend the Almighty's purposes.

Theresa helped Honoria to her feet, treading deliberately on my legs as she did so. "It's nothing." She gasped under Honoria's limp weight. "She's always having...daydreams and things. Talking frogs, violet cats, green men... I'll just help her to bed."

Miss Salamanca sighed. "Such a thoughtful girl. So mindful of her friends." Then she paused, as if a terrifying thought had just occurred to her. "*What* will I tell her father about her hair?"

She turned her most fearsome glare my way. "When you've quite finished cleaning up the mess you've made here, *Miss Merritt*, you will accompany me. No soft pillows, and no cozy dormitory gossip for you tonight."

CHAPTER

5

Next morning before dawn, I limped into my bedroom, covered in coal dust. Miss Salamanca had sentenced me to a night's sleep, or lack thereof, in the coal closet. Now she'd set me loose to get changed, with orders to hurry back and resume my punishment.

The coal closet was right off the kitchen, adjacent to Mrs. Gruboil's bedroom, so I didn't dare open Mermeros's tin during the night. He wouldn't fit in the tiny closet anyway, though come to think of it, he fit in a fish tin, so perhaps he could have managed it. But I was too angry with myself for squandering a wish and, worse, allowing Theresa Treazleton to see Mermeros, to even think of venturing another wish just yet. I needed to think more carefully. When I made my next wish, I'd be good and ready to make the most of it.

Braids? I had all night long to writhe in my own stupidity. I'd wished for *green braids* and not their entire heads of hair? Braids alone gave Theresa the chance to chop them off and hide the evidence. I

should've turned both girls green from head to toe. *Maeve Merritt,*
I heard my mother's scolding voice in my ear say, *when will you ever
learn to think?*

A younger student, Winnifred Herzig, came out her door just
as I passed by her room. Her mouth fell open at the sight of my
coal-dust-covered face and clothes.

"Run along, Winnie," I told her. "Mind your business."

"You needn't be so mean, Maeve," she told my retreating back.
"I've got as much right to be here as you."

I wasn't mean, I told myself. Just in no mood for tiny Winnie's
gaping stare and thousand questions. She wasn't nasty like Theresa
and her set, but she was one of the sort who tagged along everywhere
and spread gossip like the plague. Winnifred loved having tales to tell.

When I entered our bedroom, Alice greeted me from her bed
with a cry of concern. "You're filthy," she said, "and bruised like a
boxer. And after your lovely bath, too."

I peeled off my dressing gown and dropped it on the floor. Then
I remembered the sardine can was still in the pocket. I pulled it out.

"Miss Salamanca has me doing hard chores for another two
days," I said. "What shall I do with this? If she should find it on me,
all is lost!"

"Leave that to me," Alice said, reaching for the can. "I'll hide it
where no one can find it. Oh, Maeve! I saw everything last night. The

djinni, and what Theresa did. Heavens, what a fright that creature gave me!" She bit her lip. "I do think you were perhaps a bit hasty, Maeve."

I reached for the wash jug to pour some water for my face, then realized it was smashed into smithereens.

"What will people say when they see Theresa and Honoria?" she mused. "Hair chopped short like a boy... I shudder to think."

"Don't tell them it was my djinni," I pleaded. "We might as well let Theresa's lie stand."

"Miss Merritt!" Miss Salamanca's voice found me from downstairs. "No lollygagging! I want all the girls' boots polished before breakfast."

I spent another two days under Mrs. Gruboil's wrathful and bloodshot eyes, shoveling coal, filling wooden bins, peeling potatoes, and washing windows. Even though I was officially never with the other girls, I overheard enough to know that word of my "attack" on the precious braids had spread like smallpox through the school. Most girls took great delight in wondering what my final punishment would be—a slow roasting on a spit, perhaps? A few of the younger girls, though, seemed genuinely frightened of me, as though I were a scissor-wielding menace who might pounce upon their braids at a moment's notice.

I felt badly about that. My battered appearance only made me look more dangerous. Winnifred Herzig ducked through doorways, clutching her own plaits, whenever she saw me. Which was often. She was the kind of girl who was always there. Some people just have that gift.

A letter had been sent to my father and mother in strictest tones of warning. Let Old Sally expel me, let my father withdraw me. What did I care?

More than once when I went to dump rubbish, the ginger-haired boy across the alley took a halting step toward me, but I fixed him with a look of such malice that he hesitated and looked away.

Good. If he hadn't spied on my djinni and climbed into my room, none of this would have happened. Maybe it was the sight of my bruises that made him lose his nerve.

Two days passed, and when Sunday rolled around, even reprobates like me were forced to observe the Sabbath. I sat in church, wedged between Alice and the hard end of the pew, staring ahead at the napes of Theresa and Honoria's necks, where their short, bristly normal-colored hair poked out from under their straw bonnets. At least no green could be seen. Miss Salamanca had festooned their hats with dangling black ribbons to hide their lack of hair. It made them look like pallbearers.

On and on droned the rector's sermon, while the cold air in the drafty chapel prevented me from napping. Across the aisle, the greengrocer's two young children gaped at the green remnants of my black eye until their mother pinched them. I made droll faces back at them until they giggled, and Miss Guntherson, our thick-jawed French instructor who was not the least bit French, grimaced a warning at me. Faces, it seemed, should not be made in church. Unless you were a French instructor.

"...your things yesterday," Alice breathed in the faintest whisper imaginable. I turned to read her lips.

"What?"

"Shh," she hissed. She nodded toward the pew before us. "Theresa," she mouthed. "Found her poking through your things."

We rose for the hymn. "She didn't find anything, did she?" I asked Alice.

My roommate smiled slightly. I wondered whether it would be worth another wish to punish Theresa Treazleton properly. No, it wouldn't, but oh, if only...

The hymn began, and we all rose. Alice sang the hymn, and I admit she has a lovely voice, though I have little appetite for music. She met with a private voice instructor who came to the school each week. Theresa also had musical aspirations, but her voice couldn't touch Alice's, which pleased me to no end.

"'*What can I do for England, that does so much for me?*'" She sang out the final refrain. "'*One of her faithful children I can and I will be.*'"

That hymn always made me want to sneeze. I didn't see what

it had to do with religion in the least. Nor could I think of what England had done for me of late. And they made us sing it *so* often.

When the service was over, we filed down the aisle and out the great doors, passing by the pews of orphan boys. The red-haired boy glowered at me. I walked by with my nose held high, as though I hadn't even seen him there, the wretched thief.

Back at school, after a Sunday lunch of cold beef with mustard and buttered bread, Miss Salamanca announced visiting hours. I rose to clear dishes off the table, but Miss Salamanca stopped me.

"Your mother has written to inform me that she will be visiting you this afternoon," she said, in icy tones. "She wishes to speak with you about your recent unladylike behavior."

I sighed. I was in little mood for another lecture.

"Mr. Alfred Treazleton, our great patron, will also be here this afternoon, visiting his daughter," Miss Salamanca said. Her face looked especially gray. "I need hardly remind you that you are to demonstrate the utmost propriety in the parlor. If Mr. Treazleton addresses you, as I do not doubt he may, following your vicious attack on his daughter, you will submit to his displeasure meekly. Am I fully understood?"

I nodded. Sometimes it was impossible not to just stare at her bewildering teeth.

Miss Salamanca pressed her lips together and hid them. "If your mother hadn't chosen this particular week to call, I never would have let you near the parlor on a visiting afternoon. But it can't be helped."

We all went upstairs to remove our pinafores and tidy ourselves up for our relatives' arrivals. Alice nearly burst out of her skin with excitement. Visits from home were water in the desert to her. And for most girls. Visiting day was normally a great treat. Families brought shop-bought sweets and home-cooked tarts and little bunches of flowers and new stockings for growing girls. I knew there'd be no little presents for me. Not today. Not unless Polydora came.

The bell rang announcing the first of the visitors. We filed out into the courtyard to line up for inspection and await our guests. Miss Salamanca seemed to think we were seen to our best advantage lined up in ruler-straight rows, with our cheeks and noses pinched by cold.

Alice's grandmother, Mrs. Bromley, arrived first, escorted out of her carriage by a valet nearly as ancient and tottering as she was. She made her way across the gravel to where Alice stood, and Alice threw her arms around her, kissed her wrinkled cheek, and led her in out of the cold. I smiled. Seeing Alice with her grandmother always made me glad. Heaven knew how frail Mrs. Bromley managed not be crushed by Alice's eager hugs.

One by one, other girls led their relatives indoors to the parlor while the rest of us waited. A cabdriver pulled his horse up in the stable yard, jumped down, and helped my mother disembark. She climbed out, clinging anxiously to the driver's arm and leaving Deborah to fend for herself. Deborah called loudly for assistance until the cabbie left my mother and assisted her, too, leaving Polydora to climb down by herself. With her too-tall, too-thin frame, and her wire spectacles, such was often her fate. Helpful gentlemen were anywhere but at her side offering assistance. Fortunately, my sensible eldest sister needed nobody's help to find her way to the ground.

Just then, a shiny black carriage swept impressively into the yard, pulled by a matched set of glossy black mares with red-trimmed livery. Mother paused to gape at the carriage, forcing Polydora to snatch her out of the way while the immaculately dressed footman leaped down and pulled on the door. Out poked a tall silk hat, followed by the bald head wearing it, which head, along with the attached stout trunk, gold watch chain and all, could only belong to Theresa's father, Mr. Alfred P. Treazleton. He would have been easy to spot even if he hadn't blazoned his name in gold letters on his coach door.

He took one step onto the walk and pulled his greatcoat closed about him.

His glance took in the courtyard—the shrubs, the waiting girls, and Miss Salamanca's anxious face—with one swift look of indifference. My mother misread his benign expression for friendliness and curtsied low before him, but he strode past, not bothering to acknowledge her. Mother rose and looked about, a bit stunned by

Mr. Treazleton's absence, and adjusted her hat, pretending not to be embarrassed. My fingers curled into a fist. To ignore my mother like that! Daddy did it every day by the parlor fire, but Alfred P. Treazleton could jolly well behave like a gentleman. He was no duke, even if he was as rich as one.

I hugged and kissed Deborah and Polly each in turn and beckoned to Mother while Mr. Treazleton embraced his little princess.

"Hey! Get away, you louse!"

The cry came from Mr. Treazleton's coach driver. He reached for his whip and lashed it in the direction of one of his horses. But it wasn't the mare he was aiming for. It was the red-haired orphan boy.

The lash ripped across his shoulder, tearing his clothes and cutting into his skin. I stared at the boy and wondered why he hadn't cried out. His mouth was set in a grim, hard line.

Mr. Treazleton's footman seized him in an instant and began shaking him. "What do you mean, tampering with the master's horses?" he cried. His immaculate trousers didn't seem so impressive to me now.

The red-haired boy's cap fell to the ground, but still he remained silent. I wondered if he might be unable to speak.

"Bring the boy to me," Mr. Treazleton called.

The footman dragged the boy over and flung him down before Mr. Treazleton. He landed hard in the gravel, but scrambled immediately to his feet and stared at the giant of industry, eye to eye.

"Let's go inside, Maeve," Mother whispered in my ear. "Let's get away from this unpleasantness." I resisted her pull on my arm. I had to know what would happen.

"Oh, Daddy, that's one of those horrible orphan boys," Theresa cried. "They're everywhere you look in this ghastly place. We can't ever go outside without seeing them."

Mr. Treazleton raised an eyebrow in a trembling Miss Salamanca's direction, as though the existence of orphan boys in London was a symptom of her negligence and mismanagement. Then he addressed himself to the cowering boy.

"Touch my horses, will you?" Mr. Treazleton said. His voice, in contrast with his words, was soft, almost pleasantly conversational. He didn't have any need to raise his voice. "Do you know how easily a boy like you can work a permanent mischief on a horse?"

"She had a burr in her hide, on her foreleg," the boy said. "I wouldn't ever hurt her."

Mr. Treazleton ignored the boy. "That mare would fetch a much higher price in the market than a skinny wretch like you would."

"What's the going price on rude, fat old men?"

I froze.

So did everyone else.

For once, even I was astonished.

Had those words come out of my mouth?

CHAPTER
6

The driver snapped his whip in midair. If I were a boy, I'd have tasted its sting.

Twenty girls forgot their training and stared at me with jaws hanging down to the pavement.

Mr. Treazleton's coattails swirled behind him as he swept Theresa indoors. Miss Salamanca bobbed along after them in a state of mortal panic.

The red-haired boy took advantage of the commotion...and the footman looking the other way. He darted off in a blink.

Mr. Treazleton's driver parked his carriage in the school's carriage house. Other equipages pulled up, each in their turn, and disgorged their occupants. One by one, girls led their families in out of the cold. The bachelor brother of one of the older girls caught Deborah's eye, and she sidled her way across the gravel to where he stood, looking bored by the parade of schoolgirls. Polydora watched her go and hesitated, then set her jaw and abandoned our flighty sister to her own disgraces. She steered Mother indoors.

Mother couldn't bear to enter the visitors' parlor after my insult of Mr. Treazleton. She made it only so far as the foyer and stood there trembling. Polly and I recognized the warning signs. A fit of hysterics could be seconds away.

"If I have to find another school for the ungovernable child..." she moaned. "She'll be sacked! I'll never persuade another school to take her in.... Oh, it's a cruel fate; more than any mother deserves. Brawling with schoolgirls! Insulting shipping magnates!"

"Mother," Polydora whispered gently. "People can hear you."

Mother resorted to a softer voice, yet it still carried throughout the building. "Why won't you keep a civil tongue in your head, Maeve? Willful child! Unnatural girl! You'll be my death. My absolute death. My great-aunt Bernice, *she* died of despair when her wayward son was court-martialed in the army. Fatal grief runs in my family."

"Your *voice*, Mother," Polly shushed. "A court-martial is entirely different."

A long, gilded mirror hung in the foyer, and with my angle of view, I could spy on the girls visiting with their families in the parlor. Theresa and Mr. Treazleton occupied the central sofa, naturally. I saw Theresa whispering in her father's ear for what seemed an unusually long time. My own inner ear itched just imagining it. Whispers were so *moist*.

Mr. Treazleton's reflection pointed its fat finger straight at me. To my horror, Theresa's gaze met mine. She nodded.

They could me *see me*. And they were *talking about me*.

My blood felt hot in my veins. Theresa was filling his ear with lies about the vicious fight wherein I chopped off her braids, the cunning little cat.

Then my heart nearly stopped. Theresa opened a satchel and pulled from it something that would look like a small, hairy rodent— except it was a luminous, poison green.

I moved out of view of the mirror.

She wasn't just telling him about the fight. She was telling him about the djinni.

Well, so what if she was? Let her prattle and tattle. Mr. Alfred P. Treazleton would never believe in a djinni. But let him complain to Miss Salamanca; let Old Sally bounce me out of this school. Good riddance to them all.

Through the front window, I saw Deborah lean shockingly close to the young bachelor gentleman. He twirled his cane in midair and struck what he obviously thought was a debonair pose for Deborah's benefit. With his black suit, white shirt, and golden cravat, he looked just like a penguin at the zoological gardens. I snorted, then covered my mouth.

Mother's eyes narrowed. "That's enough unwelcome noise from you, I should think, Maeve."

"Come inside for some tea, Mother," my sister said. "A nice warm cup and a sit-down will do you good."

But my mother would not hear it. "Call another cab, Polydora, there's a lamb," she pleaded. "I cannot remain here at present."

Polly sighed and succumbed, and we went outside. A cab was soon obtained, and the driver assisted Mother up into it. Polydora had to drag Deborah away, leaving the bachelor gentleman with nothing better to do but go indoors and visit with his own sister, who was, presumably, the reason he came in the first place.

Polydora squeezed my shoulder before climbing into the cab. "Write to me, Maeve," she said. "And try to behave. Christmas will be here in no time. I'll come fetch you for the holidays."

I grasped Polly's hand in reply. She pressed a small parcel into my hand: black licorice! My favorite. Dear old Polly.

Mother spoke her farewells from the cab window by means of a lace handkerchief, which she flitted at me with each syllable.

"I should *think*," she said (*flit-flit-flit*), "that a *sen*sible girl, who's had *ev*ery attention lavished upon her, and been given the *best* and most ex*pen*sive education, could learn *not* to spread so much destruction."

At this, the brave little lace handkerchief gave up the good fight and slipped from Mother's fingers. The cabbie pinched it up from the mud and offered it to her.

"Where to, ma'am?"

Mother took the handkerchief gingerly.

"Ahem. Where to, ma'am?"

Good old Polly rescued them both. "Saint Pancras Station, please."

The cabbie sprang to action. "Righty-ho."

My sister Polly waved goodbye. Deborah craned her neck to look one more time at the bachelor gentleman, and Mother stared straight ahead, as if she might forget she'd ever come here.

I watched the cab wheels spin across the cobbled street. So much for my visit from home.

I turned heel and ran straight into someone.

The orphan boy.

He was taller up close than I would have guessed, with hair so shockingly red poking out underneath his cap that he put me in mind of a ripe tomato. Fabric from the rip in his jacket caused by Mr. Treazleton's driver peeled downward, leaving his shoulder bare.

I took a step back. I wasn't quite sure what to do. Here he was, my rival. I should have had a sharp remark for him at the ready.

"S'pose I ought to take my cap off to the elegant young ladies," he said. It was the first time he had spoken to me. The sneer on his lip was unmistakable.

Fine, then. "I don't care if you do or you don't," I said.

"We poor orphans," he said, "got no place speaking to our betters, when we owe the city of London our very lives."

I considered his words. "Is that what they tell you at the orphanage?"

"It's what they feed us. Along with our porridge."

I nodded. We girls at Miss Salamanca's School knew how it felt to be reminded regularly of our inferior, if cherished, place as females. Adored like poodles, and respected about as much. Orphans' lives weren't exactly bowls of marmalade, but I'd never imagined that they, too, were getting a daily drubbing of the soul.

"You're no different," the boy said. "Been trying to talk to you for days, but you're too proud to talk to me. You and your stuck-up airs."

Oh ho! Was that how he read matters? And after I'd defended him—risking a beating and expulsion in the process. The ingrate. My thumbs curled around my fists. I spread my feet in a fighting stance. He was tall; I could use a low center of gravity to my advantage. "Is that what you think?" I cried. "I don't care if you're a poor orphan or the Prince of Wales. You'll *never* get your hands on my..."

I caught myself just in the nick of time. Drivers and footmen from nearby carriages were starting to take notice of us. And family visitors were starting to trickle out the door. Mr. Treazleton was bound to appear soon. The boy saw them, too. He turned, poised to spring across the street and around the corner to the orphans' home. I grabbed his jacket sleeve and heard the rip grow larger as he tugged himself away.

"Lemme go," he hissed.

I wouldn't have, but I felt badly about his sleeve. I grabbed his wrist instead.

"What's your name?" I demanded.

He tried to tug his hand free, and was surprised by my iron grip. "Tom," he finally said.

I let his wrist go, but not without first yanking him close so I could whisper in his ear.

"You'll *never* get your hands on my djinni, Tom. So keep your nose out of where it doesn't belong."

Tom shook his hand free, then glared at me. "Listen well, Miss Stuck-up. Fair warning: I'll get that djinni, if it's the last thing I do. I'll never give up hunting for it. Not so long as I'm alive."

"Then I hope you can stomach a life of disappointment," I said.

"Hope you don't mind being hunted without a moment's rest," Tom said. "The moment you relax, that's when I'll make my move." His eyes narrowed. "And you know I can do it, too."

I thought of the note pinned to my bed. Here was a foe to keep an eye on.

More and more people were emerging from the front door of

the school. I could tell Tom was anxious to leave. Why didn't he? I wondered.

"You talk an awful lot," I said. "You'd better get home."

He took a long, hard look at me. When he opened his mouth, I expected another blistering attack. Instead I got a brief smile. It changed his look entirely.

"Meet me tonight," he said. "In your back garden."

I peered over my shoulder. Mr. Treazleton's top hat was definitely visible now.

"Get down!" I cried. Tommy ducked and hid behind me.

"You're barmy," I said. "I shan't meet you anywhere."

"Ten o'clock," he said in my ear. "Tonight."

I watched the visitors pouring out the doorway. When I turned back to Tom, he was gone.

And so were the licorices Polly brought me. Nabbed right out of my apron pocket.

Thief. Well, good riddance. As if I'd ever keep a rendezvous with him!

CHAPTER
7

I made my own escape under cover of the bustle of girls bidding their parents goodbye, and drivers cursing one another as they jockeyed to be first to drive away. I had to avoid the schoolmistresses and make it to my bedroom, fast.

I passed by Alice as she was delivering another rib-crushing hug to her grandmother, Mrs. Bromley.

"Meet me in our room," I whispered in her ear. She nodded.

"Is this a special friend of yours, Alice?" Mrs. Bromley's speech was elegant and refined—but most unwelcome now, when I needed to escape.

"Yes, ma'am," my roommate replied. "This is my roommate, Maeve Merritt."

"Ah! The energetic Miss Maeve you've written me so much about." The old lady beamed at me. "Tell me, my dear, are your people from London?"

I curtsied, all the while waiting in dread for the hand of a furious schoolmistress to yank upon my collar. "No, ma'am," I said. "My family lives in Luton. But my father works in the city. At St. Michael's Bank and Trust."

"Luton." She nodded thoughtfully. "I had a friend from Luton once. Charming place. The trains run there now, don't they?"

I nodded. "That's how my father gets to work." Every second's delay only worsened my panic. I had to get away. But perhaps Miss Salamanca wouldn't arrest me while I was still visiting with Alice's genteel grandmother.

The old lady gave Alice's arm a squeeze. "Alice, dear, you must invite Miss Maeve to ride those trains to London over the holidays for a visit. I'll instruct Agnes to make her tiny coconut cakes specially for the occasion. Do you like coconut, Miss Maeve?"

"Ever so much, Mrs. Bromley." I'd had dried, sweetened coconut twice, and pineapple from a tin once. I'd even had a few bananas. Fruits from the tropics were wildly delicious, so much more exciting than our English fruits, though I would always be fond of strawberries, raspberries, and gooseberries.

Mrs. Bromley clapped her frail hands together. "We shall count on your arrival, then, Miss Maeve! Our holiday won't be complete without you, so please do come."

I curtsied once more. "I will come, gladly, ma'am, if my parents

permit me. Excuse me. I must get indoors now. Miss Salamanca... wants to see me." This was no fib, alas.

Alice's eyes grew wide. "Does she?" Alice hadn't seen my episode with Mr. Treazleton.

"Come soon," I said, "and I'll explain."

Mrs. Bromley's valet assisted her gently into her carriage and bundled her tightly against the cold. I made my escape, doubling back around the side of the building to the servants' kitchen doorway, and up the maids' back staircase leading to our bedroom. One small advantage to my hours of menial punishment with the staff was that I knew all these secret escape routes.

Alice found me rifling through her bureau drawers.

"Oh, Maeve," she said. "You're not trying to summon your djinni, are you?"

I sank onto my bed. "I need it back, Alice. When the last visitors leave, Miss Salamanca will come barreling in here breathing fire. I insulted Theresa's father publicly. I may be drawn and quartered. At the very least, I'll be locked up for a fortnight. I need my djinni before she comes."

Alice bit her lower lip. "But, Maeve! It's so dangerous. The last time you summoned him..."

"I won't be stupid this time. I promise."

Alice wanted to believe me, I could tell, but was having trouble. "Shouldn't I just keep it here a little longer, for safety's sake?"

A nasty feeling came over me. I looked at Alice sharply. She was trying to keep Mermeros for herself! Did she have her own secret wishes planned?

No. Not Alice.

But why not Alice? Perhaps she wasn't quite the sweet, loyal creature I'd made her out to be.

"Why are you looking at me like that, Maeve?"

I controlled my voice with an effort. "It's nothing. I just want my djinni, is all."

Alice sighed and entered the closet. I followed her in and was amazed to see her remove a shelf from the wall, revealing a narrow gap in the plaster just large enough to poke a sardine can inside. Honoria Brisbane would never have found it in a million lifetimes. Nor, for that matter, would I.

She handed me the tin, and I immediately felt sorry for doubting her. What a strange jealousy that had been! I threw my arms around her. "Thanks, Alice. You're a dear."

I began tearing through my own things, building a small survival kit. A penknife, some paper, and a pencil. A lolly and a few toffees. Polly's licorices would've surely come in handy! As it was, I had hardly enough to keep me alive if Miss Salamanca chose to starve me. I bundled it together into a large handkerchief, along with the sardine tin.

Downstairs, the bell for supper began to ring. Alice sat down on her bed and watched me tie my bundle to the waistband of my underskirt. Apart from a little rattling, no one would ever know it was there.

"How was your visit with your grandmother?"

She sighed. "Too short. How I miss home! And Grandfather!"

Even though I'd met Mrs. Bromley, whenever Alice talked about her grandparents, I pictured them living in a house made of gingerbread and candy, like something out of a fairy tale.

"*But*," Alice went on, "Grandmother had news. She's heard back from a vocal coaching clinic in Vienna that I auditioned for. It's next spring, and I've been admitted! We're going to Vienna!"

"Congratulations!" I said. "Vienna sounds marvelous. Too bad you have to sing to get there."

Alice laughed. "We don't all hate music like you do, Maeve."

"I don't hate music," I told her. "Give me an Irish jig any day."

I looked around the room once more, making sure I had everything I needed.

Alice's face grew serious. "Maeve, you're not going to use your djinni to do something bad to Miss Salamanca, are you?"

I laughed. "Revenge didn't do me any good last time I tried it."

A new thought worried Alice even more. "You won't *leave*, will you?"

I hesitated. Using my djinni to run away *had* occurred to me. I didn't want Alice to know that, though.

I shook out my skirts. My bundle was well hidden.

She knew I hadn't promised to stay, and she shook her head sadly. "This wretched school is only just bearable when you're here. If you left..." She sighed.

"I won't," I told her. "Not today." That much, at least, I could promise.

"Be careful, Maeve," Alice said. "Do I dare ask why you insulted Mr. Treazleton?"

I could hear Miss Salamanca's step bearing down the hallway. I gave Alice's hand a squeeze. "He deserved it, Alice," I said. "He deserved it."

CHAPTER
8

Even if I'd had any wish to meet up with Tom that night in the garden at ten o'clock, I couldn't have done it. Miss Salamanca was so terrified of the damage I might have done to her school by offending Mr. Treazleton—and after my cruel attack on precious Theresa, no less—that she was too rattled to flay me alive. For once, words failed her. But not actions.

She locked me in the cellar.

If she thought girls were bound to be terrified of the spiders and shadows in the dark, damp dungeon underneath her school, she hadn't reckoned properly with Maeve Merritt. I admit I would have preferred not to sleep down there, with only bread and water, but I'd die before letting her know it. I marched cheerfully down to the little cot she'd set up for me, and sat upon it.

"What was that clinking sound?" Miss Salamanca asked.

I pressed my knees close together. She mustn't find the bundle I'd hidden in my skirts. "Nothing."

She thrust a plate of bread, a jug of water, and a painfully itchy wool blanket at me, then headed for the stairs.

"The door will be locked. You are to remain here until summoned. You are to think about your misdeeds and your vile conduct. When I return—an event which may be prolonged to no end, given your recent scandalous behavior—I shall expect to find a reformed young lady where once a wild hellion had been."

"You shouldn't curse like that, Miss Salamanca," I said.

Miss Salamanca had had a long day. She pretended not to hear me and closed the door tight. The bolt of the lock shot into place.

So be it.

I sat a moment longer upon my cot, and looked around.

The basement's sour, musty smell assailed my nostrils—mildew and coal dust and burst bottles of ancient wine, with a dank, earthy barnyard smell mixed in. A smudge of light filtered through a filthy window at street level. Twilight was sinking fast, and the lamplighters had already done their work on our street. What light did manage to trickle into the cellar was pathetically pale and weak, and it only served to illuminate a small region near my cot. Beyond it were miles of cavernous lavender-black darkness. The sound of my own scuffing feet echoed back to me from walls much too far away.

I set down the plate and rose, first hitching up my skirts to untie my secret bundle. It was a relief not to have the items poking my thighs.

Should I eat my lolly? Better save it.

I picked up the sardine tin and felt again the throbbing, leaping sensation, as though there were living fish inside. What a tiny prison for a giant djinni. I'd been waiting for a private place and time to confront Mermeros again. Why not here and now? Miss Salamanca couldn't have done me a bigger favor if she'd loaned me her personal drawing room.

I wrenched off the key again and fitted the tab through the slit on the key. One twist, and then another, and soon the damp cellar smell was overwhelmed by Mermeros's foul fishy odor. In the darkness, I couldn't see his billowing clouds, but I smelled them.

Mermeros himself appeared. A dim light gathered around his green skin. The darkness made his bulbous eyes, glimmering fish scales, and shocking white mustache and brows all the more startling.

"The dungeon," Mermeros observed. "It is fitting. At last we have come to your proper home, have we not, Girl Hatchling?"

With two rotten older sisters (not counting Polly), a gang of unwashed cricket-playing rowdies back home, and the likes of Theresa Treazleton and her tribe here in town, I knew how to let jibes and jeers roll off me. But that didn't mean I needed to let Mermeros's barbs pass by altogether.

"You know, you don't have to be such a fiend," I said. "Better manners wouldn't kill you."

He twisted the tips of his mustache between his fingertips, first one side, then the other. "Tell me," he said, "about your father. He obviously is no sultan, no pasha, no caliph. Is he a serf? A slave? Does he beat himself each day in shame at siring such a daughter as you?"

I had to bite my lip to keep from laughing. "How about you?" I said. "Does your father gnash his teeth at the humiliation of rearing a green fish-man of a son who must spend eternity doing the bidding of masters like me?"

Mermeros pumped himself up, double in size, and smacked his head on the rafters.

"You do not dare to call yourself *my* master," he said. "You are nothing more than my temporary nuisance." He yawned. "Come now, Hatchling Girl. Have you thought of it yet? Your next wish? Perhaps you would like me to arrange a marriage for you with the wealthiest prince of your land?"

Marriage! *Yuck!*

I laughed out loud. "There aren't any princes to be had," I said. "The Prince of Wales is an old man and married. His son, Prince George, got married himself a few years ago. So, you're out of luck. No, wait, come to think of it, the Queen has a few grandsons around my age. But, not for me. No, thank you."

Mermeros crumpled his nose and bared his sharp teeth.

"Princes aren't good enough for the soft-brained hatchling, eh?

Then what idiot wish will you squander today? Hurry and be done with it, for when your three wishes are spent, I leave these cramped confines and move on to a vessel more suitable for one of my rank."

This intrigued me. "You mean the sardine tin won't hold you anymore after my third wish?" I said. "Who decides where you'll go next? Think you'll be promoted to a can of corned-beef hash?"

He snapped at the air in front of my face with his fishy fangs. *Chop, chop.* "The hatchling girl is a jester! A spell cast eons ago will find me a new home, of its own caprices. It changes with the passing years. This curious enclosure," he peered disdainfully down at the sardine can, "was nowhere in existence when last I served a master. I do not prefer it. A priceless porcelain vase, on the other hand, or a lamp of bronze and gold would suit me well."

I considered this. "Vases and lamps aren't as portable as a sardine tin," I said. "You fit perfectly in my pocket. Much more convenient that way."

"Another thing that would suit me well," Mermeros said, "is a master worthy of me. Give me a warlord, a maharajah, a necromancer, and watch me work. Together, a bold master and I can bring an empire to its knees, or raise an army of the dead. But a *girl* child? It is an insult to my dignity."

I jumped up off my cot. "You're a fine one to talk about your dignity, Mr. Sardiney Djinni," I cried. "You stink worse than a London sewer, and I eat sardines for a snack. So, I'd keep a civil tongue in your head if I were you, and remember, I'm your master, like it or not." A thought struck me. "Wait. Did you say an *army of the dead*?"

Mermeros ignored the question. "Oh ho, and what will you have me do next time? Turn other little females' hair pink? Soil their dresses and stomp on their playthings? Pah!" He spit upon the cellar floor and shook his head. "If my brothers should see me, reduced to this... My shame is the shame of a thousand donkey-carts filled with rotten figs."

"The shame of *what*?" I shook my head. Too much time in a sardine can had addled his brain. "You and your shameful figs— or is it your shameful donkeys? All of you can just get yourselves comfortable for the time being."

I paced slowly around him. He rotated in midair, keeping an eye upon me always, as though I might stab him in the back somehow. Stab what, I wondered. A being made of vapor?

This made me pause. Was he solid? Or was he nothing more than smoke?

I poked him in the tattooed arm. My finger went right through his green-and-silver skin, and it burned. I yanked my hand away.

"What was that for?" demanded Mermeros.

"Nothing." My finger was fine now; no lasting damage. Was he made of enchanted fire?

I kept on pacing, and tried to think. I'd learned quite a bit already. I only got three wishes, as I'd always suspected, but it didn't hurt to hope otherwise. And once the third wish was done, he'd be gone, out of reach forever.

There was more that I needed to learn.

"Do you ever wish you didn't have to be cooped up in that can?" I asked him. "Quit being a djinni, get out of the wish-granting business?"

He sneered down at me over his thick white mustache. "I wish for that as much as you wish for death."

"Huh?"

He rolled his eyes. This fellow was a great one for making dramatic faces. "My vessel is my life and my power," he said, "and wish-granting is my existence. Take them away, and I am no more."

Interesting.

"And if someone were to wish for you to be free of the spell that binds you?"

"That is not freedom," he said. "It is murder. In any case, it is forbidden. The wish would not be granted."

"Sounds like you've got quite a lot of elaborate rules," I said. "Let me get this straight. A master gets three wishes…"

"Any attempt to wish for more than three wishes will backfire upon the master most gruesomely," he said. He smiled a ferocious, fishy smile. "You should've seen what happened to the master who tried it."

Noted. I tried not to think about blood.

"Only three wishes, then," I said. "A fixed number."

"Only three, for life, forever."

I chewed on that statement until a glimmer of meaning shone through. "You mean that if, say, someone made a wish or two, then lost you—maybe you were stolen, stands to reason people would try if they knew..." Images of Tommy and Theresa filled my mind. "If someone stole you and became your new master, and then the original master got you back—"

"No additional wishes," said Mermeros flatly. "Three is all anyone will ever get. If you were to lose me after one wish, and then retrieve me—a highly unlikely event—you would still have your remaining two wishes to use. But no more than that."

Darn. So much for the new idea I'd been turning around in my head. "That means you can't get a group of people together and just pass the djinni around, taking turns with the wishes forevermore."

Mermeros barked out a sarcastic laugh. "A group of thieves tried that once," he said. "They all went mad and murdered each other."

I shivered. How would a group of thieves even try it, if one only got three wishes? This needed more thought.

"People start out believing they will keep their word and trust their comrades," Mermeros went on. "But most find that when it's time to pass me along, they'd much rather take what they can get than remember their promises."

I considered this. It made sense.

"Strangely," Mermeros said with a smirk, "the betrayed comrades often don't take kindly to being cheated." He ran a sinister finger across his throat.

I shuddered, and returned to my review of the rules.

"No master can wish to release you from captivity."

"I am not a captive."

"Fine. No one can wish you free, because it would kill you, so it's not allowed."

"Correct." He yawned. "Can we be through? Make a wish, or leave me alone."

I gazed at his oily, fishy face. "How do I know you're telling me the truth?" I said. "Why should I trust a thing you say?"

He snorted with contempt. "It is always the same. The questions, every time." He unclipped his earrings and polished them on his scaly vest. "I am not permitted to speak untruths to my master."

Oh ho! Excellent!

"So, every word you tell me is true?" I said. "You're not allowed to deceive me?"

"I cannot speak an untruth to you."

I smiled. I knew the difference between not telling a lie and not deceiving someone. I'd have to keep a close eye on Mermeros.

"If I could lie to you," he said, "why would I tell you I can grant your wishes, and then do it?"

I laughed. "You have an excellent point," I said. "You wouldn't do anything nice for me unless you had to. You're not exactly flowing with the milk of human kindness."

He scowled and wiped his arms and shoulders briskly, as if there might be some sticky milk of human kindness dripping there.

There was something else I needed to know, and judging from Mermeros's nature, there was one sure way to get the information out of him. His pride. A bully's a bully, green or not.

"How do I know you've got the power to grant *any* wish I might demand?" I said. "There must be limits to what you can do."

A thundering growl reverberated from Mermeros's chest. Off in the remote corners of the cellar I heard scuttling, shuffling sounds. Probably mice fleeing in terror.

He flung out his hands. A roiling globe of water appeared above his right hand, with a whirlpool snaking its way through it. Waves lashed, and ocean water sprayed my face. I saw ships—Phoenician galleys and Greek triremes, with rows of slaves tugging desperately at the oars—tipping to their doom in Mermeros's maelstrom.

In his other hand, the djinni had conjured a globe of fire. And not just fire—liquid fire, seething with chunks of melting rock. Lava! He held a volcanic eruption in his hand. I peered closer, despite the heat blasting my face, and saw whole villages and cities engulfed, forests of trees sizzling like matchsticks.

Mermeros's green eyes blazed with fury. With a mighty heave, he crashed the two globes together. An explosion of steam blasted me back onto my cot, but once again, I was not injured by the heat. When I rubbed the damp and the debris out of my eyes, Mermeros was still there, but turned away from me, with his arms crossed over his chest like a pouting child.

The show-off.

I know how to handle their kind.

"That was impressive, Mermeros."

He cocked his head but said nothing. His back was still toward me.

"Your power," I cooed. "It's beyond all imagining."

Slowly, slowly, he rotated in midair until he could see my face. He still kept his lower lip thrust out in sullen indifference, but I knew I had his attention.

"Have you always been a djinni? Will you always be one?"

He took a little flask from his waistband and uncorked it, then shook a few slugs of thick fluid into the palm of his hand. He began rubbing himself all over with the ointment. It reeked of eucalyptus. I wondered if lady djinnis liked that sort of thing.

"Well?"

"No, and no," he said.

"No and no what?"

He glopped the stuff right on his shiny bald head. "No, I was not born a *djinni*. I was born a prince in an empire of such splendor and majesty that a common little female hatchling like you could never begin to fathom it."

I was too busy thinking about his second "no" to take notice of the insult.

"Then who turned you into a djinni?"

This question, I could tell, had awoken a sleeping monster inside his memories. "A sorcerer," he finally said. I had the feeling he wasn't telling me the whole truth, but the look in his eyes made me let it pass.

"Will you someday cease to be a djinni?"

"When the world ends."

"So, basically, never, then."

His bushy eyebrows rose expressively. "Stupid hatchling."

I thought of the globes of fire and water colliding and extinguishing each other, and decided not to press this point further. It was not a comfortable thought.

"You mentioned brothers. How many do you have? Are you the oldest, youngest, or middle?"

He snorted. "After five thousand years, it scarcely matters."

I waited.

He turned to face me again. "I have two brothers. They were born before me."

I nodded. "Once the youngest, always the youngest. I've got three older sisters, and I know."

Mermeros tucked his vial of ointment back into the sash around his waist. "You know nothing. When will your weak female brain understand at least that? *You know nothing.*"

I jumped up off my cot and looked him in the eye. "I know a lot more than I knew before about djinnis and wishes. So there."

A wicked light gleamed in his eyes. "Here is what you do not know," he said in a voice of velvet that made my flesh crawl. "Your wishes will destroy you."

I laughed. "You're mad."

His eyes shone with a toxic light. "They will be your undoing. Before you're done, your spirit will beg you to release me, but you won't be able to let go. Greed will take hold. Gold lust will consume you. It will infiltrate you like a cancer until it owns you, body and soul, and drives you to madness and ruin."

I took a deep breath, and then another. The hot retort I wanted to make seemed stuck on my lips, and my heart pounded in my chest. Goodness knew why. He was babbling nonsense, so, why should I care?

Finally, I composed myself and confronted the djinni.

"You don't know me, if you think that'll be my fate," I said. "You don't know me at all. You don't even know my name. I'd never be so stupid as to let wishes turn me into someone else—someone greedy and horrible. I can see how it might happen to others, but it won't ever happen to me."

Mermeros's smile stretched from one green ear to another. With a hiss like air escaping from a rubber balloon, he deflated in size and poured himself back into his sardine tin.

"That," he said, "is what they all say."

He uncurled the lid over himself tightly, and sealed it with a little *ping*. The loose metal key shot to the edge of the tin and squirmed underneath until it, too, pinged into place.

Mermeros was back in his sardine tin, with nothing but his thoughts to occupy him.

I sat on my cot in the darkening cellar, alone with my own thoughts as well.

CHAPTER
9

*G*old lust will consume you.

Madness and ruin.

Mermeros's words echoed in my ears. My tongue felt as though I'd just tasted foul medicine.

Greed? Madness? Ruin? Balderdash. This was *me*.

Gold lust? My mother would suspect it was a dirty word. She, in her way, was the queen of gold lust, always hinting that Daddy ought to be earning more money. Greed comes in all sizes.

But not *Maeve* sizes.

It wouldn't be so. I wouldn't let it be so. Neither wishes nor any other thing could make me become something I didn't want to be.

But that look in his eyes...

After so many years of past experience, could he, in fact, see the future?

Should I, perhaps, just bury that sardine tin somewhere no one would ever find it and go on with my old life? Submit to stuffy Miss

Salamanca and stuck-up Theresa? Appease my family by behaving
like a priggish, boring young lady should?

No.

No, no, no!

I had found a *djinni*.

Out of all the swarms of people in London, in Britain, in the
entire world, *I* had found a djinni. Me, Maeve. Me! How could I give
up a truly one-in-a-million chance like this?

I had two wishes left, and I'd use them well. I'd wish myself into
a life of freedom and adventure, the likes of which no British girl had
ever known. I'd travel the world and live by my own rules for what
young women could say, and play, and wear. And I wouldn't sell my
soul in the process, no matter what Old Greenskin had to say about it.

I nodded. Defiantly. In a dark cellar, with no one watching. Take
that, Mermeros.

Mermeros. Now there was a mystery for you. I tried to remember
all that I'd learned about him. Youngest of three brothers. Born a
prince of an empire of splendor and majesty. Turned into a djinni by
a sorcerer. *What did you do, Mermeros, to anger a sorcerer?* Judging from
his charming personality, probably quite a lot.

Let's see, what else did I know about him? He said he was five
thousand years old. Egads. Did that make him the oldest creature
on the planet? It must! Unless there were lots of other djinnis. He'd

witnessed most of human history go scrolling by. Empires rising and falling.

What had he said? *An empire of splendor and majesty.*

There must be pots of buried treasure near the tombs or the ruins of his ancient palace. The newspapers were full of stories of explorers digging up priceless antiquities from the ancient world in archaeological digs in far-off places.

Maybe there were other ways to find the fortune that would pay for my dreams besides just wishing for it. Wishing for money felt dull compared to wishing to be led to an ancient fortune.

Besides, I wanted to know more about Mermeros. Born a prince, made a djinni, given incredible power, and fated to live until the world's end.

You're a story yourself, Mermeros, I thought, patting the sardine can. *A story I plan to read. While I raid your ancestors' tombs. Which would just serve you right.*

But when?

Not just yet. It needed planning. But soon. Very soon.

And now what?

Time slithered on like a maggot on a cabbage leaf. It was going to be a long night. And I was much too fidgety to sleep.

I decided to investigate the nearest window. I found some old crates nearby that seemed sturdy enough for me to stand upon and climbed up to inspect the window. It was firmly secured by iron bars on the inside. Apparently, I was not the first girl to be imprisoned here. I moved on to another window and found the same thing. No escape.

Rattling the bars and casements, I didn't notice the noise at first. Then a horrid rustling, snuffling sound reached my ears. I turned. Right there on my cot was a gigantic rat! Its fangs gleamed wet under its pointy snout, and its ghastly yellow tail whipped this way and that. It had made short, crumbly work of my stale bread and was now gnawing on my lolly.

I jumped. My crate collapsed. The rat hissed. I twisted my ankle. Worst of all, I screamed.

I *loathe* rats.

A second rat jumped up on my cot and seized my lolly from the first. I froze, trapped in the skeleton of the wooden crate, and watched the rats claw and snap at each other over my sweets. Perhaps, I thought, if I stayed motionless, they'd creep off after a time, after they'd gotten all that could be eaten, and they'd leave me alone.

They waged a squeaky, bloody war over my lollipop. One knocked the other off the cot, then nosed through my handkerchief of belongings and noticed the sardine can. Before I could scream a second time, it seized the tin in its frightful jaws and waddled off into the blackness with it.

No!

What I'd give for my cricket bat. And a lamp. And a hungry stray cat. Could I actually chase after that loathsome, scuttling rat and seize my sardines back? No telling where the rat might burrow away with my tin. I shuddered. What might it do to me with those claws and fangs?

Had rats ever killed people? I was sure I'd heard stories of rats attacking prisoners.

But my wishes! My cricket team, my Grand World Tour, spirited away between a rat's teeth!

I had no time to spare. I kicked the broken crate away from my feet, grabbed a sturdy spar off its bent frame, and followed the rats into the dark.

I couldn't see. I heard their scratchy claws, crunching on the moldy cellar floor. The dark was suffocating.

Something brushed against my leg. I swung my makeshift bat.

An unnatural cry split the darkness. Like a wailing ghost.

I dropped my bat. The rats squealed.

Something whooshed in front of me. I felt it rather than saw it. I cowered, covering my face with my arms.

Something clattered to the floor. Something small, solid, and metal.

My sardines! I groped around on the filthy floor, searching for the tin. Instead, my fingers found greasy rat fur. I gasped.

Rat fur that wasn't going anywhere. A dead rat. Still warm.

I fought back an urge to retch, wiped my hands on my skirt, took a deep breath, and plunged onward.

A spark of dim light wavered across the floor. I turned. Behind me, a safety match flickered. A face appeared in the gloom, and then a candle.

It was Tom, the orphan boy. And before me, ripping shreds of its dinner off a warm rat carcass, was a huge gray owl.

CHAPTER
10

Tom. *What was he doing here? How did he get in?*

After Mermeros, no doubt.

I turned in a panic and scrambled across the filthy floor for the sardine tin. The light of Tom's approaching candle gleamed off something. It was my tin, all right—pinned into place under the owl's ferocious, taloned claw. The creature had claimed it like a prize.

I'd seen stuffed owls lots of times in people's parlors. But I'd never seen a live one. Its great eyes blinked at me, but what I stared at most was the deadly curve of its beak.

I sidled away, seized my wooden spar, and rose to face Tom.

"What are you doing here?" I demanded.

Tom's eyebrows rose. "What are *you* doing here?" He gestured toward my cot and disheveled things. "New bedroom?"

I was too angry to answer, and too worried about my sardine tin. I knew that was why he'd come. To lose my wishes to one rat, and now another! Not today, thank you.

When I said nothing, Tom knelt and made a clucking sound toward the owl. "I see you've met Morris."

The great bird swiveled its head toward Tom, then began the oddest ungainly hops and shuffles toward him. He bounced on his feet and flapped one wing while the other dragged behind him on the ground. Several long pinions were missing from the dragging wing.

As soon as he was off my sardine tin and a safe distance away, I darted for my prize and wrapped my fingers tightly around it.

"Morris?" I asked.

Tom pulled a packet from his coat and offered something to the great bird. Whatever it was, the owl found fresh rat more tempting. "For the little Morris dance he does to move about."

I wouldn't say so much to Tom, but that was a clever name. We had our own Morris dances in Luton at Whitsun Fair time. I loved seeing the dancers, all in white, hopping and skipping about in unison, waving their handkerchiefs.

Morris the owl only waved a rat's tail from its beak. Ugh.

"How did you get down here?" I asked Tom.

He seemed reluctant to answer, then pointed to the rear of the cavernous cellar. "Through the back door. Figured out how to pick the lock last summer when we found Morris."

I squinted into the darkness. "We?"

"My mate Jack and me. From the home. We found Morris in the park. He was young and had broken his wing. He would've died."

I turned to look at the owl once more. He swallowed the rat's tail in one gulp, and blinked at me.

"How does Miss Salamanca not know there's an owl down here?"

Tom grinned. "Nobody comes down here much," he said. "For the most part, Morris is pretty quiet."

"So, you and Jack come down here to take care of him?"

Tom shook his head. "Jack's gone. Went to work in a cotton mill up north."

"A free man, eh?"

His expression was grim. "That's where they send all of us once we've hit fifteen," he said. "They come each season for their new shipment of orphan lads."

Shipment. Like livestock. I remembered, then, my father speaking of conditions in those mills. Workers toiling from early in the morning till late at night, year-round, healthy or sick, with only Sundays to rest. He said they often employed children, and barely paid them enough for food and the roughest housing. The air was so full of fluff that many of them took sick in the lungs at a terribly young age.

A cold current of air brushed over me from the open door. "How old are you, Tom?" I asked.

Candlelight flickered over his face, throwing deep shadows under his nose and eyebrows. "Fourteen."

Only a year older than me, yet not much time left. I didn't know what to say.

"Are they punishing you?" Tom asked. "Is that why you're down here?"

I nodded. There was no point denying it.

"And is it because of…"

"They punish me all the time." I didn't want to talk about sticking my neck out to help him. That might make Tom think we were friends. We were *not* friends. We were rivals. Rivals for Mermeros, who was now safely back in my hand, thanks to Morris the owl.

I went back to my cot, set it up straight again, and sat on it, trying not to think about the rats that had just battled there. Tom knelt and poured the contents of a canteen into a flat dish I hadn't seen. As he did so, I slipped my sardine tin underneath my skirts.

"Is that for Morris to drink?" I asked.

Tom shook his head. "He likes to have a splash now and then," he said. "Owls get their water from the blood of their prey. We didn't know when we chose this place to hide him just how well he'd fare on all the rats here."

"I wish he'd pick up the pace," I said. "There are still too many rats here for my liking."

Tom screwed the cap back on his canteen and rose. "Funny finding you here," he said. "I was just going to stop down here and feed Morris, then go and wait for you in your back gardens."

I turned away. "You would have had a long wait," I said. "Even if I wasn't stuck down here, I wouldn't have come. Why should I?"

Tom grinned. "You'd've come."

In truth, I probably would have, but I didn't like admitting it. "Why should I?"

Tom sat down on the dirty cellar floor and clucked at Morris. The owl hopped over to him and perched upon his knee. It seemed as if those talons should have pierced Tom's leg awfully. But maybe there wasn't enough flesh on that long, skinny frame to feel the sharpness. Tom dripped a few wax drops onto the floor, then jammed his candle into the puddle.

"What's your name, then?" he said.

I'd forgotten he didn't know. "Maeve," I said. "Maeve Merritt."

"Maeve," he repeated, trying out the sound. He stroked Morris's back with one long finger. "Well, Maeve, I have a proposal for you."

"Not interested."

"I propose," said Tom, "a truce."

I waited. That self-assured expression on his face needed a wallop, I thought, but I had to play fair. No punching until truly provoked. "I'm listening."

"Good." He took off his cap. Even in the darkness, the candle-light shone off his flaming red hair. "Now, here's what I figure. You've got a djinni."

"A brilliant observation."

"That means you get three wishes. Everyone knows that's how it works."

"You seem awfully sure of yourself."

"Well, isn't that how it works?"

No point in picking a fight over this. "Yes."

He nodded. "And how many have you used?"

"Why should I tell you that?"

He held up his hands. "Never mind. Let's say you haven't used any of them yet. Let's say you've got three left. Now, I told you I was going to try to steal your djinni. But why do that? It's hardly sporting. Why be enemies?"

There was nobody I trusted less than an enemy suggesting friendship.

"Here's what I say. You share your three wishes with me—"

"What?" I knew it. The greedy mongrel. "Not a chance!"

"Share your wishes with me," he persisted, "by letting me come along on your adventures. Then, when your wishes are used up, you give the djinni to me, and I'll share my adventures with you."

I stared at him.

"That way, it's like we each get six wishes. Allies instead of enemies."

Morris hooted softly. He seemed to like Tom stroking his back.

"What do you say?"

Sharing wishes? This would keep Tom from sneaking around me all the time, trying to steal my sardine can. *If* he meant it. *If* he was sincere.

He seemed like he was. After all, if he wanted to rob me, he could've easily tried already. We were alone here in the cellar. He had the advantage of size, knowledge of the surroundings, and a candle.

But I couldn't give him Mermeros when I was done with him, because after my third wish, he'd disappear to who-knows-where. I couldn't make this promise, even if I wanted to.

But Tom didn't know that.

Hmm.

I needed to stall for time. "What makes you think I'll be wishing for adventures?" I said. "How d'you know I won't wish for...dresses and things?"

Tom laughed. It erased his sneering expression. "Girl like you? I doubt it."

I sat up straighter. "What do you mean, a girl like me?"

He was still laughing. "You know what they call you across the street?"

My fists were forming already. "What do they call me?"

"Fast-bowl Franny."

I jumped up off my cot. "They *what*? Show me who dares to call me that!"

Tom pantomimed a pitch. "The lads say that if you knew how to play cricket, you'd be a mighty fine bowler."

"Oh." I sat back down. They must've seen me throw a ball around here and there at recess. Before Miss Rosewater forbade it for being unladylike. *Fast-bowl Franny*, eh? I'd fast-bowl their wet-nosed noggins and show them a thing or two.

"So, I have a cricket arm. So what?"

Tom pulled out his little pouch and offered it to me. "Licorice?"

I bristled. "You've got a lot of nerve, offering me my own licorice, you villain!"

He only laughed. "I reckon I do."

I took a length of licorice and bit into it. "Is that what you fed the owl?"

He popped a piece between his teeth. "Morris loves licorice."

I chewed on mine. It was a good, hard, sticky one. Polly knows what I like.

"I'm right, aren't I?"

I sucked hard on the licorice to free up my stuck-together teeth. "Right about what?"

Tom popped another candy. "About you, and dresses. And adventures."

I said nothing. I might hate dresses, but I didn't like strange boys deciding I was a girl who hated dresses.

He smiled. "That's why I think we should be partners."

"*I* think you're impertinent," I said. "I've only barely met you, and you've already threatened to steal my djinni. You *did* steal my licorice. Now you want me to take you on as a partner? I don't know where you get your nerve."

Tom watched me with the same steady gaze as his owl. Maddening boy! He seemed to think he had all the time in the world to wait, and every confidence that I'd agree with him.

In fact, his proposal was an interesting one. I had everything to gain by bringing him into my wishes, and nothing to lose. Except my conscience. If I made him my partner, it'd be easier to keep an eye on him. And he might turn out to be useful. Already he'd proved himself to be watchful, daring, and good at getting in and out of places.

There was just one problem. I couldn't promise to give the djinni to him when I was done with my wishes. Mermeros had made it clear—the spell that bound him didn't work that way. When my last wish was done, Mermeros would vanish and magically reappear in some other place, perhaps halfway around the world. Perhaps he'd occupy a teapot in a China, or a chamber pot in America. That would serve him right, the arrogant old sardine.

But, again, Tom didn't know that. And if he thought we had this deal going, he'd stop trying to rob me.

That's not sporting, Maeve, said the little voice in my head that tries to ruin all my fun.

But what did "sporting" have to do with djinnis? If I didn't agree to the boy's deal, he'd probably rob me of Mermeros here and now.

What should I say to this persistent orphan boy?

I decided to put off answering.

"I'm not promising anything," I said at last. "But I will take you on my next adventure. Whenever that should be. Which I haven't decided yet."

Tom eased Morris onto his shoulder, then rose, and held out his hand. I got up and shook his. It all felt so solemn somehow and, therefore, quite ridiculous.

"Why not now?"

CHAPTER
11

"Y ou're mad!" I cried.

Tom grinned. "Nothing of the sort."

I remembered my sardine tin, lying on the cot in plain sight, and sat back down in a hurry.

"I'm not wasting a wish on a flighty impulse," I said. "Three's all I get. I have some very specific goals in mind, and I aim to use my wishes well. There's no getting them back."

He rubbed his hands together. "No, but tonight you've doubled your measure of wishes. That's nearly as good."

I hadn't said that. I hadn't agreed to exactly that. But that's how he understood the bargain. Oh, dear. If I corrected him, the battle would be on again.

You're on very spongy soil here, said my nagging inner voice. Such a killjoy.

Morris began nosing his beak through Tom's hair, as though he thought he might find a tasty mouse hidden inside. Tom didn't even seem to notice.

His eyes grew wide with excitement. "Why don't you get your friend?" he said. "The girl who shares your room? Bring her along, too. You trust her. I can tell you do. She can join the club. Then, when my wishes are done, I'll pass the djinni along to her! It'll be like we each get nine wishes."

"The girl who *shares my room*!" I fumed. "You can *tell* that I trust her? What, do you know everything about me? Have you followed me home to meet my parents, too?"

I thought I saw the faintest flicker of his eyelids then—a sort of twitch, when I mentioned parents. I could've kicked myself in the shins for such a thoughtless slip. I may not trust the sardine-and-licorice robber, but for pity's sake, he *was* an orphan.

The flinch, if there was one, vanished. "Your bedroom window is in good view from my dormitory," Tom said.

"I'll thank you not to spy on me!"

"Close your curtains more often... Ow, Morris!"

The owl had tweaked him in the ear. Tom decided he was done carrying him around on his shoulder like Long John Silver's parrot, and slid him off onto my cot. The bird hobbled back and forth between his left and right feet, then hunkered down with his head low between his shoulders. Time for an owl nap. My cot had become his, apparently. At least he should keep the rats away for a while.

Tom grabbed his candle from the floor, then seized my hand and dragged me toward the rear of the cellar. I pulled away from him and retrieved my little bundle of belongings, including the sardine tin, then followed along after him. He took my hand again and steered me through the dark, cluttered cellar. Tom's hand was wiry and tough, covered with calluses. My past experience with boys' hands was limited to times when their knuckles were plastered across my jaw.

Church bells rang out nine o'clock as we emerged out from the outside cellar door, which Tom had pried open, and up the stairs to street level. Only Miss Salamanca's bedroom windows showed any light. Through the blinds, I saw her silhouetted form bent over her writing desk. No doubt she was writing the seventh draft of an apologetic letter to Mr. Treazleton. Or perhaps she was writing shabby romantic poetry. What if she was writing shabby romantic poems intended *for* Mr. Treazleton? Now there was a tantalizing thought.

"Put out your candle or Miss Salamanca will see us," I whispered. Tom snuffed the wick between his finger and thumb.

A ghostly glow surrounded each streetlamp in the cloudy, damp night. The city itself seemed draped in a gray fleece of window-lit fog. I would have preferred a blacker night, but it couldn't be helped.

"There's my window." I pointed to one on the second story. "Alice has turned the light off. She's probably asleep already."

"I know it's your window, silly," said Tom. "I climbed that downspout pipe when I left you a note." He indicated the long iron pipe that siphoned rainwater off the roof and away from the house. I had never noticed before how close it ran to my bedroom window. "Shall I climb up and tell her to come down?"

I tied my bundle of things securely inside my handkerchief and cinched the bundle to my waist. "Don't be daft," I said. "If you poke your head in our bedroom window, Alice will scream for half of London to hear. Leave this to me." I seized the drainpipe and examined the brick wall for toeholds.

I'd climbed ropes and poles back home well enough, but then I could wrap my legs and feet around and hold on. Here, I'd have only my fingers to grab the pipe and only my toes to jam into the gaps between bricks.

Suddenly, the second story looked awfully high up.

I could feel Tom's eyes watching me. I wouldn't let him see me hesitate. I grasped the pipe and hoisted myself a foot or so off the ground.

The pipe shifted slightly. I could feel it straining against the brackets holding it in place. My toes found a gap, and I exhaled in deep relief.

"You sure you want to do this?" said Tom.

"Quiet," I hissed. "Less of your chatter."

"I'm not chattering."

I ventured one hand higher up the pipe. "Shut up!"

The light from Miss Salamanca's bedroom window cast a weak glow upon my exploits. We could *not* afford to risk making noise that she might hear.

I climbed another arm's length, and then another. Each time, just as I thought surely my fingers would give out, my feet found a place to hold on. With each victory my confidence rose. Better still, the windowsill drew closer and closer.

I managed to peek down and see Tom watching me intently. I was now directly above him.

"Look away, pig," I called, but softly. "I'm in skirts."

He snorted in disgust and looked away. "I wasn't looking at you."

"Yes, you were."

"Not like that!"

"Shh!"

I knew he wasn't, in fact. But I had to make a firm point of where I stood. Once a boy named Alphonse back in Luton made the mistake of thinking I was fond of him because I praised his cricket batting, and tried to catch me unaware and kiss me after church. I gave him a whack on his shins for it, and he steered clear after that. In case this Tom was another Alphonse, I felt it best to put him on alert.

My fingers were burning and my arm muscles screaming by the time I reached our bedroom window, but reach it I did. Opening it would be another tricky matter, as I had to lean over just a bit too far for comfort to raise the sash. The sash didn't want to be raised. Alice must have thrown the lock. Of course she did, after Tom left his note on my bed. Everything was his fault! If he hadn't poked his flaming-red head into my business, I'd be fast asleep tonight in my soft, warm bed, dreaming of my next wish.

I made one last attempt to raise the sash and nearly toppled off the drainpipe. I righted myself and clung tight while I tried to catch my breath. I could hear Tom's feet shuffling down below. Did the idiot think he could catch me if I fell?

I took a desperate chance. I leaned over and tapped gently on the windowpane. *Tap, tap, tap.*

I waited.

A spark of light appeared inside the room. Good. Alice was awake, though probably terrified. Poor girl. She was the sort of person who always had safety matches and a candle within reach.

Tap, tap, tap. I prayed she wouldn't scream.

Her face appeared in the window. She held her candle close to the glass and squinted out at me. I had a lovely view of her nostrils while I waited for her to figure out what she was seeing. Her mouth formed a great O, and she set down her candle and fumbled with the window. Wood against wood squealed terribly when the sash rose.

"Maeve!" Alice whispered. "*What* are you *doing*?"

"Hush, and help me in," I said. "I can explain."

Alice leaned out the window and reached for me with both arms. "You'll break your neck! Is that a boy down there?"

I gripped her forearm tightly with one hand, then took a leap of faith and grabbed at her with my other hand. Alice didn't weigh much. I swung out in her grip underneath the window.

She gasped as she felt my full weight.

"Brace yourself!" I cried. "Lean against the wall!"

My toes found a foothold in the brick, and I climbed slowly up the outer wall, until Alice had pulled my hands inside the window and I could rest my elbows on the sill.

There was another squeal of wood against wood. I twisted my neck to see Miss Salamanca, in her nightcap, tugging her bedroom window open.

"Pull me in!" I whispered. "Snuff the candle!"

"You! Orphan boy!" cried Miss Salamanca. "What are you doing loitering about? Begone with you. Your masters will hear about this!"

Alice gritted her teeth and made a mighty heave. I tumbled through the window and toppled onto her, where she'd collapsed onto the floor.

"Constable!" came Miss Salamanca's voice from below. "A vagrant orphan is menacing and spying on my sleeping students!"

What rubbish. I crawled to the window and peeped over the sill, just enough to see Tom running off through the dark alleyway that separated our building from his. A police whistle blew, and a stout officer took off loping after Tom.

I reached up and carefully, slowly pulled our bedroom window shut. So much for tonight's wish. I'd gone to all that trouble to escape for nothing. Now I'd have to find my way back to the cellar without getting caught.

Tom was on his own, but I had a feeling he'd manage. The headmistress couldn't have seen his face, could she? Not well, anyway. I owed him one, I supposed. Miss Salamanca was too busy noticing him to see what I'd been up to, one story up.

Which made twice today—first Mr. Treazleton's horse and footman, and now this window incident—that Tom had taken the blame for something he hadn't done.

How convenient it was, having orphans and beggars and foreigners in London. There was always someone lower down the ladder whom we could punish for fun and force, when needed, to carry our guilt.

CHAPTER 12

W hat were you thinking, Maeve?" Alice chided me. "You could have been killed, and at the rate you're going, you're almost certain to be expelled."

Lying in bed felt heavenly, especially in a bed that was one hundred percent devoid of rats.

"I know you probably wouldn't mind leaving this school," Alice went on, "but I would miss you terribly. If I can't be at home with my grandparents, you're the only thing making this wretched place bearable."

I smiled in the darkness. "Alice Bromley, you are much too good a soul. I don't deserve you as a friend."

Alice sniffed. "I wish you wouldn't say I'm so good all the time. It makes me uncomfortable. You just don't know." She hesitated. "I'm capable of extremely wicked thoughts."

I rolled over on one side. "Such as?"

I could hear her breathing quicken. "One time," she whispered,

"Miss Guntherson received a letter from a gentleman. The delivery came during class. She sat reading it at her desk when we were supposed to be working out our conjugations. Then Miss Rosewater called her out of the room for some urgent matter, so Miss Guntherson dismissed us early for recess. I lingered behind, and when the other girls had left the room, I wandered over to her desk and came *extremely close* to reading her letter."

I had to stuff my pillow over my face to muffle my laughter.

"Oh, you're wicked," I snorted. "Positively evil."

Alice sounded offended. "Just because I don't punch people like you do doesn't mean I'm always good."

"You'll never convince me, Alice," I said. "Your story rings false on many levels. For one thing, there's no man alive that would write a letter to Miss Guntherson."

"That's not nice. Although...I did get close enough to see the envelope was also signed 'Guntherson.' So, it must have been from a relative."

I could feel sleep starting to tingle throughout my toes. After such a day as this, surely I could just stay there. Couldn't I? I didn't bother with a nightdress, but settled down comfortably under my sheets and blankets.

"Good night, Alice."

"Good night, Maeve."

I lay in the dark, drifting off to sleep, planning my next wish. As for the timing, when to do it, I figured I'd just have to bide my time and wait for the right opportunity. When it appeared, I would know.

I don't know how long I'd slept—some hours, surely—when sounds roused me. I sat up in bed.

"What's that?" Alice fumbled for, then lit, another match.

I threw back my bedclothes and hurried to the window.

Sure enough, there was Tom. I opened the window and pulled Tom in.

"You can't let him in here, Maeve!" Alice hissed. She dove for her robe. "A boy in our *room*? We just can't!"

"It's all right, Alice." I heaved Tom in through the casement. "He's my friend."

It was too late to unsay it. I saw Tom grin. Well, that was it, then. In my book, once you call someone friend, you stick with it forever. Unless they turn out to be a Theresa Treazleton or a kissing Alphonse. I'm loyal, but even my loyalty has its limits.

"What time is it?" I said, still shaking off my heavy sleep.

"Four in the morning," Tom said. "More or less."

I stared at him. He seemed offensively wide awake, and cheerful. Alice, on the other hand, looked like the living dead, and doubly so for her horror at this most unwelcome intrusion.

"Who?" she stammered. "What? How?"

Of course! Alice knew nothing about Tom. I'd had no chance to explain anything to her.

"My name's Tom," our visitor said, offering a hand to Alice. She had shrunk back away from him, but after a moment's pause, her politeness won out over her fear.

She shook his hand. "I'm Alice."

He grinned. "You can call me Tommy."

So, he came back. I wondered if he'd slept at all. And now here we were together, with hours to go before anyone might notice us missing.

The time I'd be waiting for was now.

"You have Tommy to thank for insisting that we all go on this adventure together," I told Alice, just to make conversation. Alice looked deeply unsure if that was cause for thanks or not.

"We're going on an adventure?" Alice stammered. "At four in the morning? With a *boy*?"

Tom rubbed his hands together, then pulled a small pack off his back. "Well, where to, then, Maeve?" He emptied the contents of his pack onto the floor. Out tumbled a length of rope, a knife, candles, matches, and the canteen of water he'd used before. "I stopped back at the home to get some supplies for our trip. You never know what you might need."

"You move in and out of there awfully easily," I said. "Aren't there headmasters or wardens who enforce the rules? Haven't you got a curfew?"

Tom laughed, and Alice shushed him.

He answered in a repentant whisper. "Our bailiff, he's drunk most nights. The headmaster, he's a mean old goat, but he sleeps downstairs, clear on the other side of the building. I have a secret way out through the garret and off the roof. It's not hard for me to get in and out when I want."

"And what about the other boys?" I said. "Do they come and go as much?"

Tom shook his head. "Some, but not as much. They're afraid of getting whipped."

I thought of Mr. Treazleton's driver and his whip. "Aren't you?"

"No," Tom said, a little too quickly. "No, I'm not afraid."

Alice watched Tom thoughtfully. "Oh, dear," she said, "I suppose I should change my clothes, shouldn't I, if we're going on an adventure? Where are we going?"

I took a deep breath. Was I really going through with my plan? Should I wait for something better? Then again, some people waited their lives away. I, Maeve Merritt, wasn't one of them. I had a plan, and I knew just the place for it.

"I know where we are going," I said, "but I don't know where we'll arrive."

Alice's face grew pale. "Oh, Maeve... I don't like the sound of this..."

"Put on your everyday school clothes," I instructed, "and a hat and coat. Do you see my hat in the closet?"

Alice passed out the hats, and then Tom sat facing a far corner—a quite unnecessary precaution—while Alice dressed inside our closet, in the dark, with the door shut.

I instructed her not to put her shoes on, and she nearly abandoned the expedition for that scandal alone. She would not venture to parts unknown without shoes. And for a young man to see her stockinged feet!

"You must have had one gargoyle of a governess growing up, Alice," I whispered. "You worry about far too many things. Bring your shoes along—see, Tom and I are carrying ours. We're just tiptoeing down the hall to go outside. I don't dare summon Mermeros in here. I don't trust him not to wake the other girls."

"Mermeros?" Tom's eyes gleamed. "Is that the djinni's name?"

I gripped the pouch tied to my belt a little tighter. "It's only a name," I said. "It'd make no difference if he was Bill."

Alice insisted on tiptoeing behind me, with me following Tom, as we crept down the hallway, hugging the wall where the less-squeaky floorboards were. Tom didn't know his way around the building, but at least he would be less able to turn around and spy her immodest feet. I adored Alice, but, at times like this, I could throttle her.

The floors still squeaked more than I'd have liked, but we made it down the back stairs and into the kitchen. This, I knew, was risky, for Mrs. Gruboil was fond of her midnight sandwich and cider. Though probably not at four in the morning. Still, she always believed the students were determined to rob her larder. We saw no lights and risked a passage through. I reached for the latch to the kitchen door, but Tom put out a blockading arm and stopped me. From inside his sack, he retrieved a small flask, the kind some men use to keep liquor in their pockets. I sincerely hoped this wild orphan boy wasn't a very young drunk. He unstoppered the flask and dripped a few drops of liquid onto the door's hinges, and another drop onto the latch.

"What's that?" I whispered.

"Oil," he replied. "An escapist never travels without it."

I was impressed. An escapist! It paid to have friends with professional skills. I did wonder, though, where a poor orphan boy came across such useful tools.

After a few experimental wiggles back and forth, Tom swung open the kitchen door soundlessly, and the night's chill air shocked our faces. We pulled the door shut and listened for the latch to click. Then, ducking low, we stuffed our feet into our shoes and fled away on the balls of our feet, until Miss Salamanca's School for Upright Young Ladies was far behind us.

In no time, we reached the rear of the shuttered mansion behind us on our city block. The towering old pile had always fascinated me, from the moment I arrived at school. What secrets must it hold? I'd never been, but I'd long ago decided I needed to explore it. Tonight, it would be our hideaway.

By what lamplight there was to guide us, it was plain to see that this once-grand home had suffered greatly from neglect. Paint chipped off the windowsills and trim. Pavement stones were missing from the walks to the kitchen door, and dead, frozen weeds poked through.

Tom waved us toward a window. Gingerly, he loosened a glass pane that dangled in its trim, just enough to snake his fingers in and slide open the sash lock. He hoisted the window up and beckoned for me to climb inside.

Alice scanned the perimeter fretfully, but no constables appeared to thwart us.

I landed in the gloomy kitchen and beckoned for Alice to follow. She clambered her way in with Tom's help and mine, then Tom vaulted in after us and pulled the window shut.

He lit his candle and led us through a maze of spooky corridors and cobwebs to a grand gallery. Footsteps echoed differently here, reverberating back from far away and high above. Tom's speck of candlelight spread thinly through the giant space, but he moved quickly from one wall sconce to the next, lighting candles that illuminated the room, section by section.

Dusty red velvet drapes obscured the floor-to-ceiling windows and hid our presence from prying eyes outside. A checkerboard of vast black-and-white marble floor tiles stretched before us down the long, vaulted gallery. The ceilings and pillars were encrusted with plaster moldings of angels and fruits and flowers, and lining the walls were drab, dusty rectangles where huge portraits and paintings once had hung. It felt magical and grand, and terribly sad, all at the same time.

"Why have you brought us here?" Alice whispered.

"Oh, I go everywhere," Tom said. "Explore everything. An empty place like this? It's my palace, now. And it seemed like the right sort of place to begin a high adventure, don't you think?" He sat down on the floor and crossed his legs. "Right, then. Maeve, let's see your djinni."

My pulse quickened and my stomach flopped. Time to unveil Mermeros and spend Wish Number Two. I hoped I'd get it right.

I pulled the Sultana's Exotic Sardines tin from my makeshift pouch and held it, trying to rehearse to myself the best way to phrase my wish. The can leaped and quivered in my palm.

"That's it?" Tom cried. "Your djinni lives in a *sardine can*?"

"What, don't you believe me?" I said. "You've seen him yourself."

I tugged the key off the tin, fitted it over the tab, and cranked with a vengeance, and Mermeros ballooned into life on a spume of foul, mustard vapor. I took great satisfaction in watching Tom gape at him. And cough at his stench.

Mermeros rolled his eyes at the sight of me.

"Still you?" he said.

"Lucky for us both," I said.

He swam through the air, looming close to Tom, then Alice. For Alice's benefit, he bared his vicious teeth and bulged his eyes out gruesomely.

Alice screamed and darted behind a pillar.

"You stop that!" I cried. "If you want to pick on someone, pick on me."

"Don't tempt me, Hatchling Girl," he said. "Well, well." He took a lazy look around the mansion gallery. "So, it's to be a party for the babies, and I'm invited? I can't remember when I've been so favored. Will there be sugared dates?"

Tom stared at me in complete bewilderment. "What does he mean?" he whispered. "Babies? Sugared dates?"

"Never mind him," I told Tom. "He's a shark in sardine's clothing. Alice, it's all right. Mermeros won't hurt you. Come out."

Alice didn't budge.

"Come back," I pleaded. "Look at him some more. He's an ugly old fish, but once you get used to the sight of him, you won't be afraid."

From somewhere inside his vest, Mermeros produced a long, thin, silver blade with an elaborate handle. He rolled back his fishy lips and began picking at the gaps in his teeth with the sinister blade. At the very moment, Alice peeked her head around the pillar: there he was, with his great head thrown back, razor fangs bared, performing surgery on his back molars with his gleaming narrow knife and making a revolting gargling sound.

Alice squealed and hid behind the pillar once more. That reprobate watched her disappear. He put away his knife, smacked his lips, smirked, and turned to me.

"There you have it, Eggspawn," he said. "You've shown your new toy to your playmates. Since we both know you haven't the spleen to demand a wish of me, why don't you all go home now, so your mamas can tuck you into bed, and let poor old Mermeros have his rest?"

"'Poor old Mermeros' indeed," I said. "You're a brute and a bully. And you're wrong. I *have* come to demand a wish of you, so listen well."

Tom snapped to attention. So did Mermeros. The djinni's green eyes pulsated beneath his shaggy white brows. He flexed his fingers and cracked his knuckles, and then his neck and spine. Miss Rosewater, our fluffy-headed deportment and etiquette teacher, would have been horrified.

"I am all attention, Hatchling," the fraud practically purred. "Speak your wish, and it shall be done."

Last-minute doubts flickered through my mind like moths around a lantern post. I swatted them away, took a deep breath, and looked up into his treacherous eyes.

"Mermeros, hear me well. My wish is for you to convey my friends and me to an empire of such splendor and majesty that a *common female hatchling* like me could never imagine it. Take us three to the palace of your father, with all its treasures, in the heart of his domain, and let us meet him, and your brothers."

CHAPTER 13

Mermeros didn't move.

His stare bored into me. I matched his stare with my chin held high.

He was the first to blink.

Alice ventured out from behind her column. "Maeve," she whispered, "are you sure we should ask for this?"

Still Mermeros hung suspended in air.

"Some djinni this is," Tom muttered. "I thought you made your wish and then, *poof!* It happened."

Mermeros scowled, but didn't take up Tom's taunt. I had the feeling his mind was racing, searching for a solution to some problem I couldn't guess.

"This is a mistake, Girl Hatchling," he finally said. His voice was flat, neither sneering nor booming. "This will not offer you the rewards you hope."

Something about this wish had stumped the old blowhard.

"How do you know what I hope?" For once, I really felt I had the upper hand with Mermeros. He really seemed afraid. "Come on, Mermeros. I thought you were dying to see me burn through my wishes."

"Maeve," Alice said, "I think we should listen to the djinni. He would know best, wouldn't he?"

Mermeros bowed deeply to Alice. "A damsel of wisdom and beauty. I am enchanted."

Oh, for the love of heaven. After all his Female Eggspawn comments for my benefit, this beautiful damsel business was cutting things rather thick.

"An empire of splendor and majesty." Tom sounded like a boy in a trance. "We *have* to go there. I should have brought bigger bags to haul back all the loot. Maybe there's something here we could take..."

"There are other places on earth of equal splendor," said Mermeros. "Places lost to mankind, places unknown to your people in this kingdom. Let me take you on a tour of many splendid sites, ancient temples..."

The more he resisted, the more I needed to see this place.

"I have spoken my wish, Mermeros," I said. "I am the master, and you must obey."

He backed away from me, seeming to shrink in the process. He pressed his fingertips together and closed his eyes. Crystals on the shrouded chandeliers above began to tinkle.

Tom's eyes lit with excitement. "Here we go!" he cried, and grabbed my hand.

Air moved through the room, stirring the drapes, sweeping up dust and dead spiders.

"Maeve!" wailed Alice. I seized her hand and held on to both my friends.

The moving air was now a rushing gale. It snuffed out the candles in a blink. I bowed my head and closed my eyes. The floor fell out from underneath our feet. The wind spun us in circles, lifting us up, up, and up, then flinging us through the air like a cannonball.

I risked opening my eyes and saw London flash by below us. How did we manage to clear the ceiling and the roof?

Such a wonder spread below me that I forgot that question. The clouds had lifted, swept away on cold night breezes, revealing a sight no living person—except aeronauts in hot-gas balloons—had ever before seen. Only the seagulls. The clouds had lifted, and now the moon illuminated the shining curves of the Thames, ribbed with bridges. Lamplight dotted London Bridge and the high peaks of Tower Bridge. The massive palace at Westminster stood out like a mighty ship in a dark ocean, and, gleaming on its high mast, like Morris the owl's round eyes, were two clocks in the great clock tower where Big Ben chimed. There was the great dome of St. Paul's Cathedral, and the ribbon of water of the Serpentine at Hyde Park...

What a city London was!

Tom squeezed my hand. He saw it, too. His wide eyes drank it in.

"Open your eyes, Alice," I said. "Don't be afraid." The wind snatched my voice away.

And now London was gone, fading in the distance, while up ahead we raced, gathering speed at a terrifying rate, hurtling along the Thames to the Channel, where cold ocean spray slapped our faces. Alice finally opened her eyes just in time to see land charging at us. She squealed and threw her free arm over her head.

"We must be in France," Tom called through the roar of rushing air. "Halloo, Frenchies!"

"Not exactly *in* it," I bellowed back. "Look! Up ahead!"

Another blossom of small lights greeted us. A massive city spread out before us like a giant wheel. Punching through the night sky, lit by a million bulbs so it shone like polished gold, was the tower—La Tour Eiffel, the tallest structure in the world. I'd read about it, and seen pictures in newspapers, but never dreamed I'd one day fly by such a marvel, high enough to reach out my hand and touch its steel pinnacle.

"Alice, look!" I cried. "It's beautiful!"

And Paris was gone.

Faster and faster we roared across endless miles of countryside. Mermeros leaned into the wind exactly like a merman on the prow of a ship. Only there was no ship, save the pocket of air that surrounded us four; and no wake, but the billowing winds that followed us.

Now the mighty Alps loomed into view. Their snowy peaks glittered with diamonds of light from a sky full of stars. Mermeros skirted around them to the south, but still the smell of cold mountain air and snow filled our lungs. Another city passed beneath us, rimmed by mountains and a great lake. Geneva, Switzerland. Or so I thought. Thank goodness for Miss Nerquist's geography class. Learning about exotic places in the world made hers the one class at Salamanca School to capture my attention.

Soon the air changed, and became warm and green and full of fruity smells.

"Where are we now?" bawled Tom.

"Italy," I bawled right back.

City after city flew beneath our feet, mountains and lakes and rivers. Wherever we went, the moon followed us in its own mad race across the sky. It felt like those times when the moon seems to fly because swiftly moving clouds are gliding by it—but this time it wasn't clouds that moved the moon. It was our mad sprint across the world.

We followed Italy's boot for some time, then leaned out across the Adriatic Sea. And still, less than fifteen minutes had passed since we left the forsaken London gallery! Had mortals ever traveled at such speeds before? Only those with djinnis.

Alice kept a corpse's grip on my hand. Her eyes were still clenched shut.

The moon was far behind us now. Notwithstanding our breakneck speed, a change started so slowly that, at first, I doubted my eyes. But there, at about ten o'clock as we faced forward, a soft glow appeared low in the sky. Not a city, as I first supposed, but morning! A silvery-gray glow on the horizon—the pale precursor to the rising sun. It steadily grew until the first lip of the sun burst forth, searing and brilliant.

"Alice, open your eyes, please," I begged. "I can't bear for you to miss this."

Now the entire eastern sky was bathed in rosy, gentle light. Below us, sunlight twinkled off the isles of Greece like stars in a dark, watery heaven.

"Oh!"

It was Alice. She'd opened her eyes just in time for sunrise over the Aegean Sea.

As the sun rose, the vivid blue of the sea dazzled my eyes. *Achilles and Agamemnon sailed here*, I thought. Helen sailed to Troy with Paris, in graceful, oared ships that plied these dark-blue waters.

We plied the skies faster than I could think of it, and soon we were rushing over a sprawling city, smelling of clay and fruits and spices and donkeys.

"Constantinople!" I called. "We're in Asia Minor!"

The city gave way to a vast expanse of land, white beaches yielding to lush green orchards and farms, then craggy hills, and a rough brown plateau. By morning light, we could see every detail, every tree and fence we passed over, and it only made our pace seem more frantically fast. We were tearing over the world. The Ottoman Empire! Where was Troy? Did we fly in seconds over the ruins of the ancient city? If only we could go a bit more slowly! We were leaving behind so very much I wished to see.

Then and there, dangling in the sky, I made a vow. I *will* travel the world someday, I promised myself. Like Miss Isabella Bird. I will visit every country, every climate, every desert and mountain and jungle, and I will never rest till I've seen it all.

"Maeve, look!"

Alice's voice drew me out of my thoughts. She pointed to the ground below. In the midst of great valleys of rock carved out from within tall mountain peaks stood an astonishing marvel. Towering columns of pale rock rose from the ground like bleached tree trunks, but ever so much larger. Some were jagged at the top like ferocious teeth. Others were topped by a thick slab of darker rock, nearly black upon the pale rock below. These columns were everywhere, of varying sizes, yet many of them had the same thickness of darker rock astride them, for all the world like thick chocolate frosting on top of impossibly tall slabs of butter cake.

Then I remembered reading about them in geography. The fairy chimneys of Cappadocia. As old as the world itself.

And they were gone.

The air grew thinner as the sun beat hotter. Up and up we climbed, over the breast of a terrifying mountain range. I squeezed my friends' hands as it grew harder to breathe. Just when I became convinced Mermeros planned to kill us by suffocation in the upper atmosphere, he veered to the right—that would be south—and skirted along the edge of the mountain range, keeping it always to our left. The air grew denser, and I took a grateful breath, watching dark multicolored rock formations tumble past us, hundreds of feet below.

Off to my far right, in greener land, I noticed a snakelike river. As its curves followed us, mile after mile, I pictured my geography books and gasped. "That's the Tigris River," I called out. "Alice, did you ever dream of seeing such a thing?"

"No!" Alice shouted over the rushing wind. "I never did." She saw the disappointment on my face and added, "It's very nice, though."

Tom watched me closely but said nothing. There was that set look to his jaw that I was coming to recognize well. It occurred to me that he might not know anything about the Tigris River of Mesopotamia, home to one of the earliest human civilizations. He'd never admit his ignorance, but he wasn't happy about it. Tom was certainly not ignorant by nature. *What kind of dismal schooling did he receive in that miserable Mission Industrial School?* Perhaps Miss Salamanca's School for Upright Young Ladies had more to offer me than I'd given it credit for.

The green swards of river-valley land seemed to reach out to encompass us, and the mountains receded in size and distance. It was then I realized we were gradually moving lower and lower, closer to the ground.

I took a deep breath of fragrant cedar and almond-spiced air. The wind tasted like apricots. Delicious. We were flying over paradise.

More green fields rushed by, and small rivers, more visible now as our altitude dropped. It gave the sensation of falling, and I felt my stomach pitch. We were still moving terribly fast, and if we hit the ground at this speed... I watched Mermeros for some clue to his intent, but he was still as unmoving as that carved wooden merman on a ship.

"Maeve, make him stop!" Alice cried.

Tom didn't speak, but his grip on my hand tightened. The ground rushed toward us, and we weren't slowing down a nib.

He's going to kill us, I thought. But why would Mermeros bring us all the way across the world only to murder us here? He could have managed that quite capably in London.

"Mermeros, what are you doing?" I cried.

He didn't answer. We raced over trees, and huts, and baked-clay villages, and still the ground rose closer. I saw wind swaying through rushes clustering along streams, and flat, craggy fields where curly-horned goats grazed. Every clump of their beards stood out clearly. We were that low to the ground. A small shepherd boy watching us rush by got the surprise of his young life.

Alice let go of my hand and threw both arms over her face. Tom turned and looked at me. He didn't look terrified, but the next closest thing, I'd wager.

"You put us down properly, you great codfish," I ordered Mermeros. "You're a bully and a brute to enjoy frightening my friends."

And we stopped. The pocket of air surrounding us slammed to a halt inches above the grassy scruff of a barren plain, with nothing but low mounds greeting us on the horizon all about. The cloud vanished, and we landed heavily on the dusty ground.

Our legs wobbled under us like sailors' when they first set foot on land. Alice sank to her knees and clasped her hands in front of her face.

I caught a glance of Mermeros, his eyes darting this way and that. His face darkened. His bushy white eyebrows brooded low over his eyes.

"Where are we, Maeve?" asked Tom.

A flock of birds flew overhead. Twenty minutes ago, we stood in a dusty, abandoned London gallery, and now here we were, in a bright midmorning, halfway across the world.

"We're in Persia," I said.

CHAPTER
14

It was hot.

After the chill of a London December, it felt unbelievably hot.

We gasped in the heat, unbuttoned our collars, and surveyed the wasteland surrounding us. Where were the green grasses we'd seen, the riverbeds, the apricots, the pungent spice fields and savory cooking fires?

Tom stumbled as he rotated around, turning, turning, taking in the entire panorama. He stopped and took a deep breath. He seemed to be filling his entire body with desert air from toe to top.

"Beats London, anyway," he said. "Smell that air!"

The sky, the vast, enormous sky, from horizon to horizon all around, was the most breathtaking blue, except where the fiery sun baked down upon us.

Alice sat on a rock and shook sand out of her boot. "The air smells like emptiness," she said.

Apparently here in Persia, the prohibition on showing one's feet to boys no longer mattered.

"Better than soot," observed Tom.

I looked for any sign of a far-off palace, but all I saw in every direction were a few scrubby trees, and low mounds covered with desert weeds and sand.

Mermeros sat in midair with his legs tucked beneath him and his arms crossed over his chest. The sardine tin spun beside him. I expected to see the djinni laughing and gloating at his triumph over my wasted wish, but he only watched the sky, following the movement of every bird with his piercing eyes. He seemed smaller here, somehow.

"I hate to complain, Mr. Djinni, sir," Tom ventured, "but if this is your idea of an empire of splendor and majesty, it falls a little short of my expectations."

Mermeros turned sharply toward Tom and bared his pointy teeth.

"Chattel should not speak unless ordered to by their masters," he snapped.

I marched over to where Mermeros hovered. "Tom's no slave," I told him. "He's a free English boy just like any other."

Mermeros leered at me. The ends of his long mustaches bobbed. "He is an orphaned youth with no protector, awaiting purchase by a taskmaster, is he not?"

I was filling my lungs for a hot retort to this when Tom took my arm. "Forget it, Maeve," he said. "Don't waste your time on it."

"Well, you're right." I shook his arm loose. "He has done a rotten job taking us to his father's palace."

"On the contrary," said Mermeros, still scanning the sky, "I have brought you to the exact location."

Alice and Tom looked at each other. Then they looked away.

I'd done it again. Botched another wish colossally. And now there was only one left. I hadn't really considered Mermeros's age, and how passing centuries would change his homeland. What was the matter with my brain?

Tom took off exploring. "Well, let's look around then. What are you waiting for?"

Alice laced her boot back on and rose stoically to her feet. "Not for breakfast, I suppose," she said. "Why not look around? We can fit in an hour or so of sightseeing before Miss Salamanca starts missing us. Your djinni can whisk us back in time, I'm sure."

Mermeros laughed from deep in his stout gut. I didn't like the sound of it.

"Not without a wish, I won't," he said.

His mad laughter echoed in my ears.

The true horror of what I'd done crashed upon me. I'd squandered all my wishes. I hadn't thought carefully. Even for all my planning, I'd missed the most obvious details. I was out of wishes and out of luck. Unless I wanted to consign us all to a Persian exile, stranded in the desert, without supplies, money, or a knowledge of local language or customs, I'd be burning up my last wish in no time to take us safely home to England.

Mermeros's sneering lips pulled back from his vicious teeth as he howled in laughter. He beat the air with his green fists. This was the moment where I should have kicked him in the sardine can, but I was too devastated. My cricket team. My escape from school, my travels around the world. All were lost forever.

I don't cry. Maeve Merritt doesn't cry. But my eyes wanted to grow wet. And I couldn't blame the dust in the air.

An unearthly scream met our ears. A large bird flew toward us, low, swooping and bobbing over the ground like a rowboat riding an ocean swell. Its wingspan was enormous, and it dragged after it a long, drooping tail. It screamed again, and Mermeros began to tremble.

"It's a peacock!" said Tom. "I've seen 'em at the zoo in the park."

"But peacocks can't fly like that," said Alice. "Only very short distances. Like up to a tree limb."

I watched the bird approach. Its vast wings scythed through the air, propelling it forward at an astonishing speed, despite the huge, dangling tail and the up-and-down arc of its flight. It was aiming straight at us.

"That's no ordinary peacock," I said.

"How do you know?" said Tom.

"I'm not sure," I said. "Like Alice said, they can't fly like that. But also…it just *feels* different."

Alice spoke up then. "Maeve, look," she said. "Something's happening to your djinni."

Something was happening indeed—something I'd seen before, but she hadn't. He shrank himself down to size in record time, dissolving into noxious smoke and siphoning himself back into his sardine can. The look on his face, before it vanished utterly, was one of pure terror.

The bird was nearly upon us now.

The tin leaped into my coat pocket. *Coward.*

We could never outrun the peacock that was barreling straight toward us, so I pulled Alice down to the ground and threw myself over her. If it planned to attack, it would need to fight me first.

But it didn't attack. Nothing happened. I raised my head and looked up.

The peacock had halted itself in the air, not ten feet away from us. It hovered, flapping its blue and green wings till fronds of sand rose in the air and lashed our faces. It was bigger by far, I was sure, than natural peacocks could grow to be. And I was positive that natural peacocks weren't surrounded by a narrow halo of green light.

The sardine can in my pocket shuddered.

The peacock didn't pay my friends a moment's notice. It turned its head from left to right, fixing first one, then the other beady black eye upon me. It let out another piercing scream and lunged at me, halting midway. Again and again, it feinted toward me, but something arrested its movement. Whatever it was, I blessed it and silently urged it to keep up the good work.

Tom picked up a rock and took aim.

"Don't." I seized his arm. "It's too beautiful."

"It's awful!" Alice cried. "It wants to peck your eyes out, Maeve!"

"Alice is right," Tom said. "He's a fancy fellow, but he wants you for lunch."

The bird screamed once more, then snapped its great fantail wide, showing radiant swirls of green and blue and gold. Then it collapsed its fan, flapped its wings, and rose up into the sky. A final scream, and it vanished high above us in a puff of smoke.

Alice wrapped her arms tightly around her ribs. "Oh, my goodness," she said. "I don't know when I've ever been so frightened."

"That bird felt *evil*," Tom said.

I placed Alice's fallen hat back on her golden braids and rubbed her shoulders. "It's all right, Alice," I said. "He's gone now."

Mermeros's sardine tin fell silent and still. My own heart, which had been keeping time with its palpitations, relaxed also.

Tom looked around once more. "I say we should look around and explore a bit, while we can."

"But then what?" Alice said. "We'll need to get home eventually."

My heart felt like a lump of lead. "We will," I said. "I promise. I didn't drag us out here just to leave us stranded."

Tommy eyed me thoughtfully. "You've got more wishes left, right, Maeve?"

I hesitated, then nodded.

"How many?"

There was no getting around it. "One more."

He whistled. "Say, that's awful," he said, "having to spend your last wish just to get back home." He patted my shoulder. "But you'll still have more fun. Now we know to be more careful when it's my turn."

I said nothing. I couldn't. Alice watched me closely. She said nothing, but I knew questions were swirling in her mind.

Tommy looked around. "Anyway, I'm not sure I'd mind staying," he said, "if there's water and food to be found somewhere. This beats Mission Industrial any day of the week." His smile cheered me up considerably. "As for dragging us, drag me anywhere, if it means another trip like that one!" He shook his head. "Flying over those mountains and cities! Like eagles, we were. Like falcons."

Some of the terror of our peacock encounter seemed to slide off our shoulders.

"Mermeros said he brought us to the exact spot where his father's palace once was," Tom mused. "Hard to imagine there was ever a palace here, but maybe if we look around, we'll find some clues to where it was."

"Too bad we didn't bring shovels," I said. "We could have dug for buried treasure."

"I doubt there'd be any treasure left to find, anyway," Alice said. "Centuries must have passed since the palace was here. I'm sure the place has been picked over dozens of times by vandals and burglars and things."

She was probably right, especially after five thousand years, and I knew it, but I set off marching. There must be some way I could salvage this wish—this *pair* of wishes—into something more than a lovely night flight. Some morsel of treasure, a token, some tiny souvenir, even, could at least help me prove to myself, in the years to come, that I really had mastered a djinni once and taken a magical trip. That I really had been to Persia.

Had anybody in the history of humankind ever wasted three wishes so badly?

We hadn't gone four steps when we halted. Tom threw out a protective arm to block my path, and I did the same for Alice. The ground underneath our feet began to shake. Rivulets of sand began streaming down from an anthill-sized mound not three feet in front of us.

Alice's eyes grew wide. "Earthquake?"

Tom pointed to the mound and shook his head. "Look."

Something was happening. The mound shuddered, then buckled. Chunks of rubble caved out from underneath the mound. Something appeared—a rat, I prayed, or some other creature.

But it wasn't a rodent. It was a *paw*. A huge, furry paw with fierce claws violently raking the earth.

What kind of animal could have a paw that big? I didn't want to learn.

We stumbled back. A massive black snout poked out and sniffed the air. The paws redoubled their pace, and more clods of brown dirt collapsed away.

The earth growled at us. Alice made a terrified squeak.

"Whatever's down there"—Alice's voice faltered—"it knows we're here."

Mermeros's tin leaped in my pocket.

In a burst of dirt and rubble, the beast sprang from the hole. Long forelegs landed, braced to fight. Snapping jaws wove low to the ground. Quivering hackles bristled.

"A wolf!" Tom gasped. "Run!"

But we stood frozen, unable to move. The huge creature didn't spring for the kill. It only held us in the gaze of its smoldering amber eyes.

The taste of bitter dread hung in my mouth. Still, the creature made no move. It paced back and forth with a slow, deliberate gait.

We waited for the end.

And waited.

Would these be my last breaths?

Perhaps not?

Since it didn't plan to rip my throat out immediately, I took a more careful look at the beast. It was gigantic, fully as tall as me, and covered with thick brown fur tipped with gold, and something more. Was it only golden fur? I squinted against the sunlight.

It *was* more than sunlight. An aura of gold light surrounded its body. What on earth? Despite the heat, my skin felt cold and prickly.

Without warning, the monster lunged for me. I fell backward in terror. But before it could reach me, something held it back. It skidded to a stop, threw back its head, and howled.

"It's your djinni, protecting you," Alice said. Her skin looked gray and ashen.

I had my doubts. Mermeros's tin rattled a staccato beat against my thigh.

Tom stood between us and the creature, brandishing his rock weapon once more.

"Here! Get back! Get on with you!" he yelled.

Black lips peeled back from the wolf's yellow teeth in a deadly snarl. Its low, rumbling growl seemed to shake the earth.

A scream from far away reached our ears. The peacock? The wolf's ears pricked. It sprang away, loping in long, graceful strides, until, with a burst of gold, it vanished.

Mermeros's tin went limp and still inside my pocket.

"Did you see that?" Tom cried. "It just disappeared!"

"Like the peacock did." My legs felt weak, and I sank to the ground to catch my breath.

"What a marvelous animal," Tom said. "So powerful. The way it ran."

Alice sank down beside me and fanned her face. "You must be mad," she said. "It was nothing but horrible."

"Only because it wanted to eat Maeve." Tom grinned. "You can't fault it for that."

Tom's eyes twinkled at me. I laughed in spite of myself and, for good measure, kicked sand at his shoes. He laughed and hopped nimbly aside.

Now that I could catch my breath, I tried to think what to do. Persia didn't seem to want us around. *After two near misses like this, shouldn't I give up and take my friends home?*

Alice stood up and brushed the sand off her skirts. "Well, come on, then." She reached out a hand to hoist me to my feet. "Time's ticking, and the day will only get hotter. Let's explore while we can."

Good old Alice. I took her hand and stood up.

We set off, with Tom leading the way and Alice behind me, clutching my elbow. Midstride, a strange sensation passed over my body, a sort of buzzing in my teeth.

"What was that?" I asked.

Tom shrugged. "I don't know. I felt it, too."

I thought I heard Mermeros's voice sound a faraway warning in my ear, like a whining mosquito.

Alice caught up to us, then paused when she felt the jolt. "Oh! How strange." She cocked her head. "Such a perplexing place!"

"It's probably just the heat," I said. "The sun and air take some getting used to, I'm sure. Let's keep moving."

Tom reached the hole the wolf had created. He knelt and poked his head inside.

"Oh, Tom, don't," Alice said. "What if that's a wolf's den, and there are more of them down there?"

But Tom ignored her. He pulled himself up and fished in his knapsack for a candle and matches. He quickly lit his candle, lowered it down into the hole, then poked his head and trunk down in after it. I was surprised that the hole was deep enough for him to do this; from above he was a pair of legs abandoned by its own torso.

"Maeve, you need to see this," he yelled. I barely heard the muffled echoes. He pulled himself upright, then poked his feet down the hole. "I'm going in. Come along after me. The drop's not far. You won't get hurt."

And before we could say anything, he disappeared.

I peered over the edge. His flaming-red hair reflected off the small patch of sunlight that had followed him down.

I bent further down and saw light from Tom's candle wavering on faraway walls. This was no mere fox's den. There was a room down there!

I lowered my feet into the opening.

Alice seized my arm. "Maeve, say you won't do anything so foolish as this," she pleaded. "We are in *Persia*. The *wilderness*. Suddenly a wolf leaps out of a hole in the ground, and you decide you want to go *down that hole*?"

Tom's voice came echoing up from the chamber below. "You have to see this place!" he called. "Both of you! Bring my sack so we can light some more candles!"

Alice sighed and sank to her knees. She took a long look at me, then shook her head.

"I could no more stop you than I could grant a magical wish," she said. "I'll stay up here and keep watch. Don't be long down there."

I squeezed her hand, grabbed Tom's sack, turned toward the darkness, and jumped.

I landed crouching in the dark. Mine was a fighter's stance, but if a blade-wielding enemy was inches away, I'd never know it in the blackness of this space. Up above, in the sunlight, Alice's blond braids hung down around her pink face, but she was all I could see. My guardian angel of worry.

My eyes found the orb of candlelight surrounding Tom. Beyond him was only dimness. The weight of the earth pressed around me, and I took an uneasy breath to reassure myself that I still could. Tom tipped a new candle into his own and handed me the lit taper. It was only another drop of light in a sea of darkness, but it was something.

The walls, though thickly covered with dust and spiderwebs, *were* walls. This was no animal's lair, but a room built by human hands. A cellar?

Tom brushed away a swath of dirt and debris, and held his lamp up close. "Look."

I came closer. By the light of both our candles we saw, not

rough-hewn rocks, but glazed bricks, and on them, carved in relief, a splendid horse, with long, prancing legs, a graceful curved neck, and a mane wrapped in tight coils.

It was beautiful. Perfect in its detail. And thousands of years old. I reached out my fingers to explore the surface, then hesitated. Something this ancient, one didn't lightly touch, and yet it was so lifelike, I almost expected it to peel itself off the brick wall and gallop away.

A wooden torch jutted from the wall above the horse. Tom lifted his candle to it and, after much fussing, managed to light its splintered end. It gradually put forth a cautious light that only made the carving look more mysterious. Furry black spiders scattered as heat spread.

Tom scraped more of the wall, revealing another brick relief carving of a bearded man in pleated robes. His sword hung from his belt, and he carried a round shield with one arm.

An ancient Persian man. The sight of him sent chills through me.

"How old do you think this is?" I whispered.

"Couldn't say," Tom said. "Old as the world, feels like."

"This is no cellar," I said. "This is much too grand for that."

Tom cleared away more debris, revealing a procession of bearded men in pleated robes, carrying various weapons or offerings of food in their hands. All the men wore elaborate headdresses, some round, some pointy, and some flat. Their hair and beards were carved in small, tight curls. This art was unlike anything I'd ever seen in England. In the men's wide, carved eyes I saw wisdom and dignity.

"Who are you?" I whispered to a carving of a man carrying a basket of fish. "I want to know." But the brick-carved man kept his silence.

Tom unveiled carvings faster and faster. His excited eyes shone in the candlelight. "Can you believe we're here, Maeve? Have a pair of kids ever been this lucky?"

He lit more torches as we moved along, observing the costumes, hats, and objects carried by each carved figure. Light began to reach beyond the wall where we stood. Stone structures dotted the room— broken columns, and benches of sorts, and footrests. In the center of the room was a wide, flat table. An altar? On a raised platform stood the remains of a stone chair.

But my attention was riveted by the ornately carved figures on the wall, parading one by one along the endless underground. "What are they looking at?" I asked.

Tom looked at me curiously. "I don't know. Us?"

"No, silly. They're all facing something up ahead."

Tom kept stripping away the filth. We reached a trio of figures kneeling before the huge form of a man, larger by half than those gazing at him. He sat upon an elaborate chair, underneath a figure of the sun surrounded by feathered wings.

"It's a throne," I said. "And that's the king. We're inside the palace."

Tom whistled. "Splendor and majesty."

"It's an old, dusty mess," I said, "but I'm sure it was splendid once. I had rather envisioned pots full of rubies and pearls for the taking, and wagonloads of gold coins, but still..."

Tom rolled his eyes. "Anybody can have pots of rubies."

"Not quite anyone, in fact."

"This is real history," Tom persisted. "It's ancient! It's secret! Archaeologists would give their teeth for a glimpse of this."

"I'll keep my teeth, thank you," I said. "If you see any pots of rubies, be so good as to let me know."

I studied the fearsome figure of the king, looming over the others, and the three figures kneeling before him with outstretched arms.

"Who do you suppose they are?" Tom asked. "Slaves?"

I shook my head. "Too well dressed, I think." They wore earrings, necklaces, and rings, and finer clothes than any of the other worshippers. "And they're closest to the king."

"Look at this." Tom pointed above the heads of each of the three kneelers at carved figures of animals. A bird, for the one closest to the king. Next, a dog. The third one, I couldn't quite make out.

"What's that animal?" I asked Tom.

"A fish," he said. "These curved things are gills."

"Maybe," I mused, "these figures represent animal kingdoms bowing before the great king, or something."

"Or something." Tom didn't sound as sure.

I thought of a new idea. "I know! The bird—that could be air. The dog, earth, and the fish, water. The ancient elements. I read about this in a book about Persia once. Only I thought there were more of them…"

"Look here." Tom pointed above the king's head, where a flame was carved, just below the winged sun. "The king is fire."

"What are you two doing down there?"

Alice's musical voice echoed mournfully through the chamber. I'd practically forgotten about her with our discovery of the carved figures.

"We're inside the palace," I called back to her. "It's incredible! You should join us!"

"No, thank you," she sang. "I prefer to bake in the scorching sun like a pudding."

I felt ashamed then. We were pleasantly cool here in the underground palace, but Alice must be melting in the heat. If her hat didn't shade her enough, she'd burn like toast.

I trotted back to where the hole cast a patch of light over the dark room. "Alice, please come down," I called. "We're perfectly safe, and you'll burn to a crisp up there."

Alice hesitated. Then she sighed. Her boots came through the hole in the ceiling, followed by her stockinged ankles and her lacy petticoats. I half caught her as she tumbled down.

"At least it's cooler here," she observed, dusting herself off.

I tugged her toward the burning torches. "Alice, look," I said. "What do you see?"

She blinked against the dark and hung back a bit at the cobwebs and dust. But when she began following the carvings, she forgot her fear. "Oh, my," she whispered. "Have you ever seen...? What does it mean?" When she reached the figure of the king, she wrenched a torch from its socket and kept on going.

The figure of the king appeared again, this time pointing an angry finger at someone. The someone was held in the elbow grip of two other figures. Back and forth darted Alice and her torch, comparing the two pictures.

"These are princes," she said at length, pointing to the three figures with the bird, the dog, and the fish. "The king's sons."

"I wonder who their mother was," I joked. "A zoologist?"

"Very funny," Alice said.

"What makes you say they're princes?"

Alice pointed to their clothing. "I think this symbol on their sashes or belts is some kind of family mark, or crest," she said. "The king has it, and so do they. Plus, they're the only figures with stuff, um, floating above their heads."

Tommy pointed to the picture with the king pointing angrily at one of them. "So, this means the king was angry at one of his sons?"

Alice nodded. "It looks like the two other sons caught and captured the bad son. Bird and dog captured fish and brought him to the king."

"Fish son…" I repeated. "The third son of a king…"

I lit another torch and pressed my way along the seemingly endless gallery. A flappy sheet of cobwebs stirred against the wall. I pulled them away. We stared at the raised carvings underneath.

"Criminy," Tommy whispered. "Look at that!"

The king figure, looming larger than ever, pressed a massive hand down on the head of his rebellious son, stuffing him into some kind of vessel—a jar or vase. Beside him stood the other two sons, but their heads were now the head of a bird and the head of a dog.

"What does it mean?" Tommy asked.

"Can't you see?" Alice's eyes were wide lamps in the darkness. "It means Mermeros's own father, the king, turned him into a djinni."

CHAPTER
16

Inside my pocket, I felt Mermeros's sardine can flop indignantly.

"I think you're right, Alice," I told her. Good old Alice!

"That's Mermeros?" Tommy said. "He was a bad one from the beginning, wasn't he?"

"He can hear you, you know," I reminded Tommy.

He traced the king's angry expression with his finger. "Wouldn't that mean the king would have to be a sorcerer, or something?"

Something clicked. "That's what Mermeros told me. That a sorcerer made him a djinni." I continued dusting the wall free of spiderwebs. This wall was a story I was eager to read.

It finally ended at a corner. I turned and paced alongside the new wall, lighting torches as I went, but I saw nothing more than rectangular bricks. After a while of walking, I turned back, cutting a diagonal across the space to rejoin Alice and Tommy.

"What I want to know is, what about the dog and the bird brothers?" I asked. "I think... *Oof!*"

I wasn't watching where I was going. I tripped hard on something heavy and solid, and tumbled down a long, stone shape. Tommy and Alice hurried over to help me up.

"What is that thing?" Alice asked, after I shooed her away from fussing over me.

"A coffin, I think," Tommy said.

"Sarcophagus," I corrected him.

Tommy knelt down for a closer look. The puddle of weak light from my candle fell upon the sarcophagus lid. "Here's that royal symbol, again," he said. "I think this sarco—whatever you said, belongs to the king!"

"Look," Alice said. "A dog and a bird."

Sure enough, two large figures stood at watchful attention on either side of the king's royal symbol.

"Not just a dog and a bird," I said. "A peacock and a wolf."

We stared at each other.

"Does that mean the king turned his other two sons into animals?" asked Tommy.

In my pocket, Mermeros's tin began to buzz against my leg.

"That doesn't seem very nice," Alice said.

Tommy peered at the sides of the sarcophagus. "Look," he said. "A foreign army, marching. Marching at the king and his sons, with the dog head and the bird head." He crawled along the back of the coffin. "Uh-oh. Here's the king with a spear through his chest."

We scrambled around to see. There was the king, falling back in his chariot, pointing at each of his sons, who fought by his side.

"He was about to die," Tommy whispered. "He was a sorcerer. I'm sure of it. Before he died, he turned his sons all the way into a dog and a bird."

"But why?" Alice asked.

Mermeros went mad with angry vibrations. Alice shuddered. "Do you think the king's really in there? Right inside this big box?"

A wicked thought seized me. "There's only one way to know," I said. "Come on, Tommy. Help me."

We crouched down and leaned with all our weight against the stone lid on the sarcophagus.

"No!" Alice wailed. "Don't open it! You can't! I can't abide the thought of dead bodies."

I pushed and gasped, but the lid didn't want to budge.

"Don't fret, Alice," I said. "After all these thousands of years, if he's in there at all, he'll be nothing but dust."

Tommy and I strained at the weight of the lid until finally it budged a bit.

"One, two, three, heave!" I cried. With a mighty shove, we shifted the lid off onto the floor. Alice covered her eyes with her hand, then peeked between her fingers and screamed.

Tommy and I peered over the edge. A grinning skeleton leered at us. Apparently, the king wasn't dust.

Inside my pocket, Mermeros shivered in staccato like chattering teeth.

The king's head *tilted toward us.*

I gripped Tommy's arm. "He's alive!"

Tommy reached down gingerly and poked the skull with his fingertip. It moved like any other object would. I waited for a curse to strike Tommy.

"It's not alive, Maeve," he said. "Something made it move. Maybe it was us, shifting the lid around."

I took a deep breath and tried not to feel too silly. Alice slipped her hand into mine. "I thought he looked alive, too, Maeve," she said. Good old Alice.

We knelt for a closer look. Tommy reached in and lifted a heavy disk-shaped object, about four inches across, from somewhere just underneath the king's ribs.

"It's the king's crest," he whispered. "In the carvings, he wore it on his belt."

"*The sorcerer king,*" echoed Alice.

"Perhaps," I cautioned. "We're making an awful lot of guesses here."

I took the crest from Tommy and turned it over in my hand. Thin strands of what was probably once leather dangled from the back.

"Whatever it is, Mermeros doesn't like it," I told the others. "He's quivering like a jelly in his sardine can."

"There's a mystery here," Alice said. "That's for sure."

In the distance, I heard something. Something so faint that I wasn't sure I heard it at all. But with each second, the noise grew.

Alice gripped my hand. "I think we should get out of here."

"Yeah," Tommy agreed. "But let's take a souvenir." He pocketed the crest, then reached into the coffin, and pulled a heavy ring off the king's bony finger.

"That's stealing," Alice protested.

"I don't think the king will mind." Tommy laughed as he admired the ring.

"But those things belong here," Alice said. "They belong to Persia. And to this king, and his memory. They're part of his story."

"Who will ever notice the difference?" I said. "It doesn't look like anyone has known this king's story for thousands of years."

Alice shook her head. "That doesn't matter."

"Look," I told her, "I'm running out of wishes. I'm not leaving here without something. Maybe I can sell it to make the money I need to..."

My voice trailed off as my eye caught the dull glint of something dusty, but metallic, dangling against the king's bony wrist. I reached for it: a bracelet with carvings that looked like they might be writing of some kind. It made me shudder to see the king's bones bump and rattle as I slid it off, but I took it anyway.

"Maeve," Alice insisted. "You shouldn't. You're not a thief."

"I'm an archaeologist," I said. Another way of saying "thief," but with credentials.

The distant noise swelled. Breathing, beating, running? I couldn't be sure. But I didn't like it. And neither did Mermeros.

"Something's coming," I told the others. "We've got to go."

We picked our way hurriedly across the dark gallery floor, heading for the hole in the ceiling that led to the ground above. The sounds of pursuit pressed in on us like a tourniquet. We heard the call of a hunting bird and a predator's growl.

As we reached it the hole, a huge, glowing thing swooped into the cavern and cut off our escape. The peacock!

Behind us, from a long, tunneling corridor, came the tawny form of the wolf.

The peacock screamed at us. Malice glinted in his beady black eyes. The wolf's growl reverberated through brick and stone.

"Maeve?" whispered Alice. "What do we do now?"

Down here, in the dark, there was no mistaking the sinister pulse of their luminous glow. The peacock, a poison green, and the wolf, a deadly yellow.

"They can't get to us, remember?" I prayed it was true.

But it wasn't.

The peacock's feathers singed my face as it flapped the air before us. The wolf closed in on us, pacing in a circle about our feet.

"Who are you," came an ancient voice from the depths of the peacock's throat, "to disturb our father's rest, and plunder his treasures?"

"Who are you," echoed the wolf in a ghostly snarl, "to dare to bring our traitorous brother here?"

Alice whispered like one in a trance. "They're talking to us," she breathed. "They speak."

"Come forth, brother," commanded the wolf. "Show yourself, and pay for your crimes."

"Confess," shrilled the wicked voice of the peacock, "and beg for mercy."

The wolf's yellow eyes left me trembling. "Give him to us, little girl," he said, "and return the things you stole, and we will let you and your friends leave in peace."

Inside my pocket, Mermeros went as still as a corpse. As quiet as his father.

"Maeve?"

I heard Alice's voice from far away. I saw the peacock's cruel beak and its wicked eye. The wolf paced back and forth before me, pawing the ancient dust with its clawed foot, then tensed as if to spring.

Perhaps I ought to give them the sardine can.

But Maeve Merritt doesn't listen to bullies. Not on the cricket field, and not at Miss Salamanca's school. Why should Persia be any different?

I seized a lit torch and swung it at the wolf. It stepped back in surprise, then snarled. I swung it at the peacock, and it screamed.

"Maeve!" Alice cried out in terror. "Don't make them angry!"

"They've made *me* angry." I slashed the torch through the air like a sword. "We're stuck down here either way, so I see no reason not to fight back."

Tommy got a torch, too, and stood at my back, with Alice clamped to our sides.

But something was happening to the wolf and the peacock. They began shifting in shape, the peacock growing taller, and the wolf's body moving upright. Whatever they were becoming, it was far more terrifying than the vicious beasts they already were.

They were becoming human.

Glowing human forms, made of wind and fire instead of flesh and bone. *Or maybe bone as well*, I realized. Skeletal teeth grinned at us from underneath their glowing, shifting faces. From their ancient lips, a chant began its drumbeat march. Words, words fell from their mouths. I couldn't understand the language, but I could feel the malevolence steaming off them like fumes off burnt porridge. In my pocket, Mermeros's tin jerked to the ugly beat of their words. They were summoning him.

"Give him to us," hissed the one that had been the wolf.

"Hand him over," said the other, "and we'll kill you less painfully."

"Leave in peace" was no longer an option. If it ever had been.

A nasty pair of brothers will gang up on you, whether at wrestling or jacks in town, or whether they're thousands of years old and reeking of dark power. We wouldn't survive, but I wasn't going to make things any easier for these two.

"I won't hand him over," I shouted. "Not unless you let my friends go."

The ghostly forms nodded. I pushed Tommy and Alice away from the terrible specters. "Run, you two! Run!"

Alice took off, faster than I'd have thought she could go, but Tommy hesitated. "We're not leaving you, Maeve!"

At times like these—not that I've faced many of them—my fists are more persuasive than my words. I popped him hard in the face, right across his pointy cheekbone. "Go! Help Alice! *Go!*"

Tommy's eyes flashed, then he took off running. Mermeros's tin tugged hard against my dress and against his will, searching for the way out, in response to the deathly brothers' call.

I pictured Mermeros's big ugly face and his nasty fishy teeth, his fish-scale vest and his blue tattoos. These two were going to tear him to bits. And I hadn't even gotten my third wish! I was sick of people trying to steal my djinni from me. I'd found him, fair and square.

"Tommy!" I hollered. In the distant bit of light near our entry, I saw him shove Alice up through the hole in the tunnel and into the sky. He turned toward me.

I ripped the sardine tin out of my pocket and bowled it at him. Just like a cricket ball.

My form was excellent. So were Tommy's reflexes. He snagged the tin from where it skidded across the floor, then pulled himself up and out of sight.

The wolf brother and the peacock brother screamed in rage. They reassumed their animal forms, leaped forward, and raced for the opening. I ran after them, swinging my torch and singeing their tails with it. They hissed and growled, but ignored me. When the animals reached the hole leading to the outside, I dropped my torch and grabbed hold of the wolf's tail. His lunge for my friends carried me right up out of the hole with him, though the touch of him sent a painful shock through my body.

We tumbled out and onto the blinding sand. I saw Tommy and Alice running helter-skelter away from the creatures, with the peacock in pursuit and the wolf not far behind. I figured I'd slowed him down a bit. I grabbed a rock from the sand, scrambled to my feet, and ran after them.

When I was in range, I hurled the rock at the peacock, clipping his wing and making him stagger a bit. He hit the sand, then mounted up once more on his chase. Of course I couldn't seriously injure an immortal. But I'd slowed him down. Tommy and Alice pulled ahead a bit, Tommy dragging Alice by the hand.

I held my breath.

The peacock and wolf peeled away sideways in their pursuit. They'd come to the invisible barrier they could not cross. Tommy and Alice stumbled to freedom. They'd made it! Mermeros and all!

The snarling beasts whirled about and headed for me.

Not quite all.

But I hadn't fought this far to surrender now. I ran straight forward, charging the beasts. They howled in rage as they galloped toward me. I saw Tommy stand, frozen, with the sardine can in his hand. He had it now. If he wanted, he could open it and claim his place as Mermeros's master. He could leave me here, and I'd never be able to snatch it back from him.

But he didn't.

He hurled the can back at me. I snatched it out of the air just as the wolf knocked me down and the peacock sank its claws into my legs. The wolf's huge jaws opened wide and snapped at my hand that held the tin. He didn't get me, but I felt the shock of contact with his wet lips.

Before I could cry out, the air burst around me with a tremendous bang and a sulfurous cloud of stink. It was Mermeros, larger than life, and furious. At the sight of him, the wolf and the peacock screamed in rage. He bowled the wolf aside with one huge arm and batted the peacock aside with the other. They tumbled over, snarling and hissing. They leaped up and began to assume their fearsome human forms. Dark, blood-chilling words shot out from their skeletal mouths.

They were too late. Before they could complete their transformation, Mermeros had scooped me up and whisked me toward Alice and Tommy, then gathered us all up and took off soaring through the air, northward and westward, to London and safety and home.

When I was in range, I hurled the rock at the peacock, clipping his wing and making him stagger a bit. He hit the sand, then mounted up once more on his chase. Of course I couldn't seriously injure an immortal. But I'd slowed him down. Tommy and Alice pulled ahead a bit, Tommy dragging Alice by the hand.

I held my breath.

The peacock and wolf peeled away sideways in their pursuit. They'd come to the invisible barrier they could not cross. Tommy and Alice stumbled to freedom. They'd made it! Mermeros and all!

The snarling beasts whirled about and headed for me.

Not quite all.

But I hadn't fought this far to surrender now. I ran straight forward, charging the beasts. They howled in rage as they galloped toward me. I saw Tommy stand, frozen, with the sardine can in his hand. He had it now. If he wanted, he could open it and claim his place as Mermeros's master. He could leave me here, and I'd never be able to snatch it back from him.

But he didn't.

He hurled the can back at me. I snatched it out of the air just as the wolf knocked me down and the peacock sank its claws into my legs. The wolf's huge jaws opened wide and snapped at my hand that held the tin. He didn't get me, but I felt the shock of contact with his wet lips.

Before I could cry out, the air burst around me with a tremendous bang and a sulfurous cloud of stink. It was Mermeros, larger than life, and furious. At the sight of him, the wolf and the peacock screamed in rage. He bowled the wolf aside with one huge arm and batted the peacock aside with the other. They tumbled over, snarling and hissing. They leaped up and began to assume their fearsome human forms. Dark, blood-chilling words shot out from their skeletal mouths.

They were too late. Before they could complete their transformation, Mermeros had scooped me up and whisked me toward Alice and Tommy, then gathered us all up and took off soaring through the air, northward and westward, to London and safety and home.

ermeros," I asked him, somewhere over northern Italy,
"why did you rescue us?"

"I didn't," he said. "I rescued myself."

We'd been flying for some time, perhaps ten minutes, in a curious
reversal of the trip that brought us to Persia. Now, instead of racing
toward the morning sun, we were... Well, come to think of it, racing
toward the morning sun again. Leaving midmorning by the Tigris
River and hurtling backward through the stages of sunrise to reach
the darkness before the dawn. It would still be nighttime in London,
but only just. Miss Salamanca and the other girls and ladies at her
dismal school would be just waking up when we got back. With luck,
we'd slip back before they found us missing.

"If you were only going to rescue yourself, we'd be back there on
the sands, being eaten by your family," I pointed out. "A jolly good
time that would be."

"Your proper fate is the one thing my brothers and I agree upon,"
said my heartless servant. "Little girls should be eaten and not heard."

"I'm *not* little!"

"Are you of marriageable age?" the djinni asked.

"Don't be revolting," I told him.

"Then you're little."

"She saved you, too, you know, you big ungrateful fish," said Tommy.

"How many fish do you know that are grateful?" was Mermeros's snide reply.

I hadn't yet figured out what to say to Tommy. Somehow it was easier to harass Mermeros than to thank the orphan boy. He'd given me the ring and crest for safekeeping. That was very trusting of him. But why did he throw me the sardine can? Even if he'd wanted to save me, which was stout of him, he could've done it as Mermeros's new master. I knew Tommy wanted this power I controlled more than anything. Without this chance at freedom, he was one birthday away from a lifetime in a cotton mill. A short lifetime, if the stories I heard were true. He needed Mermeros far more than I did.

Yet he gave me my sardine can back. I couldn't understand it, and it irked me. In his mind, we had made a truce. I never agreed to it, but he assumed I had, and I hadn't corrected his error. Not every boy would let a truce bind them when a djinni lands in their outstretched hand. Tom must be one of those typical boys who took sportsmanship so seriously. The British cultivated them like sheep.

And now I owed Tom a favor.

"You still haven't answered my question, Mermeros," I said.

"Is it your wish that I answer you?" His voice was soft, almost gentle.

Only just barely did I catch myself. I *almost* nodded. *What a beastly trick!* What a rotten way to spend my last wish. That odious creature would probably abandon us here, in midair, over the French Alps, if I'd spent my third. The bright snow on the sunlit mountain-tops looked soft and puffy beneath us, but I was pretty sure landing in it from this high up wouldn't feel so nice.

Alice shivered in the cold air, and I pulled her close to keep her warm. Her face burned. She was bright pink with sunburn. *This* would take some explaining in a London December.

"Poor Alice," I told her. "We'll get you home and put some salve on your burnt skin."

Tommy watched over Mermeros's shoulders as the Channel rushed toward us. "So, they really were your brothers, those two, er, *things* we met?"

Mermeros nodded.

"What would they have done to you?"

It was dark now. The spray of the Channel misted our faces. Mermeros's speed slowed down to a languid pace, and we followed the silvery curves of the Thames toward London.

"My brothers think our father was too lenient when he cursed me and made me a djinni," he said at length. "They think I should be tortured to death."

"I can understand that," I said.

"Maeve!" cried Alice. But Tommy grinned.

"To answer your question, puny girl-child," said Mermeros, "since I don't care one way or another what you know, I am permitted to remove myself from danger, so long as I take my master with me." He sniffed at the word *master*.

"Then why did you bring Tommy and me?" asked Alice.

I knew Mermeros liked Alice far more than he liked me, though that still wasn't saying a lot. "You don't weigh much."

Tommy laughed. "You just didn't want to deal with an angry Maeve if you didn't."

Mermeros drifted down in lazy circles toward the courtyard of the abandoned grand home near Miss Salamanca's school. He didn't confirm Tommy's statement, but he didn't deny it, either. Well, good. I hoped I'd given the spoiled fish at least a little reason to avoid my displeasure.

He set us down on the paving stones. "I warned you, hatchlings." He cranked himself down to size and curled into lazy loops of smoke that siphoned back into the sardine can. "You have one wish left. Use it wisely."

His eyes met mine, and he smirked. I heard his words echoing through my brain: "Your wishes will destroy you... Greed will take hold. Gold lust will consume you. It will infiltrate you like a cancer until it owns you, body and soul, and drives you to madness and ruin."

They hadn't yet, had they? Was it so greedy to want to travel the world, and form a cricket league for girls?

He was nearly gone now, but his gaze fell upon his father's carved bracelet, still on my wrist, and my pocket, where I'd put the ring and the royal crest.

"You're playing with fire, little girl," he said. "You have no idea what dangers you've just unleashed. What things you've stolen, and whom you've stolen them from." With a nasty smile, he blinked out of view. "Sweet dreams."

I snuck Alice up the servants' back stairs so she could dive into bed before morning light, so housemaids or Miss Salamanca couldn't discover her missing. Whoever had locked the door last night had done a poor job of it. When she was finally situated in her room, with her face slathered with ointment, Tommy and I shimmied down the pipe once more, and he showed me his secret entrance to the cellar.

Morning sunlight had begun to crawl across London's smoky skies, and I was in a hurry to get to my cot before Old Sally discovered it empty. I tried not to think about the bloody feud the rats had fought over my bits of food on that very cot. Morris hooted softly at Tommy and waddled over to see what treats he'd brought. He had to settle for more licorice. He seemed content.

We weren't a second too soon. I'd barely reached my cot and sat upon it before the raspy door was wrenched open, and Miss Salamanca descended the rickety stairs, holding a lantern next to her face. It illuminated her long nose and hollow cheekbones to hideous perfection.

Tommy didn't even have a chance to get away. He melted into the shadows and flattened himself against a wall. I braced myself for Old Sally's scolding, and wished Tommy wouldn't be there to hear it.

Maeve Merritt isn't afraid of anything, I told myself, but having a new pal watch me be torn to ribbons by a vulture of a headmistress offended my pride. Not ashamed to admit it.

But there was no scolding. Not a stitch of what I'd been expecting.

"Well, Miss Merritt," she said, "I trust we've learned our lesson this night?"

I bowed my head so she couldn't see my face. "I've learned quite a lot, Miss Salamanca."

"As I predicted." She fanned the dank air from before her face. "Now, hurry up and come upstairs. You need to wash and eat quickly. I've received a letter from Mr. Alfred Treazleton, requesting a private conversation with you this morning."

"With *me*?"

"Yes. Odd though that must seem, with you. No doubt he wishes to address your shocking behavior toward him yesterday during visiting hours." She sucked in air around her big teeth. "I trust your night in the cellar will serve as a caution to you? If you are inclined to respond to the illustrious Mr. Treazleton, a great man of commerce in the city, and a principal benefactor of this school, with the sort of impertinence you displayed yesterday, your days at this school shall be numbered."

I suspect I must have smiled then. Or failed to hide my joy. *Leave this nightmare of a school? Yes, please!* Though I *would* miss Alice.

Miss Salamanca scowled. "They'll be numbered *long*, I mean to say. And you'll spend each of those nights down here."

Good, I thought. Then I shall have free rein every night to roam the city as I please. Until I make my final wish that gets me out of this dump forever.

Old Sally wasn't satisfied. She leaned down closer. "I know you're up to something, Maeve Merritt," she hissed. "You think you're so fearless. But all you are is an unruly, undisciplined hoyden of a girl who needs putting in her place. I've seen your kind before. And putting girls like you in their place is what I'm famous for."

Famous? Hah! Yet in spite of myself, a chill ran down my spine. I hoped Tommy couldn't see it.

"I shall join your meeting with Mr. Treazleton this morning, to personally ensure that your behavior is exemplary," she said. "Now, move along. If you repeat my words to your parents, I shall denounce you as the liar you are. Whom do you think they'll believe?"

I rose and marched toward the door, toward breakfast and a

wash, my mind seething with thoughts of revenge. She was wrong. Someone *had* heard our conversation. I had a witness to her wickedness. But, of course, Tommy's word, as a rascally orphan, was worth even less than mine.

"My dear lady," boomed Mr. Alfred P. Treazleton to Miss Salamanca, when she presented herself as my chaperone for our conversation in her private parlor an hour later, "have no fear. Miss Merritt and I will have a friendly chat, I assure you." He patted my shoulder. "This young lady has spirit, and I like to see that. It just needs molding a bit. I'm merely here with some fatherly advice for her." He waggled his bushy eyebrows at Miss Salamanca, who blushed. Disgusting and even more disgusting. "I promise, I won't bite."

Miss Salamanca looked stuck. To yield to Mr. Treazleton was to admit defeat, which tasted bitter after she'd threatened that she'd be watching me. And yet she was utterly incapable of *not* yielding to Mr. Treazleton. She turned this way and that, until her eyes settled upon the double doors to this room, and the gap between them.

I knew what she was thinking. She'd leave her parlor for our use, then spy on us from outside the door. Clearly, Theresa's father read her thoughts as well.

"Come to think of it, it's a pleasant morning," he said, "and we could all do with a bit more exercise. Why don't Miss Merritt and I take a stroll together? Not far, just toward the park." When Miss Salamanca opened her toothy mouth to protest, he silenced her with an upraised hand. "It's no trouble, I assure you. Have no fear for her safety. I shall be personally responsible for her."

"But her parents—" she stammered weakly.

"—are friends of mine," said the Great Financier. "That is to say, her father is employed at a bank in which I hold a financial interest, and I occupy a seat on the board of directors. So, I am hardly a stranger. We are connected."

Hearing Mr. Treazleton claim a connection between himself and my family would've put my mother into a swoon. When recovered, she would boast of the connection in every single conversation for the rest of her life.

Miss Salamanca sagged. "Well, in that case, of course." But her hawk-eyed gaze burrowed into mine as I shrugged my arms into my coat. "I am certain that Miss Merritt will behave herself admirably on this special outing."

"Of course she will!" Mr. Treazleton beamed at me, and out we went.

His smile was so warm it left me bewildered. I followed him out the door and across the pavement to the street. He paused to allow me to catch up with him, then took off at a pleasant pace.

"Charming day for this time of year," he observed, noting the bit of blue that had found its way through London's clouds and smoke. The day was, indeed, pleasant, with birds hopping about on bare tree limbs in the park and nannies pushing prams carrying bundled babies over the tufty withered grass and leaves.

I followed along and watched the man. He smiled at everyone he met, doffing his tall hat to ladies, young and old, and depositing coins in the gnarled hand of an elderly beggar on a street corner.

Was this Alfred P. Treazleton? His genial manner disarmed me. Where was the haughty man of yesterday, berating Tommy? Well, for that matter, men do get very touchy about their horses, and if he'd misunderstood Tommy's intentions, it stood to reason. But he was the father of the odious Theresa! Still, spoiled daughters could be the offspring of fathers who are generous to a fault. I wasn't ready to let my guard down, but I decided, cautiously, to view Mr. Treazleton with a slightly more open mind.

"Miss Merritt... May I call you Maeve?"

I nodded. People did not usually ask me what they could call me.

"Miss Maeve, then. You strike me, if I may be permitted to observe, as a bright young lady with an appetite for adventure."

He turned a penetrating gaze my way. I didn't know where to look, so I studied my shoes. His shoes, I noted, were polished to an impossible gleam.

"School must be a suffocating experience for someone like you," he went on, "all cooped up and buttoned up and lectured six ways from Sunday. Am I wrong?"

I shook my head. No, he certainly wasn't wrong. But what cause had he ever had to observe me or think about me at all?

He'd studied me more, in a couple of brief encounters, than my mother ever had in a lifetime. Maybe keen observation was required in captains of industry.

"Tell me," he said, "what sorts of adventures you'd look for if you could."

A little warning sounded in my head: *Don't tell him anything! Keep your ideas to yourself!* But why? What harm could there be in discussing my private thoughts with him? It wasn't as though they were particularly secret. If the *Daily Telegraph* wanted to run a headline tomorrow, "Schoolgirl Dreams of Girls' Cricket League," I couldn't see how that would affect me much.

"I'd like to travel the world," I said. "See all the faraway places I've read about."

"Like Miss Isabella Bird," he said. "What a marvelous plan!"

"You know about her?"

He laughed heartily. "I've read each of her works with enormous interest."

I couldn't believe we had anything in common.

Mr. Treazleton rubbed his hands together. "I myself have done a bit of traveling, in my younger days. I toured America, even. Stood at the very rim of the Grand Canyon. But now, business and family matters keep me in London most of the time."

It surprised me to think that someone as rich and powerful as Mr. Treazleton couldn't go anywhere he wanted to, anytime he wished. But I suppose a vast commercial enterprise can't exactly run itself.

"What else would you do, if you could?" he asked.

I decided I might as well say it. "I'd like to start a cricket league for girls."

His eyes widened. "You don't say!"

I nodded. He didn't seem horrified, so I proceeded.

"I grew up playing cricket every day with the lads in my village," I said.

"And which village would that be?"

"Luton," I said.

He nodded. "Of course. The trains run there now, don't they?"

"Only just. My father takes the train to work now."

"At St. Michael's Bank and Trust." He winked at me. "You see, Miss Maeve, I do get around, where the city of London is concerned." He walked along, swinging his gold-tipped cane in one hand. "Well, well. A cricket league for girls, and trips around the world. Those are some very fine ambitions."

Those were the last, positively the very last, words I expected to hear out of his mouth. Or, for that matter, out of any adult's mouth, where my schemes were concerned.

"Do you think so?" I looked up at his face. I had to be sure he wasn't mocking me.

He nodded, quite seriously. "Indeed, I do." He pursed his lips. "Of course, they would cost a fair deal of money. Especially the travel. Traveling clothes, boots, mules, horses, maps, meals, hotels, guides, ocean passage—it's uncanny how costs add up." He pretended to tally up figures on his fingers. "And to start a league, why, you'd need coaches, uniforms, equipment, advertising..." He sighed. "Again and again I find, Miss Maeve, that projects always cost a great deal more than one thinks they should."

He sounded just like my dad. He was probably saying the same thing right now about Mother's plans for Evangeline's wedding.

"Suppose I were to make you an offer?"

I stopped in my tracks. "An offer?"

"A business proposal."

He had my attention.

"I will undertake to finance your trip around the world, and your cricket league, with a lump sum payment of five thousand pounds—"

Five thousand pounds!

"Deposited to St. Michael's Bank and Trust, accruing interest until the day when you are old enough to carry out these admirable plans."

I could barely find words to speak.

"But why?" I finally managed to say. "For what? What would you get out of this?"

He watched me as though he was surprised by my question. "Your djinni, of course."

My body went still.

My djinni?

I drew back. My fingers moved toward my pocket. The sardine can wasn't there—I'd hidden it in my room, along with the other artifacts—but Mr. Treazleton's eyes caught the gesture. Now he knew where I usually kept it.

I wanted to give myself a black eye for being such a fool. All that charm and friendliness? He was just warming me up to connive me out of my djinni.

I tried to stall with a bluff. "I don't know what you're talking about."

"Oh, come, now, Miss Merritt, we haven't time for that." I wasn't Maeve anymore.

Playing a role was never my strength. But I faked a tittering laugh. "You don't believe in *djinnis*, do you, Mr. Treazleton?"

His eyes never left my face. "Should I not?"

I remembered the incident of Theresa Treazleton's braids and his whispered conversation with her just yesterday afternoon during visiting hours. She *had* told him about my djinni. And he'd believed her! The thought of *my* parents believing that I'd found an ancient spirit of power was laughable. But somehow, this man trusted his daughter.

Wouldn't that be nice? Imagine if my mother thought anything I did was worth taking seriously! I would never envy Theresa for her money nor her prettiness, but I actually envied her the esteem in which her father held her. Imagine that.

We stood on a path through the park, near a bench, and Mr. Treazleton took a seat upon it, after first dusting it off with his pocket handkerchief. He gestured for me to join him. I took a few steps closer, but I didn't sit. Staying on my feet made me taller than him. I needed every advantage I could get.

"Well, Miss Merritt, do we have an agreement?"

I swallowed hard. *Five thousand pounds. Only one wish remaining.* I pictured Mermeros billowing out of his sardine can to find Arthur P. Treazleton as his new master. He'd probably be pleased, that arrogant old fish. They practically deserved each other.

Then I remembered Mr. Treazleton's footman's cracking whip lashing across Tommy's shoulder.

No, there was nothing forgivable about that. I shook myself.

How had I come to listen to, to almost trust, this mean man? Nasty Theresa's nasty father?

Imagine this man with Mermeros's power at his fingertips. Imagine the wishes his arrogant mind would conjure up.

"I'd like to go back to school now," I told him, which, under any other circumstances, would've been a lie.

"It's quite a nice position your father holds at St. Michael's Bank and Trust," he said. "Worked his way up for many years. Finally, he can provide a comfortable living for his wife and daughters."

He interlaced his fingers and rested them atop the knob of his cane. I stared at those fat, soft fingers, afraid to find out what he was really saying. In my stomach, I already knew.

"I spoke to my old friend Edgar about him just last evening," he said. "Edgar was over at my house for supper. Oh, you know Edgar, don't you?"

I shook my head.

"Edgar Pinagree? The bank manager? Your father's superior at the bank?"

Oh. That Edgar.

"There's nothing Edgar wouldn't do for me if I asked him," said Mr. Treazleton. "In fact, I am well accustomed to my wishes being honored. I am a man of considerable reputation in this city, with a great many people eager to do me favors, though I suppose a young girl like you would know nothing about that."

I let the jab pass. I didn't care. I knew what he was about, and I was tired of being manipulated by him.

"What exactly are you hinting at, Mr. Treazleton?" I asked him. "I'm not accustomed to bullies tiptoeing around their dirty business. On the playground, they're much more straightforward. Call you names, or sock you in the chin, but at least they're honest about it."

The whoosh of a little laugh escaped him.

"Well, aren't you something," he said. "I'm not accustomed to hard negotiating with little girls still in their petticoats, Miss Merritt. You don't know whom you're dealing with."

I felt my fingers flexing into fists. Of course, I couldn't take a poke at this man as I had his daughter, nor stick him with a pin as she had me, but a fighting stance cleared my head and kept my eyes sharp.

When he spoke again, his voice still had the same friendly tone, but his eyes were as hard as flint.

"I began by making you a very generous offer," he said. "Five thousand pounds for your djinni. You appear to be uninterested. Very well. I shall make myself quite clear: I will have that djinni from you before the new year. You now have two options: give it to me freely, with no payment—that ship has sailed, you see—or don't, in which case I shall see to it that your father is sacked from his post, with his name and reputation ruined, such that he'll never secure an honest position in London again."

My head swirled and my brain felt hot. How *dare* he threaten my father? How dare he threaten *me*? Would he actually be so wicked as to destroy my father's career over my little sardine tin and its fishy occupant?

"Rest assured, Miss Merritt, that whether you give me the djinni or not, I will have it. I won't rest until it's mine. There is no possible way you can keep it from me."

He was trying to scare me. He almost succeeded.

I took a deep breath. I still had my djinni. I still had my fists and my wits. And there's one thing I know: never, ever, ever yield to a bully, nor give in to fear. No matter what.

I flashed him my most confident smile. No bluffing this time.

"I like a challenge, on the cricket field, and otherwise," I told him. "I'll be ready for you."

He snorted with laughter. "Will you, now? You have no idea what awaits you."

"I think, Mr. Treazleton," I told him, "that you don't know whom *you're* dealing with, either." And before he could lever himself off the bench, I turned and marched back to school.

CHAPTER 18

Fine words. Grand words. Bold and brave, in the moment.

But what on earth was I to do? What couldn't a man like Mr. Treazleton do to get my sardine can? What wouldn't he do? If he was anything like his daughter Theresa, he'd stop at nothing to get his way.

And Father! Poor Father, and his post at the bank! It was the one thing he took real pride in. Not his four daughters: a spinster, two ninnies, and a tomboy. He loved us, of course. I'd never doubted that. But his post was his prize jewel.

I'd told Alfred P. Treazleton that I'd be ready for him. I had better be.

He sent me a letter by the next day's post. The fat red wax seal of a *T* surrounded by laurel leaves on the envelope repulsed me. I didn't like knowing his greedy hands had touched the elegant letter paper. But

I borrowed Alice's letter opener, pulled out the note, and scanned its lines. They were nothing more than a repetition of the threats he'd made on our walk. I tossed the envelope into a drawer of my desk and tried to put it out of my thoughts.

Miss Salamanca didn't know what to do with me after my meeting with Mr. Treazleton. She couldn't quite send me back to the cellar, or the coal bin, lest he should want to see me again, so she let me return to my classes. They were punishment enough.

If I'd thought I was a leper among the other girls for socking Theresa in the eye, or chopping off her braids (and Honoria's), it was nothing to the pariah I became after publicly sassing Mr. Alfred P. Treazleton. Theresa's hatred for me sank to new depths of loathing. The other girls looked upon me as a condemned criminal, awaiting execution.

A sort of sad pity, mingled with horror and fear, was on most of their faces when I passed them by; Winnifred Herzig's especially. She seemed to dog me around, anxious not to miss anything that might befall me. I felt once more like a gladiator in the ring, with spectators leaning over their seats to not miss a single inch of my entrails once the lion ripped them out of me. I began making sinister faces at Winnifred, just to scare her off. A girl needs her privacy.

Poor Alice glowed like a summertime strawberry with her sunburn. She actually fibbed—truthful Alice! She told the teachers it was a rash, so they sent her back to her room to rest. I visited her when I could and helped her slather her face and neck with cold cream, which I pilfered from Honoria Brisbane's dressing table. No amount of cream could make Honoria look attractive, and Alice needed it, so my conscience didn't bother me in the slightest.

We kept my sardine can and the other artifacts hidden in Alice's secret spot, behind the loose shelf in the closet. I tried not to think about it, nor about Mermeros, and certainly not about Mr. Treazleton. I needed time to plan my third wish, and I didn't want to repeat past mistakes.

But Mr. Treazleton's threats worried me, so I did something rare, for me, and wrote my father a letter. I asked him how he was getting along, and how things were at work. I still couldn't fathom how Mr. Treazleton would stoop so low as to go after my father and harm his career. Fathers were supposed to be invincible.

Two days later, Polydora took a morning train in company with our aunt Vera to visit me and inquire whether I had contracted the flu. Only feverish delirium, my family thought, would make me write a letter to Father, so Polly was dispatched to check on me. She examined my eyes, my ears, my tongue, and my skin color. She interviewed me about my eating, sleeping, and homework. Was I all right? Were the teachers kind? Was I making friends? And so on.

It was Polly who raised me, really. She read me stories and gave me baths and mended my pinafores and tucked me in at night. She always missed me when I was away at school, and I missed her, too. Sometimes Polly's need to nurture someone reaches a boiling point, and I help her let off steam.

As I say, it's always a treat to see Polly, and Aunt Vera, a cheerful, clever woman who will talk about anything to anybody, is one of my favorite relatives, but, after they left, I resolved to try to write to Father a bit more often. He was busy most of the time, and fussy over money the rest of the time, but at least he wasn't silly, with a head full of nonsense, like certain of my sisters. I'll make no comment about my mother.

My mind wandered in Miss Guntherson's French class as I thought and thought about the final wish and how to spend it. I needed a wish with effects that would last for the rest of my life, since this was the finale.

Why did it have to be the finale? How could I have used my first two wishes so foolishly? I racked my brain to remember all that Mermeros had said about the thieves. The ones who tried to pass the djinni around, and instead went mad and killed each other. Well, no wonder; they were criminals, after all. I wouldn't trust Tom with Mermeros for one second. Could I trust Alice? Lend her the djinni and ask her to give one of her wishes to me? She had everything money could buy, so she wouldn't mind. Would she? Surely we wouldn't murder each other. What rubbish.

But as I thought on that plan, something turned sour inside my stomach. Yes, I trusted her to hold on to it for me, but if I were to give Alice the djinni outright, and she became its master, anything could happen. I'd no longer be in control. She might lose it, or get some silly, "noble" idea and drop it in the Thames to save me from making any more wishes.

Or what if she *changed*? What if power went straight to her head, and she forgot all about her promise to me? She might decide not to share a wish. She might not give me the djinni back. She might hog all the wishes for herself. She might get drunk on power, and then she wouldn't be shy Alice anymore, the Alice who enjoys the company of someone like me, and—

I caught myself. Alice? Was I really suspecting things of *Alice*?

My face felt hot, and my hands, sweaty. I wanted to race back to the room to check to make sure the sardine tin was where it ought to be.

I was being silly. Surely I was.

But no, I wouldn't give Mermeros away to gain more wishes. Not if it might cost me the only one I had left. My only option was to spend it well.

I thought about travel, and about my cricket league. I still wanted them desperately. They both cost money.

In fact, independence cost money, plain and simple. If a girl or woman was to live life on her own terms, she needed money of her own to do it with. If she needed her father or her husband to give her the money, then she was only as free as he allowed her to be. The money came with strings attached. Expectations that must be met.

And how could a girl earn money of her own? I was certain I had no eccentric uncles out there anywhere ready to die and leave me a fortune. It was so unfair, all rich uncles belonging to some other niece but me.

I could work for money, of course, once I was grown. But my family would look down on that. So be it; I could shrug off their disapproval. But most of the jobs available to women, and I knew there weren't many, paid very little. If I were chained to a desk or a sewing machine, figuratively speaking, or a chalkboard like Miss Guntherson, here, I couldn't very well visit the Pyramids.

Some people's lot in life was to be born into fortune, like Theresa Treazleton. Other people, like me, were born into enough for everyday, but not enough to be truly free. I looked out the window at Mission Industrial School and Home for Working Boys. Some people, I reflected, were born into nothing at all.

I should, no doubt, be more grateful. But I wanted so much more out of life. And I'd been handed a miracle, if not a rich uncle: a wish-granting djinni with one wish left for me. Why not wish myself into vast riches and be free from others' rules and wishes for me forever?

I couldn't see a flaw in this plan. But I bided my time. Two impulsive wishes hadn't exactly gone as hoped.

One puzzling thing kept on happening. Whenever I passed by Theresa Treazleton, in the dining room, in a classroom aisle, or in a corridor, she bumped into me, hard. The first time, I thought it was an accident. The second time, I thought she was clumsy. The third time, I thought she was just mean.

I guess I'm a slow learner. By the fourth time, I'd figured it out. She was trying to find out if I had the sardine can in my pocket.

My suspicion was confirmed when I came upstairs to my dormitory room and rounded the stairwell just in time to see her tiptoe out of my room, close the door softly behind her, and furtively look both ways. My heart nearly stopped. When she saw me, her face hardened.

"Looking for something, Theresa?"

"I don't know what you've done with it," she hissed, "but we'll find it. This is war."

I laughed in relief. She hadn't found it, then. My reaction only angered her more. But I ought to give some thought to better hiding places.

"You think it's funny," she said, "punching my face and chopping my hair, but you'll pay. We will get that djinni. Just see if we don't. A nasty girl like you doesn't deserve it."

She turned and stormed off to her own room.

"You think you're entitled to everything," I called after her. "You think *darling* Theresa Treazleton deserves everything her heart desires."

"I should say she deserves it more than a reprobate like you," said Miss Salamanca, popping up in the corridor just then, like a mole from its hole.

Tommy climbed our drainpipe late one night for a friendly chat. Alice still looked a bit queasy at the prospect of letting a boy into our room, but at least she didn't scream. Bit by bit, I'd win her over to my life of crime.

Tommy showed us a little leather thong he'd made to loop around Morris's leg.

"With this," he explained, "I can take Morris for an outing one of these days. In the park, maybe."

"They let you go free during the daytime?" asked Alice. "We don't get to."

"Not really," Tom said. "But things will be more relaxed over the holidays. The masters will stay up late celebrating, and mornings won't have classes. A good time to come and go."

That got me thinking about what Tom's Christmas season might look like. "What happens at Christmas at your school, Tom?"

His face stiffened. "Nothing much. Some visitors. From churches and such." He fingered the leather strap. When he looked up and saw us still watching him, he shrugged. "It's fine, you know? We're not expecting *presents*." He spoke the last word like it was an object of scorn. I knew better. To misquote Shakespeare—and see, Miss Stratford? I did pay attention—the orphan doth protest too much, methinks. He'd have to be in his coffin not to want presents.

"I'll write to you over the holidays, Tom," I told him. Least I could do. Maybe even send him some shortbread.

"Don't," he said, without looking up. "The masters would be suspicious. None of us gets mail. I'd never see the letter. They'd open it, and I'd get... Well, just don't."

He'd get in trouble for having a friend who's a girl.

"So, are we going on another adventure, or what?" asked Tom.

Alice, whose nausea had finally seemed to pass, now looked greener than ever.

"Not tonight," I told him. "I've got to think hard about how to use my last wish."

Tom's eyes gleamed. He still thought after I got my last wish, he'd be next.

"Say, Alice," he said, "what will you wish for when it's your turn?"

Alice blinked. "When it's *my* turn?"

Tom looked surprised. "Hasn't Maeve told you?" he said. "We'll all take a turn being its master."

I smelled danger. Alice gave me a very curious look. But, old sport that she is, she went along with it. As I say, she was learning every day the arts of subterfuge.

"My wish is probably impossible," she said. "I would wish to leave this school and go home to my grandparents—"

"Entirely possible," I said.

"That would just be the first wish," Alice said. "And for my second, I would wish for a pure high C that wouldn't ever crack."

"A high *what*?" Tom looked baffled.

"Music rubbish," I explained, having at least the benefit of Miss Salisbury contributing to my education. "She wants a voice that would shatter glass."

"I do not!"

"Go on," I said. "Both of those wishes seem doable."

Alice sighed. "It's the third one that probably isn't." A sad look came over her face. "I would wish that I could always live with my grandparents, and nothing would change."

Tommy and I looked at each other. We were both confused.

"You mean, you wouldn't grow up?" I asked.

"Oh, I'd grow up," she said quickly, "but they wouldn't grow any older."

High C or no, her voice cracked at that.

"You're afraid of them dying," I said softly.

"Haven't you got parents?" asked Tom.

She smiled sadly. "No," she said. "I'm an orphan, too. But I have the most wonderful grandparents. I miss them so much, being here. And when I think about getting older, I..."

"You'll have everything, Alice," I said. "Homes and carriages and money and all that anybody could want."

She looked at me as though I was daft. "And nobody to share it with?"

Oh.

"You'll have friends," I said. "I'll be there."

"Me too," Tommy said stoutly, then looked at the floor. "If that's all right."

"Of course, that would be all right," Alice said, and I could've hugged her on the spot. "But you see how it is with Theresa Treazleton, and girls like her. The people that chase after rich friends are usually not the nicest people to have around."

"I didn't know you were rich," Tommy said. "You don't, er, act the part."

"That's because she's our Alice," I said. I turned to my roommate. "You're afraid you'll have no one to trust," I told her. This was all a revelation to me. I had no idea. I'd never considered it. "Well, don't worry, Alice. I'll be there with my cricket bat, and I'll give those phony types a good crack in the shins."

Alice grinned.

Footsteps sounded outside the hall. We froze, and Alice blew out her candle. Finally, when it seemed safe, Tommy crept out the window and slid down the pole.

"Maeve," Alice whispered, when he was gone, "why did Tommy think I'd get a turn with the djinni?"

I gulped.

"Does he think he'll get the djinni when you're done with it?"

I squirmed between the sheets. "I believe he does."

"You believe he does," she echoed. "And will he?"

Egads. She was as persistent as a detective in a story. "It doesn't work that way."

"But you haven't made that clear," she said. "You're letting him think he's next."

"So he doesn't rob me," I protested.

"But, Maeve," Alice said. "Tommy thinks you're his friend. Aren't you?"

I said nothing.

"You wouldn't lie to your friends, would you, Maeve?"

She stabbed my heart. No, my conscience. "I've never told you anything untrue, Alice." Just the kind of slippery, slimy thing Mermeros would say.

"That's not the same thing," she said, and eventually, went to sleep.

Days passed, one after another, and Alice's disappointment in me was never mentioned again. We didn't see Tommy, so I put my guilty conscience out of my mind. I thought constantly about Wish Number Three, but I couldn't satisfy myself as to the exact, ideal words.

Mr. Treazleton's words and Theresa's treachery, likewise, faded from my thoughts, though I shouldn't have let them fade. My mind was soon occupied with plans for the Christmas holidays. Needlework class had shifted from embroidery to knitting, and we were all busy making mufflers and mittens for the poor boys at Mission Industrial School and Home for Working Boys. It made me laugh to think of Tommy as a "poor boy," though, of course, I supposed he probably hadn't a shilling to his name. My muffler was the worst of any girl's at Miss Salamanca's school, and, as for mittens, Miss Bickle, the needlework instructor, gave up on me altogether. Alice knitted mine for me.

Her sunburn had faded to a golden glow by the time the hallowed tradition of the muffler-mitten hand-off rolled around. The weather lost *its* golden glow and settled into a chilly winter. Just right for Advent, holly berries, candles in frosty windows, and the coming of Christmas.

On the day of the charitable home's Christmas treat, we were given an early tea, then sent to our rooms to dress in our matching plaid uniform capes and bonnets. Apparently, we would be seen at our most adorable that way, not that I gave a fig about that. I had an idea, one planted in my mind by Mr. Treazleton himself. I wanted to talk to Alice about it.

"Would you help me get the sardine can down from the shelf?" I asked her as soon as we were both in our room.

"Hush!" She gestured toward the door, where girls' footsteps tramped past our room in the corridor.

"It's just sardines," I teased her. "My favorite teatime snack on toast." I dropped my voice to a whisper. "I think I have an idea for my final wish. Want to hear it?"

Alice opened the closet, removed the shelf, and pulled the sardine can out from its hiding place, then reached for her winter things. "Go on, then."

I took the can and spun it slowly between my thumb and finger. Not fast enough to bother Mermeros, I figured. But if it made him a little bit queasy, I wouldn't mind.

How best to explain what I had in mind? I'd thought about it a thousand ways. But it all boiled down to one necessary thing, and it made for the simplest explanation.

"I'll wish for a fortune," I told Alice. "Bags and bags of money. More than I could ever need. Then I can use it to do whatever I might wish for in the future—travel, buy a home, start a cricket league for girls. What do you think?"

Alice frowned. "Money?"

She looked at me as though I had mustard smeared all over my frock. I didn't like it.

"Why, what's wrong with money?" I demanded.

She settled her bonnet over her golden curls. "It's just so... I don't know. Anybody can wish for money. Most people do. It seems like some of the meanest people do nothing *but* wish for money."

"It's not the money I want," I explained. "It's what the money will buy. I'm not *greedy*."

Mermeros's warning from the cellar flashed before me, but I pushed it aside. I *wasn't* greedy. I wasn't like those others he was talking about. Besides, who knew if he was even telling the truth about people's lives being ruined, and all that rubbish? The full truth, I mean, without slippery exaggeration. The big windbag was probably just trying to scare me, just as Mr. Treazleton had tried to do.

Alice never liked to make anyone unhappy. I knew these

questions were making her uncomfortable. "Maeve, you're not like other people. The wish to visit Persia... That was you all over. It was a 'Maeve' wish to make. Dangerous, and daring, and full of mystery." She smiled. "Even turning Theresa and Honoria's braids green. That was classic Maeve. Attack first and think later."

I laughed. It had been a waste of a wish, but worth it, too.

"I only have one wish left, Alice," I told her. "I squandered the others. Money's the best way to make all the other wishes I've been dreaming of come true."

Alice shook her head. "Don't turn into a...a *banker* now, Maeve. Don't be a miser or a moneybags. Be *you*. Do something exciting. Something spectacular."

I couldn't stop what came out of me next. Or, perhaps I could, but I didn't want to. "That's easily said when you're Alice Bromley, sole granddaughter of *the* Grosvenor Square Bromleys," I said. It was rotten of me. I wasn't sorry. "You can have anything you want, anytime you want it. If you wanted a cricket league, you could form one tomorrow."

Alice looked stung. Immediately I *was* sorry. Alice could have anything she wanted, but she didn't. Some girls took every occasion to flaunt their dresses and travels and bijoux. Not Alice. You'd never know she came from wealth.

I reached for Alice's hand. "That was beastly of me," I said. "I'm sorry. I didn't mean it."

Alice tried to smile, but her face was sad. "I know you didn't."

Trust Alice Bromley to be so good a soul that her wealth made *her* feel badly about it.

She met my gaze fixedly. "I'm beginning to think," she said, "that the things we want most in life shouldn't come as granted wishes. If we don't work for them, what do they even mean? Do they even matter?"

I was beginning to see the truth. Quiet Alice Bromley could see right through me. It was a good thing she was my friend. Even if she made me squirm.

"Miss *Merritt*! Miss *Bromley*!" bellowed Miss Guntherson's very un-French voice from downstairs. "Everyone else is ready for their errand of mercy but *you*!"

I quickly hid the sardine can under my pillow, then scurried into my winter things and followed Alice down the stairs at a trot. This third wish needed more thinking. Alice was right about wishing for money.

Was Mermeros right, too?

CHAPTER
20

We assembled in the paved courtyard where we had greeted our families on visiting day. We would assemble there again the next morning when they came to bring us home for the holidays. I couldn't wait.

The clouds were thick and heavy, moist with the hopeful promise of snow. Outside the enveloping arms of the school building, London's noises never paused, but in the courtyard, quiet hung in the expectant air.

After inspecting our appearances in the frosty dark, the schoolmistresses gave us each a candle. Miss Salisbury, the music mistress, waggled her hands to lead us in singing "O Little Town of Bethlehem." As soon as our voices began, Miss Salamanca took her lantern and lit the first girl's candle with it. The second girl tipped her taper into the first girl's until it lit. Thus, slowly, carefully, little lights spread down the line, casting a halo over each girl's face.

Yet in thy dark streets shineth
The everlasting light!
The hopes and fears of all the years
Are met in thee tonight.

Mine is not a heart of stone, despite what some people think. For that moment, with those candles, and that song, Christmas wrapped itself around me like a muffler—one knitted by someone other than me. Each girl became more, to me, than she'd been before. I couldn't stay vexed with anyone. I even felt a glimmer of acceptance of Theresa Treazleton. Miss Salamanca looked, for a moment, in lantern light, like her kindly, better, warmer self—like the girl she must've been once, if she'd ever had a mother to love her.

She led us slowly, still singing, across the street to the charitable home. Each of us walked with a lit candle in one hand and a parcel in the other: a muffler and a pair of mittens wrapped in red paper. We had each tied a little sack of sugarplums into the parcel's ribbon.

"Think of the poor, motherless boys who never get to enjoy a sweet," Miss Rosewater had said when we wrapped them. I remembered Tommy stealing my licorice, but said nothing.

London's bells broke out in their joyful, clamorous song. Seven o'clock. Time for a Christmas party. From the shouts and the steam-fogged windows of the washrooms across the way an hour before, the boys at the charitable home had faced a trying ordeal getting scrubbed and combed for the occasion. It tickled me to wonder what Tom would look like, all dandied up for a party. If there was lace anywhere, I'd never let him live it down.

We filed into the home and down a dark hallway to the refectory, where the boys ate their meals. It was colder here than at the girls' school. The corridor smelled faintly of coal smoke and burnt eggs and, well, of *boy*. Sweaty, unwashed, cricket-playing, wrestling-in-the-dirt boy. I contrasted it with Miss Salamanca's school, which smelled like starched pinafores and too many rules. I almost wished I were an orphan.

Until I saw the boys.

I'd seen them roughhousing at play, of course, but never lined up on exhibition as they were now.

They didn't need mufflers. They needed dinner.

They stood in a group, arranged by height, with the smallest lads in front, and the tallest in back. Tommy stuck out. His washed and combed hair looked as red as a Christmas apple. I knew he was a bony, lanky fellow, but it wasn't until I saw him clustered with all his mates that I realized how hungry he looked. They all did. Their cheeks were hollow, and their ankles, poking out from too-short trousers and knickers, looked like twigs.

I wondered which of them was the first to coin the phrase "Fast-bowl Franny."

Tommy wouldn't look at me.

Miss Guntherson directed us to line up and present our parcels to the orphans. At her severe nod, each girl recited the phrase she'd been taught: "Happy Christmas, and God bless you." At a scowl from one of the orphan masters, the recipient dutifully replied, "Thank you, miss, ever so kindly, for your generous gift."

I was determined to give my parcel to Tommy, so I hung back in the line until I saw a chance to give it to him, cutting off little Winnifred Herzig in the process. People were always cutting off Winnifred Herzig.

I shoved the parcel at Tommy and waited for him to see that it was me. Surely this was all a big joke to him, and we could have a laugh together about it later on. True, he'd be stuck with my muffler, but at least Alice had knitted his mittens.

But Tommy wouldn't take the parcel. He still wouldn't meet my gaze.

"Happy Christmas," I whispered. "What's the matter with you, anyway? Oh," I remembered my lines. "God bless you."

His dark glance flickered upward for an instant. It was as if we'd never gone to Persia with a djinni, as if we were back to being dread enemies.

What was *the matter with him? Were we no longer friends? Was he angry that I hadn't taken him on another adventure yet? Did he suspect I'd gone on one without him?*

Or was he embarrassed for me to see him this way?

A shadow fell over my hands holding the package. One of the orphan masters, a tired-looking man with a red face and thin, pale hair, stood behind Tom.

He rested an ink-stained hand on his shoulder. "Where are our manners, young man?"

Tommy spoke like one in a trance. His lips moved but his jaw did not. "Thank you, *miss*, ever so kindly, for your *generous* gift."

Any other time, I might've kicked him in the shins for being so testy with me. But the look on his face pulled me up short. To me, the whole business was a silly, sentimental holiday charade, but I could tell it was no joke to Tommy.

Now I understood his anger. Outside this room, we were friends. Inside it, I was one of the privileged young ladies, and he was a pathetic charity case.

I didn't see it that way at all, not one bit. But I could see how he might, and how that would sting his pride. It would sting anybody's.

All along the line, girls bestowed their gifts to the "poor, needy orphans." Girls with round cheeks, bright curls, new wool hats and capes, and self-satisfied faces. Some looked contemptuously at the boys, while others showed pity and concern, but always there was the glow of feeling they'd been virtuous and benevolent. Little Lady Bountifuls in training. For a moment, I saw what that must look like through Tommy's proud eyes. How galling, how humiliating, to be put on display to make wealthier children feel better about themselves! To remind the fortunate ones to be grateful for their comforts, while these boys shivered at night. It made me want to drop the sugarplums on the floor and tread them under my feet.

A pair of the littlest boys were of a different mind. They'd already gotten the wrappers off their candies. Now their cheeks bulged and their lips oozed sugary syrup. When the pale orphan master gave them a stern look, their guilty eyes went wide as full moons, but they sucked all the harder on their candies, lest they be forced to spit them out.

I couldn't help smiling. Tom noticed them, too, and shook his head. The corner of his mouth twitched. He couldn't stay angry in the face of those little imps. I would've slipped them extra sweeties, if I had any.

The schoolmistresses beckoned us back, away from the orphans, as though they might be contagious, and indeed, they might. Several looked quite unwell—paler and far thinner than even the other boys. I stood next to Alice as we lined up, more or less, opposite to the boys, in a formation like theirs, and Miss Salisbury stepped forward with a pitch pipe and puffed out a reedy note. An A, or something. Maybe a C. All the same to me. Time for the song we'd all been rehearsing, on both sides of the square.

A young boy stepped forward to sing the first verse as a solo. His pure voice filled the dining hall:

See amid the winter's snow,
Born for us on earth below,
See the tender Lamb appears,
Promised from eternal years.

Alice's breath caught in her throat, and her eyes filled with tears. I'm no judge of music, but even I could tell this boy should be singing at St. Paul's, not starving to death at Mission Industrial School and Home for Working Boys. But he never would sing there. He'd end up at the cotton mill like all the others. If he lived that long.

We all joined in on the chorus, and in the verses to follow, and it happened again, that old Christmas magic. Music, and candles. Darkness, and light. We couldn't be Lady Bountifuls and Poor Urchins when we sang the same notes together. We were just *we*.

Teach, O teach us, Holy Child,
By Thy face so meek and mild,

Teach us to resemble Thee
In Thy sweet humility.

We sang the last refrain, and the carol ended. Nobody wanted to move, lest they break the spell of lingering song. It tingled in our bodies. But headmistresses must be immune to such things. Miss Salamanca shooed us toward the door.

I glanced over at Tommy. Maybe the carol had thawed him a little, because he gave me a grin and popped a sugarplum into his mouth. I was glad to know we would go into the holidays as friends again.

I couldn't help thinking, as we filed out the door, that "sweet humility" had been in our midst that night. Just not necessarily in the hearts of the children who thought they possessed it.

Back at the school, our party began—more songs, then pudding and punch, and little wrapped Christmas crackers. We had hung stockings in the dining room, draped over our chairs, and girls who had written one another notes and hand-decorated homemade Christmas cards put them in their friends' stockings. Alice had given me a wrapped present—a can of kippers! I got the joke immediately. I'd given her a little drawing I had made of two swans. (I'd copied from pictures in Bewick's *History of British Birds*.) Alice had mentioned once a pair of swans living at her grandparents' country home. Apparently, they were a lot tougher than they looked. That was true of Alice, too.

Mrs. Gruboil served out the pudding and sauce. Even *she* seemed in quite a jolly holiday mood. Perhaps she'd been early at her cider jug. I devoured my plate of pudding and helped myself to dried fruits and nuts aplenty, thinking all the while of the boys across the street. Why couldn't they have been invited here to share these treats with us? Of course, that would cost the school more in foodstuffs, but surely it could be managed. If I'd thought my opinion was worth a farthing to Miss Salamanca, I would've suggested it.

At length, I grew tired and decided to leave the party. Alice followed me up the stairs to our room. I'd sat on my bed and began unlacing my boots when I noticed my pillow looked strangely crooked and my bed rumpled. Alice's, too. The papers and books on our desks were strewn about and spilling onto the floor.

"What happened?" whispered Alice.

It was then that I remembered my sardine can, under my pillow.

I threw the pillow aside. I hunted behind the mattress, and between the bed and the wall. Under the bedclothes. Beneath the mattress. In every other inch of the entire room. Twice.

Mermeros's sardine can was gone.

CHAPTER

21

Alice and I stayed up half the night searching for my sardine can, and even after we took to our beds, I could only stare into the darkness at the ceiling. The Persian artifacts were undisturbed in their hiding place, and if I'd had the sense to leave the sardine can there, I'd still have that, too.

I should've wished for the money while I had the chance. I should've wished for anything.

When Alice woke in the morning, I confronted her with my theory. I sat on the edge of my bed and fiddled with the artifacts despondently, sliding the ring on and off my finger.

"Do you remember us talking about my final wish, and money, last night?"

She nodded and rubbed her sleep-fuzzy eyes. "Mm-hmm."

"What if someone overheard us?" I told her. "Theresa, or one of her friends?"

She blinked herself more awake. "Oh, I was so afraid of that!"

"I know." I hung my head. "I was careless. It was stupid of me."

Alice rose and began her preparations for the day. "Poor Maeve," she said. "That would mean Mr. Treazleton has Mermeros already."

"Or he will," I said, "once he meets Theresa today at pickup time."

What Alice said next proved what a good friend she is, for she holds obedience and rule-following to be angelic virtues. "Do you, er, want me to distract Theresa this morning while you search her room?"

Hoofbeats and carriage wheels sounded outside. We had to run out to the landing in the corridor for a window view of the front courtyard. There it was, Mr. Treazleton's carriage, and descending from it, a stout, magnificently dressed older woman.

"That's Theresa's grandmother, the Widow Treazleton," Alice whispered in my ear. "She's an acquaintance of my grandparents."

I stared at her.

"Distantly," she stammered. "We don't dine with them, if that's what you mean."

"They're picking her up early," I said. "Taking no chances with Mermeros. Come on, let's stop her!"

Then, Theresa appeared in the courtyard. We were too late. Footmen took her luggage and stowed it atop the carriage. Before she got in, she turned and surveyed the entire school with a self-satisfied expression. She glanced at my window, saw me watching her, and favored me with smug little wave.

"May she break out in pimples," I muttered as she drove away.

And there it was. Before we were even out of our nightdresses, Theresa was gone. My sardine can, no doubt, clutched in her little valise. All morning, my mind watched the roll of her carriage wheels, over and over, bearing away all my hopes.

A cab discharged us at St. Pancras Station: Aunt Vera, Polydora, and I, along with an old man in a homburg hat who kept winking at Aunt Vera, and a ginger-whiskered fellow in a bowler hat who wouldn't even look at us.

Polly and my aunt had come to fetch me late in the morning to whisk me home for winter holidays. Aunt Vera was in a jovial mood and gave me a tin of gingerbread, but I could barely taste it. Polly was feeling festive, too, but she could tell right away that something was wrong.

"What's the matter, Maeve, dear. Are you ill?" She peered into my eyes and made me stick out my tongue when we were still in the school courtyard, where my bags and I had been waiting for her arrival. I didn't appreciate the public examination.

"Just tired," I told her. "I had trouble sleeping last night."

Polly stroked my cheek. "Poor darling," she said. "We'll get you home, feed you, and tuck you right into bed."

Now I followed Polly and Aunt Vera through the crowded train station like one in a trance, while the porter Aunt Vera had paid followed us with our luggage in tow. St. Pancras Station was a splendid building, but I couldn't enjoy it today. Biggest room in the world, they called it. The soaring heights of its iron-and-glass roof made us travelers nothing more than scurrying ants. Usually it made me feel like I was falling, in the best of ways, though my feet were firmly on the ground.

This close to the holidays, the place bulged with travelers and their parcels, even at midday. Carolers sang with collection baskets displayed for some worthy charitable fund. A brass quartet played holiday tunes in another corner of the station. The tea shops had draped bunting and paper cutouts in their doorways. Sellers of newspapers and hot chestnuts wore sprigs of holly pinned to their hats. And nobody seemed to begrudge the poorer folks clustered around heating stoves. Not at this time of year.

But what did I care? Christmas was ruined. School holidays were ruined. My entire future was probably ruined.

Aunt Vera purchased our tickets, then steered us toward a tea shop. "We have half an hour before our train," she said. "Let's take a little refreshment while we wait."

I nibbled at a dry biscuit and watched people pass by without really seeing them. *Where in all of London could my sardine can be now?* Out of all London, I'd been the one to find it the first time. I'd never stumble upon it again by sheer luck, that was plain. After the new owner's three wishes were spent, Mermeros would probably vanish and reappear in Timbuktu.

I'd had a *djinni*. A real, magical, wish-granting djinni. Just like in the stories. What had I to show for it now? Theresa's chopped braids and Alice's sunburn. The memory of an adventure, but what good are memories? A few shabby antiquities. Useful to a museum, but not to me. I'd brought them home with me. They mocked me with bitter recollection of what might have been, if it weren't for my big mouth.

I'd had a djinni, and I'd lost it. I'd let Mermeros slip through my fingers like the wiggling sardine he was. I had only myself to blame. (If I ever found out who else I had to blame, they'd get a taste of my fist.)

"Maeve? Maeve?" Aunt Vera was saying.

I blinked awake. "Yes, Aunt Vera?"

"Penny for your thoughts?" She smiled at me.

"I'm sorry," I told her. "What were you saying?"

"I was asking what friends you've made at school. Last time we visited, I never had a chance to ask."

I didn't mention Tommy. Not even cheerful Aunt Vera would want to hear that I was fraternizing with orphans, for one thing, and boys, for another.

"My particular friend is my roommate," I told her. "Alice Bromley."

"Ah! The Bromleys are a fine old family," Aunt Vera said. "They live in Grosvenor Square. I met Mrs. Bromley at a charity benefit she hosted at her home once. Oh, the hothouses! She has the most exquisite flowers at her tables, and fresh strawberries year-round."

"She's invited me to come visit Alice over the holidays," I said.

"Splendid! Now that's a very fine connection to cultivate, Maeve."

I wanted to groan. As if my friendship with Alice was a hothouse flower, needing cultivation. I'm not so false, and neither is Alice. If she was, she could fawn after Theresa Treazleton. I didn't like Alice because I *ought* to; I liked her because I did.

"If your mother's too busy to take you—and if I know my sister, she will be, what with all this wedding folderol—I'll take you to see Alice," Aunt Vera said. "I can always do with a bit of shopping in town."

I wondered if she was more keen to shop, or to have occasion to visit Grosvenor Square. But Aunt Vera wasn't too terribly much of a snob. She was nowhere near as bad as Mother.

"Did you know, girls, that after his father nearly bankrupted the family estate, the present Mr. Bromley made a fortune for himself in buttons?"

That got my attention. Alice had never mentioned it. We'd been friends for months, sharing a room the entire time, and Alice never once spoke of where her family's wealth came from. Many girls would talk of nothing else.

"Buttons?" asked Polly. "Is there a fortune to be made in buttons?"

"Of course there is," Aunt Vera declared. "Just look around this tea shop at all the buttons on bodices, on men's waistcoats and jackets."

It was true. Fashionable ladies' dresses and coats were positively studded with buttons, many of them elegant and elaborate. Spread that button count across London, across England, and there were more than enough buttons to maintain an elegant London townhouse *and* a country estate, swans and all.

My button-hunting gaze rested upon the back of a man's head, seated near us. His ginger hair was combed slick, and his bowler hat sat in front of him on the table. He turned to one side, and I caught sight of his whiskers. It was the man from our cab. *What were the chances that he'd be right here*, with half of London, it seemed, jostling about St. Pancras? Then again, there at another table was the older gentleman with the homburg hat. Naturally, folks would look for tea before continuing their journeys. Nothing surprising there. The old man's waistcoat had five buttons, at least.

We drank our tea and ate our biscuits, then Aunt Vera glanced at the time and shooed us toward the platform. "Let's find a compart-ment, girls," she said. But by the time we'd reached our train, a long queue had already formed, and the dining car and private compart-ments were full once we got onboard. The only spots remaining to us when we boarded were in the general seating cars.

We sat facing each other. Aunt Vera pulled out her knitting, and Polly opened her novel and adjusted her spectacles. I looked out the window, facing the rear of the train, but I saw little as we slid out of the station. The horses, carts, dogs, bicycles, delivery boys, hawkers, vendors, shoppers, and stores that would ordinarily command my attention held little to interest me now.

Without my djinni, my future would be to remain at Miss Salamanca's school until I grew too old or they threw me out. And then what would I do with myself? Sit about at home, listening to my mother talk about table linens and neighbors' hats forever? The day would soon come, if it hadn't already, when cricket with the lads would not be an option. The only escape from that prison was too disgusting to think about. Marriage, eventually. Thank goodness Polly hadn't been hauled off to that particular kind of execution yet.

Our train car was full of people of all shapes and sizes. Most of the men's faces were masked by newspapers. One man lowered his paper and looked directly at me, before he realized I was looking back, and then he vanished again.

It was Mr. Ginger Whiskers.

I stared at his newspaper, and at the heavy gold ring on the hand holding it over his face, as though my eyes could penetrate the *Daily Telegraph* and read his thoughts.

Odd. Was it merely one coincidence after another, him taking the same cab, the same tea shop, the same train, the same car? It could be.

But what if it wasn't?

I turned this thought over in my mind. Might this man be an admirer of my sister Polydora? My sister Deborah used to say no man would ever take a fancy to spinsterish Polly's spectacles, but that was just Deborah being Deborah.

Could it have anything to do with Aunt Vera? Unlikely.

Could he be following me? Why would a man follow a thirteen-year-old girl? Unless he were sent by Mr. Treazleton. But Mr. Treazleton already had my djinni. So, he'd have no reason to send someone to spy on me.

It must be my imagination, I told myself. His presence here was a mere coincidence, and nothing more.

But when he got off the train at the Luton stop, just as we did, and disappeared into a cloud of engine steam and coal smoke, I had a hard time persuading myself of that.

CHAPTER 22

Going home on holiday presented me with a curious conundrum. On the one hand, it was marvelous to be away from the wrath of Miss Salamanca and her minions, the Miss Gunthersons and Bickles and Salisburys and Nerquists (though I did enjoy the latter's geography class). On the other hand, going home dropped me right into my tangled web of sisters, plus my fussbudget mother (though Polydora was always a good sport). It was hard to know which I liked best, or least, home or school. I'd need a third hand to break the tie. I did wonder, would a third hand be somehow useful in cricket?

But Christmas was Christmas, and family was family. Dejected though I was, I resolved to try to put on a brave smile and enjoy the season if I could, after being robbed of all my hopes.

True to her word, Polly fed me a bowl of soup and tucked me straight into bed that afternoon.

I knew I'd slept because, when I got up, I had to face the bitter truth that I *hadn't* gotten even with Theresa Treazleton for stealing my djinni for her daddy by knocking out her two front teeth and stringing them onto Mermeros's shark-tooth necklace.

I hate it when beautiful dreams turn out not to be real.

I got up in time for dinner, sadder but wiser, and went downstairs to greet my family.

Even if I was in no mood for it, and even if Mother, Deborah, and Evangeline were too full of wedding fuss to care about it, Christmas had arrived at the Merritt home.

Jenkins, the housekeeper, and Polly had been at work for days, stringing garlands of evergreen along the banisters and draping wide velvet ribbons along the mantelpiece of the drawing-room fireplace and along the tops of all the draperies. Extra candles glimmered in all the rooms, and a wreath hung in the front picture window. The house looked like a wonderland, and smelled of pine and cloves and cinnamon. It almost made me forget my troubles, for a moment.

Then we gathered in the dining room, and the old family nonsense broke the bubble and returned life to normal. Nobody can stay forever in wonderland, anyway.

Polly was her usual cheerful self, with bits of news to share about people we knew in Luton—babies and weddings announced, puppies born, relatives returning home to celebrate the season. Somehow, Polly kept tabs on everyone without being a gossip in the slightest. Dad seemed lost in his thoughts. Mother was still vexed with me for my transgressions at school. Whenever she looked at me, which she mostly avoided doing, she pinched her lips together as though she'd tasted a lemon. Fortunately, Evangeline's impending wedding diverted most of her attention.

Deborah was in raptures about the pale-rose-colored brides-maid's dress that had been ordered for her. To hear her describe it, you'd think *she* was the bride, and the wedding her own, an obser-vation also noted angrily by Evangeline. The blissful bride-to-be could think of nothing else but Rudolph, her intended, who joined us for supper. It didn't take me long, after listening to him natter on to Father about the Irish taxation question, whatever that was, to decide he was the dullest chunk of brick ever to propose to someone's older sister. Apparently, the Irish had been overtaxed, and Parliament planned to pay them back, or something, or so the *Daily News* reported. I was happy for the Irish, but very sorry for myself, needing to be seen and not heard during such long, tedious talk.

What Rudolph didn't notice, but I could see as plain as day, was that Father was in no mood to think about the Irish taxation question, nor any other matter not directly on his mind. Ordinarily, my father loved this kind of talk. A man of finance and business, he devoured the morning papers on the train to work and the evening papers on the way home. I should've thought having a son-in-law who was as much of a news-eater as he was warmed his banking heart to no end. But Dad was out of sorts and very low in spirits. Christmas apparently hadn't affected him much.

"Are you unwell, dear?" my mother asked him, during a pause when Rudolph took a bite of pork.

"Hmm? What's that?" Dad looked up as if roused from sleep. "Oh. Perfectly well. Just a conversation with Mr. Pinagree and...well, some troubles at work."

Mother brightened. "Oh, *that*. I shan't worry, then. There are always troubles at work."

"*That*," said Deborah, "is because banking is so incredibly dull. They need to stir up troubles just to give themselves something to do."

Mother didn't notice Dad's expression then, but I did. His face said these weren't ordinary troubles, and that it would be nice, now and then, if his wife and daughters took certain things more seriously. I itched to ask him what was the matter, but this was not the place nor the time. In any case, Dad would think I was a lunatic if I started asking him about his employer.

Was Mr. Treazleton the cause of my father's difficulties? It was hard to imagine what else might cause them. Daddy was so diligent and earnest about his work. He'd never give an employer cause to wish he weren't there.

I wished I could do something to help. But if I'd really cared enough about helping, if I'd really been a loyal daughter, I would've given Mr. Treazleton the sardine can and spared Father any troubles at the bank. I was a hypocrite and a fraud, with no djinni to show for it, and now Father would pay a terrible price. What would happen to us then?

Three days later, on Christmas Eve, we attended a gathering at Aunt Vera's home. She liked to throw parties, and her husband, Uncle Edgar, never minded the expense where celebrations were concerned. His big belly proved it. He ought to have trimmed his hat with holly and dressed as Father Christmas. So my sisters and my parents and I, as well as Rudolph, other relatives, neighbors, and friends all gathered for a late supper and games at their house. Normally I wouldn't be allowed to attend this, being too young, but Mother made a Christmas exception. Polly played carols on the pianoforte, and we were a merry bunch. Even *I* got into the spirit of the occasion and played the part of an imp in our little Christmas tableau. My pretty cousin, Penny Anne, was the Queen of the Faeries. Naturally. More power to her. I'd rather be an imp anyway.

We returned home late, and I went upstairs to the room I shared with Polly. When I opened the door, my stomach sank. Yet again. As Miss Guntherson, my French instructor, would say, déjà vu. My bedroom, ransacked. My window, left open. My curtains, fluttering in the cold breeze.

"Thief!" I cried. "Someone has burgled my bedroom!"

Mother, Father, and my sisters came trip-trapping down the hall and crowded into the doorway. We gaped at the sight.

"Evangeline," Father ordered, "check the other rooms and see if there's been a burglar anywhere else."

"Don't make *me* do it, Daddy!" she cried. "What if I'm attacked? What if the burglar is still *here*?"

"Ring for Jenkins," Mother said. "She'll go with you."

"Now, Mother, we need not wake the servants," said Father. "Let them rest. It's Christmas."

"There's no burglar," Deborah scoffed. "This is just another of Maeve's tricks."

My vision flamed red. "It is not!"

"Didn't you say someone stole something from your room at school?" she retorted.

Polly came to my aid. "Maeve would never do something like this maliciously."

Mother pursed her lips. Clearly, she had her doubts.

Jenkins rose without us ringing for her and appeared with a candle, with her housecoat wrapped tightly about her. She and Evangeline took off on their brave exploration. Father inspected the windowsill and looked around the room at the disheveled bedclothes, the scattered papers, the dangling drawers of the bureau and desk.

Polly searched through her own things. "I don't seem to be missing anything, Father," she said. "My necklaces, my porcelain jewel box, my change purse—they're all here."

Father's eyebrow rose. "Maeve? What are you missing?"

I sifted through my belongings, my mind racing. Surely the thief could only be after one thing: my sardine can. I didn't have it, of course. So the thief was someone who didn't know I'd lost it. Mr. Treazleton *must* know. What new enemy had I acquired?

The man in the ginger whiskers, of course. My heart went cold.

"I'm not missing anything, Daddy," I told him.

Evangeline returned, breathless, with Jenkins at her heels to give her report. "No other room in the house is disturbed," she said, "except the old nursery. Someone has dumped out the toy box and cleared all the dollies off the shelves."

Mother and Deborah folded their arms across their chests and stared at me.

"I didn't do it!" I yelped. "Why would I do such a thing?"

"There's no one else who would," said Deborah. "And no thief would be so stupid as to muss up your room and the nursery, and take nothing."

"This is your wretched idea of a joke, Maeve." Evangeline entered the fray. "I call that a beastly thing to do. Especially at Christmas!"

My fingers curled into fists. But I couldn't sock my grown sisters.

Especially not with Mother and Dad standing right there. Besides, it would be like striking old ladies. They were about that helpless.

But it still stung to have them suspect me so. Their own baby sister.

"Father," said Polydora in her smooth, calm voice. "Hadn't we ought to summon a policeman? I'm certain Maeve wouldn't do this as a prank."

Father poked and prodded at the windowsill. "It does seem," he said, "as though someone did use a ladder here."

Take that, Deborah. My nose might've poked a hole in the ceiling, and I'm not too proud to admit it.

"Jenkins, would you wake Henry and ask him to bicycle to the station and send over an inspector?"

Jenkins disappeared down the dark hallway, followed by Deborah and Evangeline in a shared huff of indignation. Mother drifted off to her boudoir, lamenting that we would all be murdered in our beds.

"Thank you," I told my father as he passed by me on his way out the room.

He stopped and looked me directly in the eye. "You didn't do it, did you, Maeve?"

I shook my head. "No, sir."

He patted my cheek. "Then I believe you."

He may have been a fusty, dull banker, but my father leaped high in my heart then and there, and hasn't ever fallen since.

"Why don't you gather up your bedding, and Polly's, and make beds for yourselves on the downstairs couches?"

I hurried to do as he'd asked.

As soon as I'd made the beds, I slipped down the stairs to the coal cellar, candle in hand, and dug at the base of the coal bin with a shovel. There it was, undisturbed—the tin of gingerbread Aunt Vera had given me, now devoid of gingerbread, containing the Persian king's crest, bracelet, and ring. Though I felt certain these weren't items any thief knew of, I still wanted to be sure they were safe. Satisfied that they were, I climbed the stairs, washed up, changed into my nightdress, and went to sleep.

I woke early in the morning to voices in the breakfast room and wandered in to see Polydora seated at the table in earnest conversation with a uniformed police officer. Father stood near the windows, half listening and half reading the paper.

"There was an intruder," the officer was saying, "but as nothing appears to have been taken, and we have no leads on who the intruder might have been, there's not much more that we can do."

Polly nodded. Her eyes were bright behind her spectacles, and her cheeks unusually pink.

"We're most obliged to you for coming out to attend to this matter, Constable—"

"Hopewood," the officer said. "Matthew Hopewood."

Polydora held out her hand. "I'm very pleased to make your acquaintance."

She certainly was. I'm no expert in such matters, but it seemed to me that Constable Hopewood was equally pleased. He had a broad face and serious eyes. When he smiled, he seemed like a likable sort.

Romance was for the birds, but anybody who liked my Polydora had excellent taste, and I couldn't help but approve. Besides, wouldn't it be spit in petty Deborah's eye if spectacled Polly found a beau before she did?

"It was most kind of you to come investigate this matter on Christmas morning," my sister said gently. "Depriving you of your family holiday, no less."

Officer Hopewood rose. "Oh, that's all right. I don't have any family. Least, not nearby. I have an aunt and uncle up near Oxford."

"No family to spend Christmas with!" Polly repeated sadly.

"In that case," my father said, peering over his paper, "you must have Christmas breakfast with us."

When they appeared and discovered our guest, Mother and Deborah seemed rather put out by Father inviting him. Evangeline didn't care one way or another, as her precious Rudolph joined us for eggs and bacon and kippers also. But I didn't mind a bit. In fact, watching Polly blush as she poured the constable's tea, and watching his eyes never leave her face, I almost forgot my lost djinni and the ginger-whiskered man. And when Father insisted that Constable Hopewood extend his visit through dinner, and Polly turned the color of Father Christmas's big red coat, it was the best Christmas present he could've given me.

Besides, of course a certain sardine can. But on Christmas Day, I tried hard not to think of that.

CHAPTER

23

Aunt Vera rang the doorbell at 20 Grosvenor Square and pinched her cheeks to give them a bit more pink. I rolled my eyes and pretended not to notice. Behind us, the park bustled with activity, even in late December.

An elderly butler, tall and gaunt, answered the door. At the sight of me, a small smile appeared on his lips.

"Ah. Miss Merritt. And her mother?"

"Her aunt," said Aunt Vera. "Mrs. Vera Lindsey."

The butler bowed slightly and beckoned us in out of the cold.

The front foyer was certainly grand. I could tell Aunt Vera was a bit cowed by it. A sweeping staircase, soaring ceilings, beautiful plaster carvings. I clamped my arms tight to my ribs, lest I accidentally bump and smash one of the dozens of porcelain vases and marble busts.

Then Alice came running down the curved staircase, followed more slowly by her beaming grandmother, and the place stopped feeling like a museum immediately.

Alice greeted me with a hug. "I'm so glad you're here, Maeve! I've been counting the days 'til you arrived."

"Me too." That was no exaggeration. Passing the holidays at the wedding-planning headquarters was more than a body could take. I envied Father for his ability to escape each day, even to a gloomy old bank.

Mrs. Bromley greeted Aunt Vera warmly and led her into a little salon for tea and sandwiches. I knew Aunt Vera would be telling anyone who'd listen about this visit for a month of Sundays, but I didn't mind.

We'd arranged that I would stay the rest of the holidays with Alice until it was time to return to school. That would save my family needing to take another trip on my behalf.

Alice showed me through the drawing room and down a back stairway, straight to the kitchen, where a smiling cook had a platter of the long-promised coconut cakes and tall glasses of milk waiting for us at a gleaming countertop. We demolished them in short order, then went up to Alice's bedroom, which overlooked the park.

"Have you any new theories about what happened to Mermeros?" Alice asked me earnestly.

I shook my head. "I'm certain Theresa Treazleton has him." I told her about the ginger-whiskered man and the burglary of my bedroom in Luton.

Alice frowned. "But, then, that makes no sense," she said. "Mr. Treazleton would've had the sardine can by midday, at the latest. There would be no reason for him to send someone after you."

"He threatened that he'd have the djinni by the new year," I said glumly. "Theresa herself said, 'This is war.'"

"Oh!" Alice clapped her hand to her forehead. "I forgot. I got a letter from Cynthia Murray, whose family is friends with the Brisbanes, you see, and Cynthia said that Honoria told her that when Theresa left the school to head for home, her face burst out in the most frightful case of boils. She's been avoiding every holiday event because she doesn't want to be seen!"

I hadn't much heart even to laugh. "Serves her right, doesn't it?"

"I don't know," Alice said thoughtfully. "Does anyone deserve that?" Her maid came to the door, and Alice went and spoke to her about something.

That's when it hit me. As I'd watched Theresa leave, *I'd wished that she'd break out in pimples.* And almost immediately, *she did.*

My spine began to tingle. Did I have some power of my own to grant wishes, now? Was I becoming a bit of a djinni, too? Was it my trip to Persia that had done it?

"I wish for my sardine can back," I said softly, under my breath.

Nothing happened. Maybe that was too much to ask.

"I wish for those curtains in the window to sway," I whispered, considering that to be a pretty harmless request. They didn't move.

Maybe the magic had to involve people? "I wish for that freckle on the back of my hand to disappear," I said. "Or even fade a bit," I added, by way of a compromise.

Nothing. Those must have been coincidental pimples after all.

Alice showed me all around her grandparents' town home, then we went downstairs so I could say goodbye to Aunt Vera and meet Mr. and Mrs. Bromley properly.

When Aunt Vera had gone, Mr. Bromley, a spry gentleman with a twinkle in his eye, asked us what we planned to do first.

"Papa," Alice began (for so she called her grandfather), "we want to go to Mr. James Pascall's candy shop."

Did we? Well, why not? I nodded my agreement.

"At St. Paul's Churchyard, Papa. You know the one?"

"Young ladies and sweets!" cried Mr. Bromley. He winked at his wife. "Ladies of any age, and sweets!"

Mrs. Bromley smiled. "You'll take them, won't you, dear?"

"I wouldn't miss the chance," said he, "to squire such handsome young ladies around town. Indeed not."

Handsome? Well, imagine Deborah's response to that.

Mr. James Pascall's candy shop in the vicinity of St. Paul's Churchyard was like nothing I'd ever seen. This was no paltry apothecary's shelf of lozenges and lollies. This was a carnival of bright-colored sweets, a parade of delicious flavors. Shelves groaned under long rows of glass jars filled with colorful bonbons that seemed to stretch for miles. We stayed too long, sampling sweet after sweet until it was almost too much, then left clutching little sacks of candies and picked our way along the sidewalks. Mr. Bromley planned to take us to his gentlemen's club, where we could join him for luncheon in the dining room. It all sounded terribly fancy and intimidating, but I promised myself I'd eat hearty and otherwise keep my mouth shut.

We'd meandered several blocks when a curious shingle hanging in front of a small, lower-level storefront caught my eye. "The Oddity Shop," it read. "Mysteries, Marvels, and Wonders from Beyond the Seven Seas. We Buy and Sell Rare and Wondrous Things. Mr. Siegfried Poindexter, World Traveler, Chief Buyer, Proprietor."

I halted in my tracks. Alice knew my thoughts immediately.

"Papa," she said, "may Maeve and I visit this shop for a moment?"

Mr. Bromley polished his eyeglasses with a handkerchief and squinted at the sign. "But, my dears," he protested. "Lunch!"

"We won't be long," I promised. "I just want to see what a world traveler looks like. I plan to be one myself someday."

"Well, who's to say you can't?" Mr. Bromley chuckled. "Go on, then."

We all went down the steps and inside the store. After the rainbow brightness of the candy shop, this dim and shady store felt grim and strange. A glaring owl perched on a branch made me scramble to a stop.

"Morris!" I gasped.

"Who's Morris?" asked a voice from somewhere in the shadows.

"Oh..." I stammered. "Just an owl that I know."

"You know an *owl*, Maeve?" asked Alice.

"He's Tommy's," I explained.

"Who's Tommy?" asked Mr. Bromley.

"A friend of ours."

Alice's eyes grew wide.

"How are you friends with a *boy* named Tommy, at Miss Salamanca's School for Upright *Young Ladies*?" asked Mr. Bromley. "This is not the first time I've suspected that supervision there must be sorely lacking."

Oh, I'd done it now. Well did I know girls were *not* supposed to socialize with boys. Ever. Until they were eighteen or so, coming out into society, chaperoned within an inch of their lives, and only meeting the most suitable of men. Whatever that meant. From what I could tell, it meant the most boring ones. I'd been ignoring propriety ever since my hands first gripped a cricket bat. But now I'd dragged Alice into my vices. I had to try to fix it.

"Tommy is an orphan who lives across the street from the school, at Mission Industrial School and Home for Working Boys," I said. "He's *my* friend, but Alice has met him. It's my fault, though."

I looked up to see the shopkeeper watching me with interest. He was a short, robust man of middle age with a tanned, bald head and thick muttonchop whiskers. Mr. Bromley, however, watched his granddaughter.

"Maeve has been very kind to Tommy," Alice said softly. I wouldn't put it that way, but I appreciated what she was trying to do. "He's very clever, and quite respectful. He's just in a most unfortunate situation, in that unhappy home."

"At his next birthday," I piped in, "he'll be sent to work in a cotton mill."

Mr. Bromley's face melted into sympathy. "The poor young man," he said. "Any one of us could share his fate, had we not been more fortunate."

"Pardon me," said the man with the muttonchop whiskers and the checkered vest, "but did you say this clever young orphan owns an owl?"

I nodded. "A live one," I said, "with a broken wing."

"I should very much like to meet this Tommy of yours," said the man, "if by so doing, I might also meet Morris, his owl."

"Are you Mr. Siegfried Poindexter?" I asked.

"In the flesh."

"Grandfather," Alice asked, "could we come back tomorrow and bring Tommy and his owl?"

Mr. Bromley took a step back. "Well, now, I say… It seems unlikely that the masters at the home…"

"Please, Grandfather," Alice persisted. "It would mean so much to him."

"I'll make it worth his while," added Mr. Siegfried Poindexter. "I'll buy that owl of his, and give it a good home, right here in the shop."

Mr. Bromley hesitated.

"What do you want with an owl?" I asked.

Mr. Poindexter turned to me. "Owls are good luck," he declared, as though this should have been obvious. "The ancient Greeks believed they brought protection." He smiled. "Mostly, I just like them. I've had this stuffed fellow, here, for years. But a real, live owl? That would be something."

What could be better for Morris? If Miss Salamanca discovered him there, and she was bound to, eventually, she'd summon someone horrible to get rid of him by any means necessary.

I turned to Mr. Bromley. "Won't you, sir, help us bring Tom and his owl here? It's a good deed for the orphan *and* the bird."

That cinched the deal.

"Of course, we shall." Mr. Bromley nodded decisively. "I'd like to get a good look at that charitable home, while I'm at it. A friend of mine is on a committee to better the living conditions of young orphans and unfortunates in the city. I could give him an informal report, don't you know."

I couldn't help smiling. "I'll save my licorices for Tommy," I said, pocketing my candy sack. "They're his favorite. Morris likes them, too."

"Does he, now?" Mr. Siegfried Poindexter smiled.

"Sir," said Mr. Bromley, "were those scarab beetles I saw in the window?"

"Indeed, they were," said the world traveler, chief buyer, and proprietor of the Oddity Shop. The two men walked toward the front of the shop, leaving Alice and me free to browse around.

By the light of green-shaded lamps, I poked about the store, looking at items in glass display cases. I saw pots and vases, bracelets and earrings, headbands and daggers, all looking ancient and strange. It reminded me of the objects we took from Mermeros's father's sarcophagus—the crest, the bracelet, and the ring, still packed in my gingerbread tin, now stowed in my carpetbag in Alice's bedroom closet.

Would Mr. Siegfried Poindexter buy those from me? For how much? Perhaps I could salvage something from my lost and wasted wishes. Enough to travel around the world? Probably not. But possibly enough to start a girls' cricket team. If we didn't care too much about proper uniforms and provided our own gear.

"Maeve, look," Alice whispered. "Aladdin's lamp, he's calling it."

She pointed to an ancient-looking oil lamp made of brass. I read the placard, "'A replica of Aladdin's lamp, once the home of a powerful djinni.'"

We looked at each other in wonder. "Does he believe in djinnis, do you think?"

A footstep sounded behind us. "I believe in all sorts of things," said Mr. Poindexter.

I turned to look at him. "Me too."

He smiled. "I see you appreciate antiquities. One doesn't always find young people so interested in relics from the ancient world."

"I think they're fascinating," I said. "In fact, I have—" I cut myself off.

Mr. Poindexter prompted me to continue. "You have...? You have antiquities at home, perhaps?"

I might as well tell him. I'd have to, if I planned to sell them to him.

"I have a bracelet, a ring, and a royal crest that once belonged to an ancient king of Persia," I said, then held my breath.

His eyes grew wide. He tapped his chin thoughtfully. "How do you know they belonged to an ancient king of Persia?"

I tried to think what to say.

"There's an awful lot of fraud and forgery in the antiquities business," he said. "I have to be on my guard against it always."

"They're authentic," I said. "I know without an ounce of doubt."

He folded his arms across his sturdy chest. "How?"

I had to back up this claim, and I couldn't produce any evidence. Nor could I think up a more convincing lie than the unlikely truth.

"I found them myself," I said. "I traveled to Persia, and was part of a, er, dig, and I took these things from the king's own sarcophagus. From his very bones."

Mr. Siegfried Poindexter watched me closely. "From his very bones," he repeated. "Is your father an archaeologist? An uncle, perhaps? Or an aunt? Women seem to be joining the search for rare treasures in growing numbers."

"Do they?"

He nodded. "So? Who's the scientist in your family?"

Alice saw her grandfather heading our way, so she went over to intercept him and draw his attention elsewhere.

I tried to think of what to say, but imagination failed me. I didn't know enough about archaeology to fool someone like Mr. Poindexter. And if he might believe in djinnis, he might believe the truth.

"No one is." I told the man, watching his reaction closely. "I traveled to Persia myself. With the aid of a djinni."

I'll say this for Mr. Siegfried Poindexter: He didn't mock, or scold, or dismiss me. But I could tell he doubted me. Who could blame him?

"Can you prove it?" he asked. "Do you still have the djinni?"

I shook my head.

"That's a shame," he said. He winked. "I would pay a small fortune for a real, live djinni of the lamp."

So would Alfred P. Treazleton, I thought bitterly. They could form a club.

"How much would you pay for authentic royal antiquities?" I asked.

"That depends," he said, "on their authenticity. And I'm an excellent judge of that. If they are what you say they are, they'll be worth quite a bit. Can you bring them tomorrow, when you return with your friend and his owl?"

I nodded.

He held out his hand. "Then, Miss Maeve—did I hear rightly that your name is Maeve? It will be a pleasure doing business with you."

CHAPTER
24

T hat night, as we lay in the feather beds in Alice's nursery, I reminded Alice about Cynthia's letter, Theresa's pimples, and my muttered curse. I told her my theory, and how my attempts to test it had failed.

Alice sat up in bed, thinking hard.

"Maeve," she said, "when you said that about Theresa and pimples, weren't you wearing the sorcerer's ring?"

My body went cold and prickly all over. Much like that strange sensation we had passed through in the Persian deserts. I got out of bed and dove into the closet where my luggage was stored. There was the gingerbread tin, and in it, the sorcerer's things.

They looked so drab and dull, sitting there in the dark room. Like dusty museum relics. Not like objects of power. I put the ring on my finger. It swiveled around loosely on my much-smaller finger than the sorcerer king's had been.

"Imagine if this works," I said. "Who needs to worry about djinnis and their three wishes? With a ring like this, we could do anything. Maybe I won't sell it to Mr. Poindexter."

"Maybe," said Alice doubtfully. "We don't know for sure."

"We need another experiment," I whispered.

Alice moaned. "Not again! I don't want hideous pimples or green hair!"

"We'll do this safely," I promised. "We'll think of something harmless and simple."

Alice sighed. "There's nothing I could say that would stop you, is there?"

I laughed. "No. But I don't want you getting hurt."

Alice lit the lamps, and I concentrated hard on simple options.

By the bay windows overlooking the park stood a small round table.

"Let an apple appear on that table," I said.

Nothing happened.

"Make the lamplight shine more brightly in this room," I said.

No change.

"Make that spider in the corner start crawling along the ceiling," I said.

"Spider?" squeaked Alice. "What spider?"

"It's tiny," I told her. "I thought, maybe, the spells might only work on living things. But apparently not."

"Are you sure the spider is alive?"

I crossed the room for a closer look. "Definitely," I said. "She's weaving her web."

"Living things," Alice said thoughtfully. "Living things…"

I sat on a soft chair in front of the fireplace. "What if the spells only work on people?"

Alice winced. "You're going to try to spell me, aren't you?"

"Not without your permission," I said. "I do have somewhat of a conscience, you know."

"Somewhat," Alice muttered.

"Here," I said, holding out the ring. "You spell me."

She shook her head. "With my luck, I'd accidentally freeze your blood or break all your bones."

"Well, haven't *you* got a gruesome imagination," I said. "Tell you what. What if I spell your hair to grow an inch longer?"

She looked extremely doubtful. "If this spell backfires, I'll be a regular Rapunzel."

"Good," I said. "Then we can sneak out of our dorm room much more easily when we're back at school."

She shuddered. "I never understood, in that fairy tale, why her scalp didn't hurt dreadfully."

"It just goes to show," I said, "that writers don't know very much. I'll bet the Brothers Grimm never had anyone yanking on their pigtails. What do you say?"

She began undoing her braids. "All right. I'm trusting you, Maeve."

Good old sport!

"Wait," she said. "The Brothers Grimm would never have *had* pigtails."

"They were German," I told her. "You never know what happens on the Continent."

She loosened her hair, fetched a ruler from her desk, and stood before a mirror. She held the ruler straight across her upper arm, at the exact place her hair ended.

The time had come. *How had I worded it before, exactly?* I clutched the ring to my finger.

"May Alice Bromley's hair grow an inch longer," I said.

Nothing happened. Foiled once more. Alice's hair stayed resolutely the same.

For a moment, I'd almost gotten excited again. We both went and sat in the soft cushions by the bay windows, with a view of the street and the park below. I dropped the ring in the gingerbread tin, where it landed with a *clink*.

"Maeve," Alice said softly. "This, er, sorcerer king. He doesn't seem to have been a very nice person at all."

"Like father, like son," I said. "Chip off the old block. The apple doesn't fall far..."

"No," said Alice. "What I mean is, what if his magic only does harm? Wishing pimples for Theresa wasn't a very nice thing to do."

A power created for the sole purpose of doing harm? Who would be so low?

A king who ensorcelled his sons—all three—into an eternity of servitude, perhaps.

The sinking feeling in my belly told me Alice was right. Even before I had any proof.

"Wish me harm," Alice whispered, handing the ring.

"No!"

"Something small," she urged. "Like a toothache."

I shook my head. "I wouldn't even wish a toothache on Theresa Treazleton." Not that I was an angel, but toothaches are agony. Nothing small about them.

"When I wished pimples on Theresa," I said, "I was furious at her. If your theory is true, about this being a mean sort of magic, I just wonder if it might not rely on that. On real anger or hatred being part of the spell." I elbowed Alice playfully. "I couldn't hate you for anything."

We sat and looked out the window. The streets were quiet, and the park, too, at this hour. Grosvenor Square was a posh neighborhood.

By the light of a streetlamp in the park, though, we saw an old man walking slowly along the path. His figure was stooped and bent.

Suddenly, along came another figure, someone younger and much more fleet of foot. Just as the old man was leaving the safety of the light, the younger figure pounced. In the distance and the darkness, the struggle was confusing, but there was no doubt in our minds: the younger man had robbed the older one.

Off the thief shot, like a cannonball, leaving his victim without a coat or, presumably, a wallet.

A surge of anger rushed through me. "Make that man trip," I said. "Let him twist an ankle, and let the constables catch him."

Down went the villain, as though a giant club had swept his feet out from under him. Two constables came running from the shadows and tackled the man, calling out something that sounded encouraging to the shivering victim left behind. We watched as the thief limped away, pinned between the two constables, after giving the coat and wallet back to the old man.

Once again, I dropped the ring into the tin with a *clink*.

"It worked," Alice said in wonder.

My whole body shivered. "I don't ever want to do that again."

"That wasn't a coincidence, was it?" said Alice.

I shook my head. "That was me. I felt it."

Concern for me showed on Alice's kind face. "He deserved it, Maeve," she said. "You didn't hurt him badly. You didn't do anything wrong."

"I think I did." I put the lid on the tin and buried it once more in my luggage. "That ring is deadly dangerous."

"Even if you used it to, you know, help with crimes and things?"

How many times had I wished I could better teach brutes and bullies a lesson! But not this way.

"If I did," I said slowly, "I'd become Mermeros's father."

Alice regarded me strangely.

"I don't mean his actual father," I said. "I mean, someone ruthless and powerful and cruel. Someone owned by their anger."

We went back to our beds and returned to the shelter of our blankets.

"Why do you say so, Maeve?" she asked.

I sat up on my elbows. "Because I *liked* it, Alice," I said. "Just like I *liked* turning Theresa's braids green. It felt good, in a nasty way." I sank back into my pillow. "It terrifies me."

Alice was quiet for a long time.

"Maybe I'd start out thinking I could only use such power for good causes," I went on. "For justice. But I'm the sort who gets mad at people all the time. And if I had the power to hurt others just by wishing it? It's already gotten me into trouble too often. Whether with my wishes, or my fists."

I thought maybe Alice had fallen asleep.

"If Mermeros's father wanted an apple on his table," I said slowly, "or a brighter lamp, or whatever he might want, he could threaten someone with agonizing pain if they didn't get it for him."

"Power changes a person, doesn't it?" she said softly.

I nodded in the dark, though she couldn't see it. "Hurting others to get what you want makes you evil," I said. "I can't sell these artifacts to Mr. Poindexter fast enough."

"But Maeve," Alice said, "if you get rid of them, what if someone terrible gets them and uses them cruelly?"

I was trying not to think of that myself.

"The odds of that happening," I told her, by way of reassuring myself, "are so small as to be insignificant. No one would know where they came from, nor what they can do. These pieces will end up in a museum, or in some collector's glass cabinet."

Alice didn't sound convinced. "I hope you're right."

CHAPTER
25

We stood in the vestibule of Mission Industrial School and Home for Working Boys across the street from our school and eavesdropped as Alice's grandfather persuaded the head orphan master that he should be allowed to bring Thomas, surname unknown, on an outing. The orphan master didn't seem pleased to hear that Tommy had been fraternizing with girls at the school across the street.

"That one gets out too much as it is," he grumbled.

Mr. Bromley coughed. "I'm sure that my good friend, Sir Henry Bates of that London Orphans' Commission, would be thrilled to hear of your generosity in allowing this young man a special treat with his friends."

The headmaster summoned Tommy. He appeared looking wary, but curious, and shook Mr. Bromley's hand.

"Am I in trouble?" he whispered.

"No," I told him. "You're in for an adventure."

"Another Maeve adventure?" He grinned. "Let's go!"

Tommy grabbed a coat from one of dozens of pegs in the entry-way and followed us outside.

"Now," Alice said, "you need to fetch Morris."

He stopped and stared at me, then at Mr. Bromley.

"Oh, that's all right," Alice told him. "Grandfather knows about your owl."

"But…" Tommy blinked repeatedly. "Why do you want Morris? What's going on?"

"We've found someone you need to meet, Tom," I told him. "Someone eager to give an owl like Morris a proper home."

Tom looked unconvinced, but he nodded slowly. "It won't be easy to slip in and out of the cellars in broad daylight without being seen."

"No fear," I said. "The school is closed, and the mistresses and staff are still away on holiday."

"We'll stand guard," Mr. Bromley said. "Hop to it, young man."

I handed Tommy some licorice. "Here," I said. "Lure Morris out with this." He made a wry face at me, then laughed and popped a piece in his own mouth.

We sat waiting for him in the carriage. A young woman passed by, quite near us, and gazed up at Miss Salamanca's School and then down again at a paper in her hands several times, looking quite perplexed. Mr. Bromley opened the door to the carriage.

"Can we help you, miss?" he inquired. "Are you lost?"

The young lady turned and curtsied. "Thank you, sir. I'm looking for Darvill House. The employment agency said it was near here. Do you know of it?"

"Darvill House," repeated Mr. Bromley. "Can't say that I do."

"It's the mansion behind this building," Alice said, "on this block, but on the opposite side."

"It is?" I was surprised. I'd never heard of Darvill House.

"It's the place where we—" Alice cut herself off quickly. "But surely nobody is hiring there," she said. "It's empty and quite run-down."

She meant the empty mansion, with the spooky gallery. The place from which we'd embarked on our journey to Persia.

The young woman, who had a very friendly, likable face, grinned. "Thank you, miss," she said. "I'll look into it, all the same. Can't afford to let an opportunity pass."

"No, indeed," said Mr. Bromley. "We wish you good luck."

"Who could be interviewing for positions at Darvill House?" I wondered aloud.

In only a few minutes, Tommy returned, bearing a blinking Morris on one arm. The bird ruffled his feathers and hooted in agitation, but he allowed Tommy to carry him into the carriage. Our driver looked quietly horrified.

"Morris is the most interesting traveler I have ever had the pleasure of riding about London with," declared Mr. Bromley. "And I once rode with the Lord Mayor."

Once Morris was situated—no easy proposition—we rode through the alleyway that ran between the girls' school and the boys' home, passing by the grand derelict mansion.

So this *was Darvill House.* Derelict no longer; an army of workmen scampered about on ladders and scaffoldings, like sailors flying through the riggings of a merchant vessel.

"Look, Maeve," Alice said. "That young woman was right. Someone *has* taken the old mansion and is fixing it up."

"It'll take a maharajah's fortune to do it properly, by the looks of things," Mr. Bromley observed.

Tommy peered out the window as London flashed by our eyes. Despite the congested streets, in very little time, we reached the Oddity Shop. I felt a load lift off me as we arrived. Finally, I could be rid of these wretched objects and make some money in the bargain. A sorry ending to my djinni adventure, but better than nothing.

Alice's grandfather helped us all out of the carriage, then entered the curious little store, holding the door for us. Tommy and Morris went first, then Alice. I was next to step down into the fascinating little shop, when a strange sound froze me to the pavement.

A cry, a wail. Somehow both a hiss and a scream.

The London sky, always gray and smoky, went black and still. A shadow passed over me, but when I looked up to see what huge thing had flown by, I saw nothing. An icy chill sliced through me, colder than any wind off the Thames.

I couldn't move. All around me London shuffled by, horses and carts and people, plodding slowly, like dead men walking.

Through the shop window, I saw Mr. Siegfried Poindexter greet Tommy and Morris, but far away, thickly, as if through treacle. They didn't realize I hadn't followed them inside. It felt like a dream that becomes a nightmare. A dream where your friends forget you exist.

"Help me!" I called out, but the sound was snatched from my mouth as if by a hand. They never turned. They never heard me. It was as if I wasn't even there.

I'd been erased from London. Erased from the earth. Except for Morris. His wide owl's eyes watched me closely. I could feel it. It felt—I'd swear—like Morris was the only thing keeping me alive.

The eldritch scream uncurled behind me like a cracking whip. Slowly, painfully, I turned around.

A man walked toward me.

But not a man. The haggard shape of one, rigid, as if framed of tree limbs. Draped in raggedy black clothes, a shabby old suit and coat, that billowed as if they enclosed a cyclone.

Was there even a body? There was a face. His eyes settled upon me, black as tar pits, empty as night. A hat slouched low over his head. His skin was white, like teeth, and his nose, two livid holes.

Winds whipped around us both.

Three things I knew: He was not alive. He was evil. We'd met before.

He raised a long arm and pointed his bony fingers at my face. "You," he said, his voice, like rocks shifting at the bottom of an ancient tomb. "The things you carry are mine. Give them back."

I stared at the fiend.

"Give them back," he repeated. His fingers flexed, grasping air. "My talismans. They belong to me."

"What *are* you?" I cried. The wind snatched my voice from my throat and flung it away.

"Give them back."

I tried to move away from him, but my feet wouldn't budge. My hands moved as though forced by an unseen power toward the bag where I kept the gingerbread tin.

"Tell me who you are," I shouted again.

He advanced closer. His gruesome lips moved over his mouth, then flickered out of view, revealing long, broken teeth. His face wavered between flesh and skull, as if it couldn't decide. Teeth, and a skull, that I had seen before.

"You know what I am," he said. "You know *who* I am." His hand clutched my elbow, and cold—cold, so cold it burned—shot down to my fingertips.

"You may be a sorcerer," I gasped, "and you may have been a great king. But you're nothing but a bully. Just like your rotten son."

No, I thought. Far worse than his rotten son. He made Mermeros look like Father Christmas.

Even as I spoke, my hands opened my sack and pulled out the tin of their own will. Of *his* wicked will. I struggled against the inexorable force. I was losing sensation in my entire arm and shoulder. If this deadly cold spread throughout my body, I was finished. I turned, with effort, to again see Morris's great owl eyes upon me. Their golden depths were the only suns in this deathly world.

"How did you find me?" I cried to the specter before me.

He laughed. "Fool," he spat. "I care nothing for *you*. I left my sons to guard my realm and its treasures for all eternity. Should anyone disturb them, I will always find my talismans, even if I must rise from the underworld to reclaim what is mine."

I glanced into the store again, at Tommy and Alice, Mr. Bromley and Mr. Poindexter. Happy and smiling, oblivious of my doom and theirs.

"You've used them, haven't you?" he hissed. "I can smell it on you. It made you so very easy to find. Did you enjoy it? Do you want to drink the wine of power one more time?"

"You're sick," I cried.

"You're weak," he spat back.

"Speak your name," I cried.

"Shall I?" he hissed. "It is an ancient spell of power. If I utter it, the very rocks would crumble. These buildings would topple and crush poor fools inside."

Maeve Merritt doesn't back down. She doesn't give in to bullies. She refuses to play their games.

But my friends' bright faces through the window, unaware, smote my heart. I'd endangered them once before in Persia, when first we tangled with Mermeros's family. I couldn't do it twice. Once was already too many.

Morris blinked at me. *Go on*, he seemed to say. *Do it.*

With my last shred of will, I removed the gingerbread tin from my pouch and handed it to the wraith of the sorcerer king, and with it, my last hope of all my dreams.

His bony fingers punctured and peeled back the metal of the tin as if it were wrapping paper. He seized his precious things, and their metal clinked against his bones. Cradling the relics in his hands, he closed his eyes and inhaled deeply, slowly, like someone savoring a delicious fragrance. My flesh crawled at the sight.

The sorcerer king, dressed as a vagrant, fell to dust before my eyes, and a great shape, dark and winged, leaped into the air from the spot where he'd stood. With one final shriek that rent the sky, he gathered into himself the cold darkness that had surrounded us, and surged away. East, and south, if my bearings were reliable.

And he was gone.

I gasped as sensation returned to my frigid arm, like a hundred thousand stabbing needles. I tumbled down the stairs and into the welcoming warmth of the Oddity Shop, and hurried over to its potbellied coal stove. Morris's neck swiveled as he followed my movements.

"Oh, there you are, Maeve," Alice said. "Mr. Poindexter and Morris are making great friends." She took a closer look at me. "What's the matter? You look as pale as the grave. Have you seen a ghost?"

My teeth chattered. I turned away so she wouldn't see me and draped myself over the stove as close as I could without touching it. "I'm all right," I managed to say. "Just a cold wind outside, is all." Just a cold wind that keeps snatching my hopes and carrying them off in the whirlwind. I don't like admitting it, but not all the blurriness in my eyes was the result of the cold.

I heard Morris hoot across the room, and looked over to see him occupying the perch formerly held by the stuffed owl. I went to his perch and pulled a licorice from the pouch I'd brought. He nipped it from my fingers and nibbled at my open palm.

"Thanks, friend," I whispered.

"Who?" he replied.

I very nearly hugged him. But that might not be safe for either of us. I returned to the warmth of the stove. This cold, I feared, might never leave my bones.

Mr. Poindexter was arranging the stuffed owl on a high shelf and talking with Tommy.

"What you really need to see, my lad, is New Zealand," he told him. "A land of wonders, it is! Pools of water so blue, so green, like you've never seen. Mountains! Fjords! Volcanoes! Caves of glow-worms, strange lizards and kiwi birds..."

Perhaps Tommy was part glow-worm, too, for his eyes shone like the caves the shopkeeper described. Mr. Poindexter's stepladder wobbled just then, and the stuffed owl slid off the shelf. Tommy deftly caught it and handed it back up to the man.

"You've saved me a heap of trouble," he said. "Too bad you weren't here this morning to catch the pottery I knocked over in the back storeroom."

"I wish I had been," Tommy said. "I...I could come help out, you know. Any time you wanted." He caught himself, and stared at his feet.

"Well, now," said Mr. Poindexter. "That is indeed something to consider." He situated the owl, wiped his hands on his trousers, and descended the ladder. Seeing me watching them, he made his way over to the stove.

"Young lady," he said, "were you able to bring those Persian artifacts you described to me yesterday?"

I couldn't answer him. My throat wouldn't work, and I couldn't look him in the eye.

Tommy and Alice gathered in to listen.

"That's brilliant!" Tommy said. "That bracelet and ring, and that what-d'you-call-it, they should be here, in this shop!"

Alice prompted me. "You brought them, didn't you, Maeve?"

I nodded. "I brought them," I told the dark wood of the floor, "but I lost them. Just now."

"You *lost* them?" Tommy groaned. "How did you manage that?"

"It wasn't my fault," I said, my anger rising. "Their original owner took them from me. Just now."

Tommy and Alice's jaws dropped.

We all stood there, glued to the floor by awkward silence.

Tommy broke the spell. "But you've got your djinni," he said. "Just make a wish and get them back."

His eyes grew wide, and he clapped his hand over his mouth. He'd mentioned the djinni in front of Mr. Poindexter.

"It's all right, Tom," I said. "I told him about it." I wanted to crawl under the stove and stay there. "But it's no use. I lost that, too." I swallowed hard. "Someone stole it from me at school."

Tommy closed his eyes and kept very still. I knew what he was thinking—he didn't steal the sardine can when he could've, and now it was beyond his reach forever. That's what I'd be thinking if I were him. And that he was a fool to trust a friend. Maybe not even a friend.

Tom had talked of adventures, but he needed Mermeros to save him from a short life in a cotton mill. My big mouth and stupid mistakes hadn't only cost *me* my hopes.

I couldn't bear to look at him.

Alice had the goodness to take Tommy by the elbow and lead him away to a different part of the store to explain the ugly truth to him, leaving me alone with Mr. Poindexter. I waited for his scorn to fall upon me. He just stood looking thoughtfully at me for a long moment.

"Young lady," he said.

I waited.

"It's a wonderful thing to dream big dreams."

The lack of reproach in his voice disarmed me. I looked up into his muttonchop-whiskered face.

"It's an even more wonderful thing to imagine impossible, beautiful, strange, and exciting dreams." He gestured to the store. "None of this would be here if I didn't dream and imagine, too."

I knew a setup when I heard one. I waited for the punch.

"It doesn't do, however," he said, "to tell falsehoods about your dreams. Not to others, and not to yourself."

I took a deep breath to tell him what I thought of his patronizing sermon.

I found that I couldn't.

Much as I hated admitting it, I knew his intentions were kindly. Would I believe my stories, if I hadn't seen all that I'd seen? A djinni, a sorcerer, a deadly ring, a magic trip to Persia? Of course, I wouldn't.

He rested a hand on my shoulder a moment, then walked over to where Mr. Bromley stood beckoning him with another urgent question about scarab beetles.

I don't cry, as a general rule, but I wanted to weep for Tommy.

I thought of Mr. Poindexter's words, his expression, his voice. My thoughts shifted to my father's face, watching distractedly as we opened our Christmas gifts, keeping a brave smile on, all the while counting the cost and chafing over why things had turned so ill with him at the bank and his manager, Mr. Edgar Pinagree. If I'd given Mr. Treazleton the sardine can, just as I'd given the sorcerer his artifacts, my father wouldn't be in trouble now.

True, the sorcerer king was, shall we say, more persuasive.

But if I'd thrown that reeking sardine can back in the dustbin when I found it, there never would've been trouble in the first place.

As for my dreams, my cricket team and my world travel—did they even matter now? Weren't they just youthful, selfish fancies compared with other people's more serious needs?

We finally left the shop, with Tommy promising to return to help Mr. Siegfried Poindexter, and Mr. Bromley promising Tommy the roast beef lunch of a lifetime. I followed the others into the carriage with my heart made of lead, splashing somewhere around in my stomach. Morris's eyes watched me go. I wanted to take him with me and secretly cry in his feathers.

The last thing I saw through the carriage window, just as the horses began to move, and the wheels began to spin, was the peering face, the searching eyes, and the bowler hat of the ginger-whiskered man.

CHAPTER
27

The rest of my visit with Alice and her grandparents passed quickly, in hazy colors, like a dream. The memory of the sorcerer king still made me shiver, but as days slipped by, I figured that if he'd wanted to magically disembowel me, he'd have done so by now. Gradually, I stopped assuming every man in London had ginger whiskers. Though more than a handful of actual gingers gave me a momentary fright.

I stewed endlessly over my lost djinni. It would take a miracle, I knew, but when I returned to school I was determined to get it back. That resolve settled upon, I tried to enjoy the rest of my holidays.

The Bromleys were as good as gold to me. We took outings to the menagerie, to the Crystal Palace, to the Serpentine, to some very clever pantomimes. They proffered sweets and treats and parties galore. Evenings of checkers, chess, Hearts, and Old Maid in the drawing room. A grand party to ring in 1897.

After our New Year's Eve party, as we got ready for bed, Alice handed me a small wrapped present. My heart leaped into my throat when I ripped off the paper. Sultana's Exotic Sardines!

"My djinni!" I whispered. "I can't believe it! You had it all along?"

Alice's eyes grew wide with alarm. "Oh, Maeve. It's not your djinni. I...I just happened to see the exact same tin in a shop window, so I bought it for you." She blushed with embarrassment. "I wasn't trying to trick you. I thought it could be a, um, a memento."

I tried to smile, so she wouldn't feel badly. What had I been thinking? If Alice had Mermeros, she wouldn't have concealed the fact from me.

"Should we open it and see if there's a djinni inside?" I said.

Alice couldn't hide her relief. "Only if you're in the mood for some fish."

Too soon, the day came. Mr. and Mrs. Bromley climbed into a carriage with Alice and me and drove us back to Miss Salamanca's school.

I hated to leave. Their friendly welcome had almost made me forget my troubles. I understood better now why Alice loathed leaving home and attending Miss Salamanca's school. If I had grandparents this warm and loving, I'd wish I could live with them forever, too.

The early January day was unusually warm and bright, with glistening drops of melted frost dangling from spindly tree branches in the parks. The pretty day might almost have made me forget I was returning to Miss Salamanca's School for Upright Young Ladies. But I knew the truth. I was returning to fire and brimstone. And to Theresa Treazleton herself, a devil in training. My only consolation was the hunt for the djinni. Back at school, I could put my quest into motion.

"Well, I never," Mr. Bromley said to his wife as we neared the school. "Take a look at that, Adelaide."

He pointed out the window at the swarm of workmen hammering, roofing, patching, and painting the old mansion that shared an alleyway with the school: Darvill House. A steady stream of tradesman and deliverymen marched in and out the door, bearing furniture, rugs, pillows, drapes, culinary items, food shipments, cases of wine, houseplants, grandfather clocks, marble mantelpieces, and framed works of art.

"Darvill House, in use again?" wondered Mrs. Bromley. "When I was young, it was a grand old home."

"They've fixed it up in record time," observed Mr. Bromley. "An astonishing pace!"

"Who's taken it?" Mrs. Bromley asked. "Surely this must be discussed about town."

"I haven't the faintest," Mr. Bromley said. "Most peculiar..."

"Maybe it's an American millionaire," proposed Alice.

"Or a cousin of Tsar Nicholas of Russia," I added.

We stopped in the school courtyard, and the driver helped us all out.

"Why, look!" Mr. Bromley pointed eagerly across the way. "There's your friend, Thomas, Alice." He waved Tommy over.

I blew out my breath. Tommy would probably have plenty of hot words to fling at me, and I'd best prepare myself. But after he'd greeted Mr. and Mrs. Bromley, and Alice, he simply looked at me.

"Hello," he told my shoes.

"Hello, Tom."

I waited for the attack to hit me like a fist to the jaw. But it didn't. The disappointment and betrayal in his eyes hurt far more than anything he could've said.

"It wasn't your fault that the djinni got stolen," Tom said. "Bad things just happen sometimes. That's the way it is."

Somehow, I felt he wasn't only talking about my lost sardine can. Tom had long practice in disappointment.

"See you," he said at length.

I nodded. "See you."

Miss Salamanca came gliding out to greet the charming, the gracious, the affluent Bromleys. "My dear sir," she purred. "My dear madam. *Dearest* Alice." I poked my head out from behind Alice, and Miss Salamanca's face took on a strangled look.

"And Maeve." She pulled herself together and smiled for the Bromleys. "How good to see you." She cast a sidelong glance my way. "All of you."

She beckoned us indoors and offered tea to Alice's grandparents. "You girls run along to the dining room," she told us. "Cook is serving refreshments there for returning pupils."

We went to the dining room gladly, and found a woman we didn't recognize setting out plates of cut sandwiches and little tarts made with raspberry jam. She wore a cook's uniform, and an apron tied tightly around her plump waist.

"Afternoon, young ladies," the woman said. "Hungry, are we?"

"Who are you?" I blurted out.

"*Maeve!*" scolded Alice.

The woman smiled. "It's a fair question. I'm Miss Plumley, and I'm the new cook. The former one gave her notice right before Christmas."

I shook my head. "Mrs. Gruboil's gone?"

"So it seems," said our new cook. "The school's loss is my good fortune."

"Oh, she's no loss," I told Miss Plumley. "Don't worry about that."

Alice hid her eyes behind her hand. "*Maeve!*"

Miss Plumley chuckled. "That's all right, Miss—"

"Alice," I told her.

"Miss Alice. Very nice. Don't worry about your friend." She winked at me. "I think we'll get along like two yolks in an egg."

I turned my head at a small sound and saw Winnifred Herzig nearby, clutching a small bread-and-butter sandwich and watching me with anxious eyes that darted back and forth between me and Miss Plumley. Oh, that Winnifred! I was sick and tired of her mincing around me anytime we met, as if I were some three-headed monster.

But I'd told myself I'd try to be a bit kinder in 1897, so I gave her a smile. "Happy new year, Winnifred!" I told her.

She blinked several times, blew her nose, and fled the room, leaving her half-eaten bread-and-butter sandwich in broken bits on the floor.

As I say, most people ignore Winnifred Herzig, but it's not as if she gives them no reason to.

Pleasant weather decided not to prolong its visit. All the next day, a cold and miserable winter rain slanted along the windowpanes. Londoners hunched down inside their coats and turned up the collars to endure the misery. Very much, I thought, like the way I had to face each day at Miss Salamanca's school.

In needlework class, when Miss Bickle wasn't looking, Theresa brandished her four-gauge needle at me. As if I could forget her stabbing me with it. The beast! The vicious, thieving, prissy beast. Her pimples seemed mostly to have healed up, but one spectacular one lingered right on the tip of her nose.

I'd made up my mind, staring at that blemish that turned her nose into a rhinoceros's horn. I was going to get that sardine can back at any price. I had one wish left, and I intended to make the most of it. I didn't know how I'd break into the Treazleton home and snatch the can back, but I'd find a way.

I reminded Theresa what my fists look like. She swallowed, and focused intently on her stitching. *That's right, little spoiled princess. You're lucky I don't knock your teeth in after you stole my djinni.*

I looked out the window to see a man leave Mission Industrial School and Home for Working Boys, open an umbrella, and hurry down the street. I didn't trust my vision at first, through the blur of weather, so I sidled over to the window for a better look. I was right. Mr. Siegfried Poindexter of the Oddity Shop was hurrying away in the rain. I wondered what on earth he could be doing there, and what could be so important that it would bring him out in such weather. His expression seemed thunderously angry and upset. I hoped Tommy wasn't in any kind of trouble. Maybe Mr. Poindexter merely hated bad weather.

After dinner at midday, during our twenty-minute break before classes resumed, I sat in the common room on my dormitory floor reading a book Alice had lent me by Mr. Dickens, *Nicholas Nickleby*. It was a topper of a story. I was right at the part where Nicholas stopped his nasty headmaster, Mr. Squeers, from abusing a poor boy by whacking him with a stick. *Great stuff!* I was so engrossed by it that I didn't hear the telltale clack of Miss Salamanca's heels until she stood before me.

"Miss Merritt," she said. "You have a visitor." She stalked away before I could ask her any questions. Or whack her with a stick.

Miss Salamanca ushered me into her office where my visitor awaited. It was Mr. Alfred P. Treazleton. Shipping magnate, captain of industry, noted philanthropist, father, and thief. Coldhearted, stone-hearted, pernicious thief. Summoning me here, no doubt, to gloat at his triumph over me and boast of the magnificent, glorious marvels Mermeros was conjuring for him, perhaps even now.

He rose and shook my hand. "Miss Merritt. How nice to see you looking so hale and hearty."

I curtsied and said nothing until Miss Salamanca, standing behind the eminent donor, jerked her head in his direction and scowled at me ferociously.

"It is good to see you as well, Mr. Treazleton," I said, to spare Miss Salamanca a crick in the neck, though she deserved one.

Mr. Treazleton turned toward my headmistress, who replaced

her scowl with beaming tranquility faster than one could say "school benefactor."

"Miss Salamanca, would you be so good as to allow me a brief, but private, interview with my young friend? It continues the conversation we began before the holidays, but the weather today is too inclement for another stroll."

It was almost worth being shut up with this man to watch Old Sally squirm, caught between propriety, curiosity, and the unstated rule that whatever Mr. Treazleton wants, Mr. Treazleton gets. He won. Of course, he won.

When the door had shut, Mr. Treazleton rested his palms and leaned his weight on the knob of his walking stick—a favorite pose of his. What would happen if I knocked it out from under him? Might he topple to the floor? Now *there* was a picture.

"Why do you smile, Miss Maeve?"

I bit the inside of my checks. "I'm not smiling."

"Could it be, perhaps, because you think you have gotten the better of me?"

I bit down harder. What could he mean? Every instinct told me to keep my face flat and reveal nothing until I knew more.

"I will come right to the point," he said. "You're a clever girl, much too clever for your own good. Clever women, I find, though charming at first, become miserable, frustrated, nervous creatures before long."

That monster!

"Because they're suffocated in tight dresses, imprisoned at parties, and forbidden to use their brains, I imagine," I said. "Because they must always defer to some *pig* of a husband."

He made a dry laugh. "At last, you see what women are fit for," he said. "You've been paying close attention in Miss Rosewater's deportment classes. One wouldn't know it, upon observing your manners."

What on earth could he want with me? To toy with me, like a cat with a captured mouse?

"You said you would come right to the point," I said, "but you've hardly done so."

He laughed again. "It's a shame you weren't born a boy, Miss Maeve," he said. "I'd bring you on at the firm next year and make a great man of you before long."

I saw my opening and I took it, and I twisted the knife as it went in. "Is that how you feel about Theresa? Is it a shame *she* wasn't born a boy?"

His mouth hardened. "I'll thank you to keep a civil tongue in your mouth."

I nearly stuck my uncivil tongue out at him, but I was a tad too old for that.

"What is that you've come for, Mr. Treazleton? I'll need to return to class momentarily."

He gave me a withering look. "Let's not pretend we don't know, shall we?"

"Actually, let's do just that," I said. "What do you want?"

He banged the heel of his cane on the floor so violently I nearly jumped. "I want—" He realized he was speaking far too loud, so he shifted to a strained whisper. "*I want that djinni, and I want it now!*"

My mind spun.

Could he be toying with me?

But why on earth would he?

He didn't have it. He didn't have it! *Who did?*

It wasn't Theresa who stole it?

Mr. Treazleton believed I still had it!

A glorious vision burst before my eyes: The Treazletons didn't have my djinni. Perhaps it was still right here at Miss Salamanca's School. If it was, I'd sniff it out like a cat sniffing, well, sardines.

But there was Mr. Treazleton, glaring at me. Was there any good I could squeeze out of a situation like this? Oh, why hadn't I spent more time letting Aunt Vera teach me whist, instead of cricketing with village boys? Then I might be better at forming strategies, and keeping a straight face to conceal devious plans.

"In case you need further persuasion, Miss Merritt, I shall make my intentions fully clear to you. I have already planted the seed of doubt about your father's scruples, his honesty and integrity, with my old associate, Mr. Edgar Pinagree, manager of St. Michael's Bank and Trust. All that remains is for me to offer confirming proof that your father has mishandled bank funds for his own gain, and he'll be sacked, never to be hired at an honest establishment in Britain again."

My fists, my old friends, leaped to my side. Fat good they'd do me here.

"You know my father hasn't mishandled a farthing," I said through gritted teeth. "You know he hasn't. He wouldn't. He's not that kind of man."

Mr. Treazleton shrugged. "Is he? I couldn't say. I hardly know him. Nor do I care." He tapped my shoulder gently with the edge of his cane. "What I do know is that his daughter is so greedy, so stubborn, and so selfish that she would ruin her father's career in order to keep a whimsical plaything she fancies."

Oh, there were so many retorts I could make to this, I didn't know where to start. Silently, I fumed and raged, boiling inside my own skin like a potato in a hot oven. I wished for a moment that I had the old sorcerer's ring still. I could call down some diabolical punishments upon Alfred P. Treazleton without a second thought.

The sorcerer king. On second thought, he may keep his evil, far away from me. Next to him, Mr. Treazleton might as well have been made of pillow down.

He interpreted my silence as defeat. "Now. Miss Merritt. Will you produce the djinni, and we can put this whole unpleasant business behind us?"

I took a deep breath, grasping at the ether for the words I needed. I wanted to sound quite grown-up and official.

"I am not able to produce it at this moment," I told him. "For... safekeeping, I have placed it somewhere where I am not able to obtain access to it without some difficulty." This might be a vaguely true statement.

His eyes narrowed.

"Are you lying to me? I can always tell when people lie to me."

I prayed he was bluffing. "Do you think I'd be such a fool as to keep something so valuable lying around, within anyone's easy reach?" That was precisely the fool I'd been. But Mr. Treazleton didn't know that.

"Very well, then," said he. "I shall return to the school tomorrow morning, under pretense of needing to speak with the headmistress about matters of business. I shall be here by eight o'clock, before your classes begin."

I nodded.

"I shall expect you to come to the headmistress's office with a package for me. You can say that it's, oh, let's see..." He puckered his lips in thought. "Say that it's a book you borrowed from Theresa, and then I asked her to give it back to me."

"That's a pretty flimsy story," I said. "Do you really expect Old Sally to believe that?"

His eyes bulged. "'Old Sally'?" He grimaced as if my rudeness was a bitter taste in his mouth. "Frankly, I don't care a fig what 'Old Sally' thinks. Bring me the package. If you don't—if I get back into my carriage with no djinni in my possession—I will drive straight to St. Michael's Bank and Trust and give Mr. Pinagree more than enough proof of your father's perfidy. He'll be out on his ear before nine thirty in the morning."

We glared at each other. He clutched his cane so vehemently that for an instant I thought he planned to strike me with it.

"Do we understand one another?" he said.

I reached for the doorknob. "I can't begin to guess what you're capable of understanding, Mr. Treazleton, but as for me, I believe I understand you as well as I need to."

And before he could sputter and rage at me, I opened the door and left him there.

CHAPTER
28

For the rest of that day's classes, I was worse than useless. Miss Guntherson rapped me on the knuckles with a ruler in French class for not paying attention to the imperfect subjunctive conjugation of *se souvenir*, to remember. As if I would ever remember how to use it. Or care. All I could think about was: if Theresa Treazleton or one of her minions didn't steal my sardine can, then who did?

If whoever took it opened it, they would discover Mermeros, and their lives would never be the same. They, themselves, would never be the same. I was certain of it. I wasn't the girl I'd been ten minutes before I found Mermeros in the dustbin.

This caught me up short. I *was* different. I'd changed. *Had Mermeros been right?*

Never mind.

If it wasn't someone in Theresa's crowd who had my djinni, it could be any girl. But that girl would be different now. She'd be… excited. Scheming. Planning. Distracted. Devious.

Just like me.

I studied each girl in French class, and in deportment, and in maths. They all looked the same to me. No one seemed to be stewing in a deep secret. They looked like girls who resented returning to school after winter holidays.

Just like me.

At teatime, I watched the table where the instructors took their tea together. Miss Plumley made a special point of drizzling their scones with melted butter and honey. She was no fool. Getting the teachers on her side was a wise move.

What if I had it all wrong? What if it wasn't a girl who'd found my sardine can, but a teacher? Perhaps a teacher had overheard me talking to Alice about sardines?

But why would a teacher remain on Miss Salamanca's penny-pinching payroll if she'd discovered a djinni? If I were old enough to make my own decisions, without parents telling me what to do, and I'd accepted employment here, then found a sardine can with a djinni inside, I'd give notice in a trice.

Oh. Oh my.

What if someone had found the sardine can but *not yet discovered Mermeros*? What if they'd never opened the can? What if they'd just put it back somewhere where food belonged?

What if even now it sat on the larder shelves?

I could barely hold still. Imagine. Imagine! What if it was that close, and right within my grasp?

As soon as I could slip away from my plate of toast and cup of tea, I raced downstairs, but two kitchen maids, stirring pots and basting mutton, blocked my path to the larder and left me no choice but to try my search later that night. I didn't know how I could stand to wait. My only consolation was that dinner was delicious. Succulent mutton, not even a little bit burnt. Miss Plumley was a vast improvement.

After dinner, I pried a novel out of Alice's hands and, in my most hushed whisper, told her all about my talk with Mr. Treazleton. Her eyes grew wide as moons.

"But if he doesn't have it…" she whispered. "Maeve, what does this mean?"

I took both her hands in mine. "I think it means someone stole the sardine can, and they have it still. I suspect they haven't opened it. I think, if they had, we'd know."

Alice shook her head in astonishment. "But, why take it, if you didn't know what it was, or if you didn't plan to eat the fish? What other reason could there be for stealing a tin of sardines?"

"A prank?" I said. "Or someone who thought the sardines belonged in the kitchen? I plan to search the larder tonight after lights-out."

"Maeve, you can't," Alice protested. "You've already gotten into trouble too many times. Miss Salamanca will expel you if you're caught poking around the kitchen, after all your other incidents."

"I have to, Alice," I said. "If I don't find that sardine can, my father will be sacked tomorrow. His life will be ruined. And I'll definitely be kicked out of school. No matter what, I'm going sardine fishing tonight."

Alice groaned and flopped back on her bed cushions. "I'm turning into a criminal," she moaned. "What will my poor grandparents think when they lock me up in Newcastle?"

I laughed. "How are *you* turning into a criminal?"

"Well, someone's got to come with you, of course," she said, "to make sure you don't get caught. I believe that's called being an accomplice to the crime." She made a wry face at me. "You're a bad influence on me, Maeve Merritt."

"Yes, but you've got to admit, I'm never boring."

She rolled her eyes. "You might want to try it sometime."

We tiptoed down the back stairs toward the kitchen in our stockinged feet, keeping to the edges of each stair to reduce the creaking. This routine was becoming all too familiar. Perhaps Alice was right. Perhaps I was leading her down the slippery slope to a life of crime. I could just see drawings of us in the London newspapers, as a shocking pair of criminals, robbing kitchen larders of their supplies of fish.

"This is hardly amusing, Maeve," Alice whispered. "Stop giggling."

We reached the bottom stair and were headed toward the kitchen when the sound of low voices and a closing door pinned us to the spot. Alice gestured to me to go back, for heaven's sake, but I crept farther down the corridor. I wanted to hear who was talking. I heard Alice sigh and tiptoe along after me.

"You poor thing! You're soaked. Here, have a seat by the stove, and I'll put the kettle on."

It was Miss Plumley's voice. I heard the strike of a safety match and the whoosh as she turned on the gas stove and lit the burner.

"Th-thank you, miss." It was a woman's voice, sounding like a young one, and sniffling. Crying, even.

"Have a biscuit, dearie," urged Miss Plumley. "Have all you like."

I hoped she wouldn't want too many. I needed this impromptu party to end quickly.

But the crying woman wept all the harder. "You're too good, ma'am. And me, a stranger!"

"Oh, tut-tut. None of that," said Miss Plumley. "I'll have a nice cup for you as soon as the kettle's hot. Meanwhile, tell me, who struck you like this? Was it your young man?"

I inched closer to the kitchen. This was getting interesting. *A young man, striking a girl on the streets of London? Right outside my school?* I'd sock him, if I saw it happen.

The young woman's indignant voice rose. "I never! I'm respectable, miss. I don't have a young man about anywhere."

"Hush," whispered Miss Plumley. "You'll wake the students."

"*She* did this to me," sniffled the young woman.

"Who's she?"

"My mistress," sobbed the younger voice. "My wicked, horrible mistress!"

Alice and I exchanged glances. Alice mouthed words at me. "Is that...?"

I bit my lip. Her voice almost *did* sound familiar, but I couldn't think how.

Miss Plumley was shocked also. "Your mistress struck you *across the face*? Hard enough to leave a *mark*?"

Alice gasped. I turned and held a finger over my lips.

"That's right," said the young woman—a servant, it seemed.

"You mean to tell me," said our incredulous cook, "that the lady of that house, there, the one where no expense has been spared to deck it out fit for a queen overnight—*that's* the lady who struck you like...like some brawler in an alleyway?"

The other person blew her nose. "She's no lady," she said angrily. "She may dress like one, but she was never raised by the proper sort. Speaks like a barmaid and swears like a sailor. To see her eating at the table makes a body lose her appetite, I can tell you that. And lazy!

She's the laziest thing you ever saw. She won't so much as reach over to her own dressing table to fetch a mirror, but what she rings the bell for me to get it for her!"

"You poor girl," Miss Plumley said in a soothing voice. "I never heard of such a thing in all my life."

"When she's vexed, she hits me. With a hairbrush, or a paperweight, or anything nearby."

The teakettle began to sing, and footsteps moved about the kitchen. I heard water being poured into a cup.

"Is that what happened tonight, then?"

"Yes, miss," the unfortunate servant said. "I dropped a tray and broke a china plate. When I'd picked up the tray, she snatched it from me and struck me with it. And this isn't the first time."

"It's the most appalling thing I've ever heard," Miss Plumley said. "To strike your servants! To use objects as weapons. It's shocking." I heard the clinking of china. "Sugar?"

"If you don't mind," the young woman said gratefully. "I'll never go back. I won't. She can keep my wages, but I'm through working there."

"Of course, you are," Miss Plumley said. "You ought to summon the police. That's what you ought."

The younger woman blew upon her tea to cool it.

"Who is your mistress?" Miss Plumley asked. Just what I would've liked to ask myself.

The younger woman clinked her teacup on her saucer. "She calls herself 'Baroness Gabrielle'...something—something French, but I'm certain she's not saying it right. She talks like a vegetable hawker off a stall in Covent Garden. If she's French, then I'm a poodle. If she's a baroness, I'm the empress of France."

France hadn't had an empress for quite some time, and the previous empress was now a widow living in England, somewhere in Hampshire, but this was not the time to point that out.

I heard some plates and dishes rattling about. "Are you hungry for something more substantial than biscuits? I have cold mutton and good bread. I could make you a sandwich."

"No, thank you, miss, I ate earlier." The young woman laughed bitterly. "Baroness Gabrielle is awfully fond of cold meat sandwiches." She took a noisy sip of tea. "And that's not the only thing queer about her. She has a closet in her bedroom, locked up with half a dozen keys, which nobody can enter, under penalty of getting sacked. What's she got in there, do you suppose? A dead body?"

Somebody rose to their feet.

"A dead body's what I'll be, come morning, if I don't get to bed right away," Miss Plumley said. "Come along, dearie. There's an extra bunk in my room, and you can get some rest there. In the morning, we'll figure out what's best to do to help you."

One more long, noisy sip of tea. "You've been ever so good to me, ma'am," the girl said. "I don't know how to thank you."

Alice tugged desperately on my sleeve. We only just managed to slip around the corner and exit the hallway before Miss Plumley and her grateful charge left the kitchen and headed toward the cook's sleeping quarters.

We waited a moment or two to make sure no one returned, then crept into the kitchen and searched the larder from top to bottom. Every shelf and cupboard and drawer in the entire kitchen, too. I found delicious things and disgusting things and mysterious things and boring things, but nowhere was there a sardine tin to be found.

We tiptoed back upstairs, out of ideas, and out of time.

CHAPTER
29

We opened the door to our room only to find Winnifred Herzig sitting at my desk and doodling on my ink blotter. She jumped like a nervous rabbit when she heard us come in.

"Winnifred!" I said. "What are you doing here?"

She wouldn't look up at me, but chewed on her lips and drummed her fingertips.

"What is it, Winnifred?" Alice asked, much more gently than I had done. She put her arm around the younger girl. "Tell us, what's the matter?"

"That's right, Winnie, tell us," I said. "Has someone been mean to you? We'll teach them a lesson."

Winnifred shook her head vehemently. She clenched her hands together on the desk, but her fingers squiggled like fish in a net.

"I've been the rotten one," she whispered at last. "I'm so sorry, Maeve!"

Finally, she looked up at me.

"Sorry for what?" I asked.

She scrubbed at her eyes with the back of her sleeve. "For getting you expelled!"

Alice turned to me. "Have you been expelled, Maeve?"

"Probably," I said, "but no one's told me yet."

Winnifred's bleary eyes opened wide. "But...I heard you! Just tonight! Talking about getting expelled!"

I folded my arms across my chest. "What were you doing, Winnifred? Eavesdropping at our door?"

Poor little Winnifred looked stung. "I...I didn't mean to."

I stared at her.

"Mostly I didn't mean to," the sheepish creature admitted.

Alice's gentle frown was probably far worse than a punch in the nose from me. "You mustn't listen at doors, Winnifred," she said. "It's not ladylike."

I swallowed a laugh. "That's right, Winnifred," I said. "Alice and I would never *dream* of listening at doorways to *private conversations*."

Alice blushed crimson.

Winnifred looked up at us both. "Then...you're not angry at me?"

I sat down on my bed. "We will be," I said, "if you make a habit of it. But this time, you're forgiven." A twitch of her eyebrow made me pause. "*Have* you been making a habit of it, Winnifred?"

She squirmed.

"Winnifred," Alice said severely. "Do confess. It's better that way."

Winnifred buried her face in her hands. "It's just that I've been so worried about you," she sniffled. "I heard you say 'sardines' and 'expelled,' and I was just so terribly sure—"

A terrible coldness came over me. "So terribly sure of what, Winnifred?"

Winnifred peeped out from between her fingers, then hid her face in Alice's shoulder. "See? See? She is angry with me! I knew it, and now she'll chop my hair off! And...and knock my teeth out!"

"Whose teeth have I ever knocked out?" I demanded.

"Maeve." Alice held up a hand to shush me.

I restrained my voice, though it just about killed me to do so. "What about sardines, Winnifred? What were you going to say about that?"

Winnifred pried herself away from Alice's protection and faced me. Her lip jutted out defiantly. "It's not all my fault, you know, Maeve." She sniffled once more. "You started it."

"Started *what*?"

"Shh!" Alice hissed. "You'll bring down the headmistress upon us!"

Winnifred took a deep breath. "It was the night before winter hols," she said. "We went over to the Industrial School, or whatever they call it. Remember?"

I nodded. "And?"

She swallowed hard. "And I was there, ready to present my muffler and my sweets to the one orphan boy who's..." She paused.

A wicked laugh bubbled up from down in my belly. "Who's what?"

"Never mind," Winnifred said hastily.

I wouldn't let the poor girl go free. "Who's handsome? Is that it, Winnifred?"

Winnifred turned orange. Alice patted her on the shoulder.

What a lark! Wait till I told Tommy there were girls here who thought he was handsome! Wouldn't his stomach turn at the thought?

"Well, anyway," I said, "you were ready to present your offerings to an orphan, never mind who—"

"And then you cut in front of me," she said angrily. "Like you always do. Like everyone always does. I get so sick and tired of it!"

I grinned. "That's the spirit, Winnifred! Stand up for yourself! Don't let anybody push you around."

The color drained from Winnifred's face. "Well, as to that," she said, "I decided I wouldn't. Or at any rate, I decided I'd take my vengeance." She clasped her hands nervously on the desk once more. "So, I, uh, that is, I, um..."

"Out with it!" I cried, earning another shush from Alice.

Winnifred clenched her fists. "I told Mrs. Gruboil you were hiding sardines in your room. Sardines you'd probably stolen from the larder."

I saw red, and purple, and silver, and black.

"*You did what?*" Alice cried. Now she needed shushing.

"I heard Maeve talking about them that very evening, right before we went over to the boys' home," Winnifred explained.

"Eavesdropping at our door again?" asked Alice.

Winnifred nodded.

"I was just so angry at you," Winnifred said. "But I never meant to get you expelled."

So, Winnifred ratted on me to Mrs. Gruboil—the miserable cook who burnt everything, and bossed us around, and who was always suspecting us girls of stealing food from her larder.

The cook who had given notice over the holidays and not returned to the school!

I rose and held out a hand to Winnifred. I needed to get her out of here. "I'm not expelled, Winnie, so there's no harm done. I forgive you. Let's shake and be friends, shall we?"

"*No harm done?*" echoed Alice, eyeing me strangely.

Winnifred shook my hand like someone lost in a daze. "Are you sure?"

"Sure as sugar," I said. "All's well. Thanks for telling us. Stop listening at our doors. Off to bed with you now, before you get into trouble."

I bundled her out the door, with her repeating her apologies every step of the way, and thanking me for being so forgiving. Forgiving? What a joke. I'd like to have boxed her ears in. She'd cost me Mermeros. But at least now we knew something we hadn't known before.

I shut the door and locked it, then faced Alice.

"Do you realize what this means?" I whispered. "Mrs. Gruboil! That's why she didn't come back to the school after Christmas!"

Alice nodded mutely.

"So now all we have to do is figure out where she is," I said breathlessly. "She must've left a forwarding address. Maybe you could ask Miss Salamanca for it. Or, if we had to, we could rummage through her desk and papers…"

I paced the room, my blood pumping with excitement. The hunt was on once more.

"You won't need to do any of that," Alice said.

I stopped my pacing. "How's that, again?"

"You won't have to search for where she's gone," Alice said, "nor travel far to find her."

I shook my head. "Explain, please," I cried softly. "You're making me dizzy."

"The voice," Alice said. "The young woman talking to Miss

Plumley. I think it's the same person who asked us for directions to Darvill House days ago, remember?"

I was about to explode. "That's very nice," I said, "but what of it?"

"Your sardine tin," she said softly, "must be in the locked closet in the mansion next door. Mermeros's new master is this 'Baroness Gabrielle,' the ill-tempered lady of the house who strikes her servants. Formerly Mrs. Gruboil, the school's cook."

CHAPTER
30

I really and truly was leading Alice into a life of crime now, and no mistake. We were about to burgle a baroness's mansion. Not a true baroness, but I doubted the magistrate would care one way or another about that.

If we didn't end up as career criminals, I decided, Alice and I should become a pair of detectives. She could sleuth out the mysteries, and I could sock the villains in the nose. That was a smashing bit of deduction on her part there. I'd been too caught up in the poor servant girl's story to see what ought to have been obvious.

We waited until the lights of the school had gone dark, as far as we could tell, then slipped down the stairs and out the back door. Bitter wind blew through my cloak and hat. We kept low and close to the school until we'd left it behind us by a good distance, then ran along the back alleyway toward the mansion, abandoned no longer. Two lit windows upstairs blazed into the dark night, like the baleful eyes of a monster, daring us to step closer. Probably Mrs. Gruboil's bedroom.

Where to break in? How to locate the closet? How to get past its many locks? I hadn't exactly rushed outside with a plan. Just rushed outside. Typical me.

We lurked in the darkness and watched. A stout shadow passed before the curtain, sat down on what must have been a bed, and lay down for the night. A lamp was blown out, and the two bedroom windows went dark. Only the reddish glow of a hearth fire lent any light to the room.

"Well," I said, "we know we're looking for a closet in Mrs. Gruboil's bedroom, and now we know which room that is. So we're off to a good start."

Alice hugged her arms tightly to her body and shivered in the cold.

"A good start," she said, "except that the house is locked, the closet has several locks, and no doubt the bedroom is locked as well. And the mistress of the house is still awake."

"Let's hope not for long," I said.

"You two don't ever sleep, do you?"

A voice in my ear made me jump out of my skin.

Tommy laughed.

I whirled upon him. "You're hardly in bed yourself."

He shrugged. "I'll sleep when I'm old. Besides, I'm too excited to sleep."

"Nice muffler," I told him.

He rolled his eyes. "It's a bit lumpy and holey," he said. "But the mittens are tops."

Alice and I exchanged a look.

"Maeve has surprising talents," Alice said kindly. "Now, what has you so excited, Tom?"

He grinned from ear to ear. "A couple of days ago, Mr. Poindexter from the Oddity Shop came to the orphanage and took me for an outing to his shop for the day. Talked about maybe taking me on as an apprentice."

"How wonderful!" Alice clapped her hands. "You must've made quite an impression on him."

"If you worked for him, you wouldn't have to go to..." My voice trailed off. I didn't even want to say the words: "the mill."

"I'd get to live there, and everything," Tommy said. "We had the *best* day. He took me for a big lunch at an inn, and he showed me everything in his shop and told me about all his travels. He's been *everywhere*."

"Was that today?" I asked him. "During all the rain?"

Tommy looked at me, puzzled. "Nah. Three days ago."

"Ah," I said. "Has Mr. Poindexter visited you since?"

He shook his head. "No. Why do you ask?"

"It's nothing." I remembered seeing the Oddity Shop owner

marching off angrily, but I waved the subject away with a mittened hand, then thumped my friend in the arm. "That's tops. I hope it works out for you, Tom."

"I get to visit him again tomorrow," he said. I could feel his excitement, even through the cold. "I really think he means to take me on. And maybe I could travel with him on his next adventures!"

Alice smiled. "And look after Morris."

"That's right." He looked around him. "But say, what are you doing out here so late?"

We explained to him about Mrs. Gruboil, and about "Baroness Gabrielle," and what the servant girl said, and how Alice had pieced it all together. It would be just the sort of petty, spiteful thing for someone like Mrs. Gruboil to do—to wish for a fortune so she could live like a grand lady, right under the nose of her former employer. And to turn mean and cruel on the taste of a little bit of power, and beat her servants, when she'd been a domestic servant herself not long before.

"So that's the plan?" Tommy asked. "Break in, and steal the djinni back?" He elbowed me. "You owe me that sardine can when you're done with it, mind. Wishes, here I come!" He laughed. "'Course, if Mr. Poindexter hires me on at the shop, I won't mind so much if I don't get it now." He took of his cap to scratch his red-haired scalp. "Funny thing. Mr. Poindexter was asking me all about your djinni, Maeve, and your antiquities, and our trip to Persia."

"Did you tell him everything?" Alice asked.

Tommy nodded. "I figured since Maeve had told him about it already, there was no point in being secretive," he said. "He seemed very interested in it all. I thought, if any adult would believe all this, it's him."

"And did he believe you?" Alice asked.

Tommy shook his head. "Nah. But that's all right. Doesn't matter."

I hoped he was right.

Tommy blew on his fingers and rubbed his hands together. "We'd best get a move on, before we freeze to death," he said. "C'mon. Let's get your stinky fish-man back, Maeve. Then we can take another fantastical journey, all right?"

We stared at Darvill House. Was it just a few weeks ago that we climbed into this empty place, summoned Mermeros, and flew to Persia? Back then it was empty, spooky, and wonderful. Now it felt like the Queen herself might live here, with all the royal retinue. Armed guards especially.

As for how to burgle a locked mansion, I had no idea.

Tommy stepped closer to the building and examined its brick-work and exterior pipes. "I could climb this, no problem," he said. "You could, too, Maeve. And you, Alice, could be our lookout. Then we just pop in through the windows."

"Oh, don't climb," Alice cried. "You'll fall to your deaths!"

"Not Maeve," Tommy said. "She climbs like a monkey."

"But surely the windows will be locked," Alice said.

"Maybe they will," Tommy said, "and maybe they won't. It's a chance we'll have to take."

"But Mrs. Gruboil will wake up if you rattle the windows," Alice protested.

I took off my mittens, flexed my fingers, and tested the sturdiness of the pipe. "Let's just hope she had plenty of wine with her supper," I said. "She'll sleep like the dead. She snores, anyway. She might not hear a thing."

Alice caught my arm. "Don't do this, Maeve," she begged. "It's bound to go wrong. You could be terribly hurt. And if you're not hurt, you're certain to be caught. Let's think of something else, tomorrow." She snapped her fingers. "I know! We could find a way to dress up as upstairs maids and go dust her bedchambers..."

I squeezed Alice's hand. "Tomorrow's too late," I told her. "If I don't stop Mr. Treazleton, he'll get my father sacked first thing in the morning. His career will be over."

Tommy halted. "You're not giving him the djinni, are you?"

I felt sick to my stomach. Tommy had trusted me all along to give him the djinni next.

"Not if I can help it, Tom," I said. "I'd far rather use a wish to stop Mr. Treazleton than just hand it over to him." Even still, I was misleading him. After my third wish, the djinni would vanish away. Tom didn't know that, but I did. Sometimes a lie, even an accidental one, or a lie that comes from *not* speaking up rather than speaking, gets too big to fix. Or so it felt to me. If I hadn't told him already, I didn't see how I could now. And if we didn't succeed in getting the sardine tin back, there'd never be a need to admit to what I'd done.

Still. I had to help my father. It was my fault his livelihood was in danger. I had to make it right.

"Come on, Tom," I said. "Mrs. Gruboil's bound to be sleeping now. Ups-a-daisy."

I started climbing toward one window, and Tommy took the other. My fingers were stiff with cold, which didn't reassure me any. I forced myself not to look down, but just to study the bricks and mortar before my eyes. Fortunately, this building had a good deal more ornamental brickwork and stone inserts than Miss Salamanca's school. I had more to hold and step onto. Some of it was old and crumbly, though, and once my left foot gave way underneath me altogether. I only barely caught myself. I heard Alice gasp down below.

Tommy reached his window before me and climbed into its deep well. He tugged at the windows, poked and prodded at their frames. Nothing.

I said a little prayer, just in case—who was the patron saint of burglars, I wondered?—and continued my climb. Finally I reached the window, and with shaking hands and knees, I climbed onto the deep windowsill.

These windows were tall and side by side, opening outward like double doors. I could see a brass lock mechanism, a sort of rotating crescent blade holding the two sides together, by a glint of light from a streetlamp. It was locked, but only barely. The circular mechanism hadn't been rotated all the way.

I pressed my head against the glass and listened for any sound. Nothing but Mrs. Gruboil's rhythmic snores. I'd know her anywhere.

I pried my fingernails into the strip of wood on the inner edge of either window. On Mrs. Gruboil's next snore, I tugged the windows toward me. They moved, just a smidge. I waited for another snore, and pulled again. Back and forth, back and forth, I tugged at the windows, begging the brass mechanism to loosen and yield.

On and on she snored, and on and on I tugged. I could've sworn the windows were swinging out a tiny bit farther now, and I was pretty sure the brass rotator had budged a bit.

"It's no good, Maeve." Tommy's whisper floated across to me on the night wind. "It's locked. We can't get in."

"I can," I whispered back. "Hold tight. Once I get in, I'll let you in."

Back and forth, snore after snore, I worried away at that window until I was certain I was making progress. Once Mrs. Gruboil snorted herself half-awake. I froze in terror, but soon her sawing noises returned to their normal rhythm.

The windows moved, little by little. The brass locking mechanism strained against my pull. I was starting to lose all sensation in my fingers.

And it gave. The windows opened. I nearly fell backward to my death.

But I caught myself and held the windows mostly shut, lest the cold wake Mrs. Gruboil, while I planned what ought to be the best way to stealthily go in.

"Hurry, Maeve," Tommy whispered through chattering teeth.

The clocks in the grand house began to chime for midnight. I used the noise as a cover to slide myself gently into the house. A thick carpet cushioned my footfall. I pulled the windows mostly shut behind me, then tiptoed to Tommy's window.

He stood hunched and shivering on the window ledge. I threw the lock and pushed one side's window open wide. Tommy edged toward it, and I slowly opened the other window.

He stumbled, and fell! I lunged forward to snatch at him.

I caught him by the muffler. My horrible, loose-knitted muffler! I vowed that if Tommy survived, I'd take needlework class more seriously from now on.

He'd slipped below the window ledge, but he found his grip, took a deep breath, and climbed up the last few feet of bricks once more, with me pulling so hard on his muffler that I nearly choked him.

When Tommy was safely deposited on the carpet, I pulled his window shut, and we tiptoed toward the fire. Mrs. Gruboil's loud snore from the canopied bed in the corner nearly made Tommy jump. It occurred to me that, although he knew we were burgling a woman's bedroom, it might not have fully dawned on him that that would mean there was a woman in it.

We crouched beside the hearth for a minute or so, thawing our icicle limbs. He stared, aghast, at the large, shadowy, blanket-covered form of Mrs. Gruboil, through the sheer bed-curtains.

"I never knew women snored like men," he whispered. He looked more horrified than when monsters chased him in Persia. "Our schoolmasters sound like train engines."

"Not all women sound like that." I felt a need to defend my half of the world's sleepers.

When we were warm enough, Tommy stretched before the fire like a sleepy cat, then pointed to a door, dimly lit by the fire, festooned with locks. I nodded to him, and he went to explore the door while I went searching for a ring of keys.

I tried to think. If I was a greedy, grasping, bitter older woman who had found a djinni by robbing a student's dormitory room, and I'd chosen to live near that girl's school where, heaven knew, she might well try to come after it, where would I hide the keys I used to keep my precious djinni safe?

I'd keep them on my person at all times. On a key ring. More likely, a chain around my neck. And if I were the size of Mrs. Gruboil, I could hide them in the bosom of my dress, and no one would ever be the wiser.

But I wouldn't want to sleep with them there. At night, I'd hide them where no one would think to look. A place where, if someone looked, I'd be sure to wake up.

Under the mattress? Under her pillow?

I tiptoed over toward the bed, assessing the difficulty of pulling back the curtains and sliding my hand underneath her pillow without getting caught. A small bedside table with a drawer gave me momentary hope. I ever-so-carefully pulled the drawer open. On a flat ceramic dish sat her false teeth—*faugh!*—some fingernail clippers, and a used handkerchief, but no keys.

Why couldn't something be easy, just for once?

I stared at her sleeping form. It was too dark to see much, but Tom, sensing my predicament, added some bright-burning kindling to the fire and it cast a bit more light about the room. It also burned with a loud crackle, and Mrs. Gruboil began to stir in her sleep.

I didn't move. She rolled over on her side, facing toward me, and *the key chain flopped out* from the neckline of her nightdress.

There they were, dangling from a bit of silk cord running around her neck.

I reached for the nail clippers from the drawer.

My body cast a shadow over her, so I couldn't see well. I couldn't prop my elbows on the bed, or she'd wake up. I had to cut the keys free without her noticing, and *without cutting her*. I didn't dare breathe.

They keys lay on the mattress, right in front of her. I tugged them toward me ever so slightly and slipped the lower silk cord between the blades of the nail clippers. One snip, and the cord was cut. *Success!* But when I pulled the keys away, the cut cord slid around her neck, and she murmured in her sleep.

I waited.

I had to cut the cord again. The top part. Not below the keys, as I'd just done, but above them. And the "baroness" had begun to snore.

My fingers shook. The cord wouldn't cooperate and stay between the blades. I squeezed the clippers, and they squeaked. I was ready to abandon all, but I managed one more attempt, and the cord fell, cut in two.

I tiptoed slowly over to the closet. I fanned out the keys, six of them, for Tommy, and he pointed to the keys he thought most likely to fit the four locks on the closet door. Each click made our bodies clench with terror. But each click brought us closer and closer to my sardiney djinni.

One lock left. My heart pounded and my breath came fast. We'd done it! We'd found Mermeros! Like a needle in a haystack the size of London, we'd done the impossible and found one vitally important little tin of fish.

The key twisted. The latch clicked. The door swung open.

And out fell an avalanche of metal pots and pans, plates and cups, spoons and forks. The clang and bang and gong of them would've woken the dead.

They surely woke Mrs. Gruboil. She sat up, shouting and cursing, and fumbled for a package of safety matches—and her false teeth—and lit a pair of candles. Then she seized a bell and jangled it furiously.

"Help! Thieves!" she screamed. "Intruders in my bedroom! Fetch the police!"

That business done, she shuffled her body out from under her blankets and approached where Tommy and I stood paralyzed. She held the candle up to my face and let out a long, slow chuckle.

"Well, look who's here." The gloat of triumph on her face looked like a toad's, if toads could gloat. "Little Miss Trouble, and she's brought her no-good friend. Pull up a chair, Miss Maeve. I've been expecting you."

CHAPTER
31

They arrived in record time, those constables. I suppose if you're a baroness, or as rich as one, they come when summoned, jolly quick.

I hoped Alice had had the good sense to get far away from this place and in from the cold. As for us criminals, Tommy and I sat on soft chairs by the fire. "Baroness Gabrielle" hadn't exactly bound and gagged us, but she might as well have done. A butler, a footman, and a housekeeper were at her door within moments of her screaming. Now they surrounded us with their glaring eyes.

But not before I'd seen what I came to see. By the light of a growing collection of candelabra, I saw the prize. Inside that closet, perched like a rare jewel on a cushion of velvet, enthroned upon a small table, was my sardine can. Sultana's Exotic Sardines, Imported.

I won't say that I'm particularly clever, but I did receive a little flash of genius. When the servants appeared in the doorway, and Mrs. Gruboil turned from castigating us to go give them their orders,

I coughed loudly, to cover the sound, then I dropped her ring of keys into the embers smoldering in her fireplace grate. They sank and disappeared into the red heat like sacrificial maidens disappearing into volcanic lava to appease an angry heathen god.

The closet door was still open.

I made my last move.

"Tommy," I whispered. "My pocket. Make the switch."

He didn't sputter, nor ask stupid questions. A man of action, was our Tommy. He belonged on jungle expeditions, not in Mission Industrial School and Home for Working Boys.

I turned my body somewhat so the others couldn't see him reach into the pocket sewn into a side seam of my cloak. He pulled out my secret weapon and slid it up his sleeve. Then he stood, watching the adults warily, and stepped toward the pile of pots and dishes, tripping and falling spectacularly on the floor in front of the closet.

"Baroness Gabrielle" Gruboil whipped her head around. "Back in your chair, orphan!"

Tommy extricated his long, lanky limbs from the jumble of cookware. "Yes, ma'am. Apologies, ma'am." Quick as an eel, he sat back down and slipped something underneath the cushion of my chair.

"Surround them," barked Mrs. Gruboil. "You, Jackson, and

you, Fredericks. Watch them like hawks. Don't let them move a muscle."

They favored us with their most intimidating grimaces while we waited for the officers of the law to appear. Appear they did, two of them, looking puffy with fatigue and irked that their snoozing at the police bureau had been interrupted by actual police business.

The older, shorter of the two officers took a probing look at us. "Your intruders are *children*?"

"That's right, Officer," said Baroness Gruboil. "That one there, the girl, is a bad sort."

The taller, younger officer with the fat mustaches, rubbed his forehead. "She looks like any other schoolgirl to me." He turned to me and said gently, "What's your name, young miss?"

"I'm Maeve Merritt," I said meekly. "I'm a student at Miss Salamanca's school."

"Trust me, Constable," said Mrs. Gruboil. "I know this one. She's rotten."

The elder officer cocked his head. "The report on this property said you'd recently moved to London after years on the Continent and a long visit to America," he said. "Days ago, in fact, which beats all. So how could you possibly know this girl?"

The baroness coughed. "I mean, I've seen her about. In the schoolyard." She screwed up her nose and mouth. "It's easy to see she's the sort that's always causing mischief." She gestured to Tommy. "Running about, up to no good with those dirty orphan lads!"

I heard Tommy's angry inhale, but I leaned my foot against his in warning.

"Officers," I said, "what the lady says is true. I am, I confess, a troublemaker."

The mustache twitched, and the older officer's eyes twinkled behind his spectacles.

"And how is that?" the older officer inquired.

"Well," I said slowly, "back when this house was abandoned, my mates and I would come here sometimes to play games."

The older officer leaned over toward me. "That's trespassing, that is."

I bowed my head. "I know. It was wrong of me." I gestured all around me. "But as nobody was living here, and we weren't damaging anything, I didn't see any harm in it."

The younger officer frowned. "You're not saying you didn't realize anybody lived here *now*, are you?"

"No." I sighed. "It's just that... Well, it all feels very foolish, now..."

"No doubt," he interjected.

"...but we resented the fact that this house wasn't available to us to play in anymore," I said. "So, I challenged my friend Tom to a dare. We would see if we could get into the house, and get out again, without getting caught."

"Don't believe this one," snarled Mrs. Gruboil. "Listen to her, officers! She's a liar, bold as you please!"

The older officer turned to her. "What did you say your name was, your, er, ladyship? Your full and legal name?"

Mrs. Gruboil drew herself up tall and indignant. "What is that supposed to mean? What has my name to do with anything?" She held her nose high. "Who are *you* to question me?"

The younger officer swelled with official pride, ready to tell Mrs. Gruboil exactly who they were to question her. I interrupted him.

"Please, officers," I said. "We're very sorry. We'll be in ever so much trouble if the school finds out about me, and Mission Industrial School finds out about Tom."

The older officer folded his arms across his chest. "I should think you would be."

I thought of Aunt Vera's dog and tried to give my best pleading puppy eyes to the older officer. "Please, Officer. May we go home? We promise we'll never, ever disturb this fine lady again." I turned to Mrs. Gruboil. "Please forgive us, madam. It was a stupid prank, and it was very wicked of me to suggest it." I gestured to Tom. "Tom tried to talk me out of it, but I called him a chicken if he didn't do it."

A sudden fit of coughing seemed to seize both officers at once.

Mrs. Gruboil's red face contorted with rage. "You cunning little fox, you won't get away with this so easily!"

"Now, madam," the older officer said soothingly. "Has anything been stolen?"

Mrs. Gruboil huffed as she stormed around the room. She made a show of checking every cupboard and jewelry box. Then she marched over to the closet and looked inside. She let out a slow, relieved breath.

"It appears not," she told the officers. Then her face hardened. "They opened this locked closet of mine!"

The tall officer leaned over to peer inside it. "The closet where you keep nothing but a can of sardines?"

A few of the other servants, clustered near the door, tittered.

"What I keep in my closets is my own affair," Mrs. Gruboil snapped.

"Come along, you two," the taller officer said to us. "Turn out your pockets for us, and don't give us any trouble."

We each pulled out the linings of our pockets. What few belongings Tommy carried so obviously belonged to a grubby boy that nobody questioned them.

Good thing I'd gotten rid of those keys.

"There," said the older officer. "I think we'll just return these two young people to their proper homes. We'll show ourselves out."

Mrs. Gruboil's brows lowered. She leaned over me to whisper in my ear. "I'm watching you," she said in a low voice. "If you ever bother me again, you'll wish you hadn't."

I gathered up my mittens and my muffler, straightened my chair cushions, and untangled my cloak from its carved armrests. Tommy followed my lead and let the police officers shepherd us out the door.

"I hope we've learned a lesson tonight," the tall officer said. "This sort of business leads to very unhappy ends. You'd both best say your prayers, and change your ways, and leave this foolish behavior behind you."

"We will, Officer," Tom said.

"Good show." The senior officer proffered a hand for each of us to shake in turn. "Off to bed with you, and think twice before doing something like this again. Next time, I'll warn you, we won't be so soft on naughty behavior."

"There won't be a next time, Officer," I vowed.

"See to it," he said. "I suppose you two miscreants know how to let yourselves back indoors without getting caught?"

Tommy grinned, winked at me, and melted into the night, heading toward Mission Industrial School and Home for Working Boys. I turned heel and headed for the back entrance to the school that I'd left unlocked.

I found Alice there waiting for me, pale as a ghost with worry.

"Thank the Lord you're all right, Maeve!" she whispered. "When I saw all those lights go on, and heard all the screaming, I was afraid Mrs. Gruboil would summon Mermeros and have him chop you to bits! Feed you to sharks, even!"

I gave her a hug, and we headed upstairs. "No such luck for the sharks," I whispered, "though Mermeros would've loved that. Now, hush, if you don't want us getting caught."

"No djinni is worth all this risk," she whispered as we made our stealthy way up the stairs. "I say we abandon this nonsense immediately."

I pulled open the door to our room and quietly, we slipped inside.

"I mean it, Maeve," Alice insisted. "This djinni business has got to stop. I'm through."

I pulled Mermeros's squiggling sardine can out of my cloak pocket. "You want to miss out on all the fun?"

Y ou got it back!" Alice cried softly. "You're a wonder. How ever
did you find it? And how did you manage to smuggle it out
right under their noses?"

"An excellent question," said a man's voice. "Alas, there's no time
for an answer."

And before I could make a peep or swing my fists, iron fingers
pried the sardine tin from my hands.

"Help!" Alice screamed. "Intruder! There's a man in our room!"

I sprang toward the dark figure, my fists flailing. I grabbed at
handfuls of hair and punched a back in what I hoped were the
fiend's kidneys.

"Give that back, you villain!" I yelled.

Alice kept on screaming, but managed to strike a safety match
and light a candle.

He was the man with the ginger whiskers!

His dark eyes took us both in murderously before he darted for the window and wrestled with the lock. I tackled him afresh and tore at his coat pockets, but he shoved me aside roughly. I'd felt the flat weight of the tin swinging in his coat pocket, though. I dove for the pockets again, but he boxed my ears. His heavy ring probably left a mark on the side of my face.

Alice rushed to my side and pushed hard at the man. They scuffled back and forth. I think he was so surprised to be attacked by a pink-cheeked, blond-haired cherub that he wasn't sure how to strike back. He'd had no problem shoving me. But Alice was relentless. My corruption of her was complete.

He darted toward the door, but I managed to trip him so that he stumbled. Voices and footsteps running toward the door made him pause, and he darted back toward the window and pried up the sash. He looked down the drainpipe toward the ground, far below, hesitated, then swung himself out the window, hanging from the ledge. Alice rushed over and pounded and pried on the man's fingers.

"Alice!" I cried. "Are you trying to kill him?"

"Kill whom?" demanded Miss Salamanca, bursting through the door. "What's all this screaming about a man in the room?"

"Here, at the window." Alice panted and pointed. "He was in our room!"

Miss Salamanca went to the window and looked down. "I don't see anybody."

Alice and I ran to the window to see for ourselves. I pointed down below. "Don't you see that shadow, Miss Salamanca?" I said. "That's him, getting away!"

"How could he have gotten away so quickly, Maeve?" Alice asked.

I wondered the same thing myself. "Slid down the pole, I expect."

"Or never was there in the first place," Miss Salamanca said darkly.

More teachers came pouring into the room, wrapped in blankets over their nightdresses. Curious girls followed them in droves. Miss Salamanca shooed everyone back out the door. When it was just the three of us, Miss Salamanca glowered and took a deep breath, priming herself to deliver a fatal verbal blow. She looked, if it was possible, even more gaunt and forbidding in her long nightdress, robe, and cap.

"What is the *meaning* of this outburst?" she demanded. "You wake the whole school in the dead of night, with an invented story about a man in your room, putting the entire staff and student body into an apoplexy of fright, and for what? Some attention-seeking stunt? A cover for some misdeed of yours?"

Poor Alice. She'd had a terrible night. And she wasn't used to scoldings as I was—or to having her story doubted. Her eyes grew red and filled with tears.

"But we're *not* making it up, Miss Salamanca," she protested. "There really was a man here. I swear it."

"Well-bred young ladies never swear," said our kind headmistress.

The bell rang down below, and Miss Plumley, in her housecoat, showed two police officers upstairs. We heard their deep voices and their heavy boots on the stairs. Miss Salamanca went out into the hallway to confer with them.

"*Psst!* Alice, Maeve. Everything all right?"

We turned to see Tommy's bright-red hair poking up from his head, which hovered in the window opening.

"I heard the screaming," he said. "Something about a man?"

All my frustration and anger washed over me once more, like a bucket of cold water dumped over one's shoulders in a bathtub.

"He got away with the sardine tin, Tommy!" I sank down onto my bed and buried my face in my knees.

"No!" He let out a low whistle.

Out in the hallway we heard Miss Salamanca's voice. "I assure you, Constables, that there's no need to investigate."

"Good," I whispered. "Old Sally's getting rid of the bobbies. Here, come on in, Tom, before you freeze to death." I reached him an arm and pulled him inside.

"Which way did he go?" Tommy said. "Could I catch him, do you think?"

"He's a big man, Tom. He'd beat you to a pulp."

Alice darted back to the door in a panic. "Maeve, if they find Tommy in here—"

I looked up to see why she'd stopped talking. There, framed in the doorway like a portrait of three avenging angels, were Miss Salamanca, the tall constable with the mustaches, and the older officer with the spectacles.

"Well, well," Miss Salamanca said coldly. "It appears I was in error, Miss Alice. It appears there was a *male*"—she sniffed—"in your room after all." She pointed an accusing finger at Tom. "Officers! Arrest this intruder!"

Any friendly warmth, any patient kindness we'd seen in the officers' eyes before, was gone. The taller policeman thumped his club, over and over, into the thick palm of his hand.

Alice didn't recognize the policemen, of course, so she ran to them for help.

"Officers," she said, "this isn't the man who was in our room. It was a tall man, in a long black coat and a bowler hat, with a ginger beard. He stole something from Maeve!"

It's impossible not to love Alice, unless you have a heart of stone, and I thought I saw the shorter officer's frosty expression melt.

"What did he steal, sweetheart?" he asked her.

Alice's confidence faltered. She looked to me for help.

"A tin of fish," she said softly.

"A tin of fish," he repeated, with the air of a man who didn't hear that story every day.

"A tin of fish." Miss Salamanca fumed with scorn. "Officers, their tale is preposterous. It's some vain attempt to divert our attention from the fact that they've invited orphan boys into their bedroom."

The taller officer lifted his cap and scratched his scalp. "A tin of *fish?*" he echoed. "That's what that phony baroness had in her special closet."

The other officer elbowed him in the ribs. "Something fishy going on, I'd say."

Miss Salamanca didn't care a fig about fish, nor about jokes. She pointed her lethal gaze at Alice. "I must say, Miss Bromley, it grieves me to see *you* stoop this low. Maeve's behavior doesn't surprise me at all, but you! *Such* a good family. It just shows you never can tell." She sniffled tragically. "It also shows me my error in keeping a pupil like *this* one"—she nodded in my direction—"for as long as I have. She infects my other students with her wickedness." She dabbed the corners of her eyes with the sleeve of her housecoat. "I hoped I could help her change her ways."

Balderdash, she did.

"What kind of fish?" the tall officer asked.

Miss Salamanca's face twitched. "How can that possibly matter?" she cried. "Officers. I will deal with my pupils, and write to their parents, and set things to rights here in my own way. But this boy"—she skewered a knobby finger in Tommy's direction—"this boy is an intruder. Breaking and entering. Stealing, no doubt, from my school. Harboring wicked intentions regarding these young ladies."

Tommy's cheeks bloomed red-hot. It looked like he was ready to explode.

"He's my friend." I didn't care what Miss Salamanca thought anymore, but I needed the police to hear it. "He only came when he heard us screaming about the man in the room. He came to help."

The officers looked at each other, then at Tommy, then at me.

Miss Salamanca crossed her arms across her chest. "This one's a troublemaker, Officer," she told the older policemen, pointing to me. "Whenever there's mischief in the school, you can bet your life's savings that this wretched girl is behind it."

The taller officer nodded. "I'd take that bet."

"Quiet, Rogers," the other said. Rogers. So that was his name. "I don't doubt you're right, ma'am, but as you say, I'll leave her in your..." He swallowed hard. "...capable hands. As for you, young man," he said to Tommy, "twice in one night is twice too many breaking-and-entering incidents for my liking. We're taking you down to the police bureau with us, lad. You've got some lessons to learn, and a night or two in a cell will teach them right quick." He reached for Tommy's collar. "We'll report this to Mission Industrial School first thing in the morning. Come along with you."

Tommy's face was blank as he passed by me and out the door, each arm gripped by a police officer. I watched his back disappear around the door to the stairwell, the rip in his jacket still flapping from where Mr. Treazleton's driver had lashed him with a whip. *What happened to boys at the Industrial Home who got into serious trouble?* It couldn't be good. *Would they send him off sooner to the cotton mill? Keep him locked up on bread and water until he reached fifteen?*

Poor Tom.

He should've stolen my djinni the first time he had the chance. Becoming my friend instead of my enemy was the worst decision he'd ever made.

CHAPTER 34

Miss Salamanca locked me in the coal closet for the night. Of course, she did.

I will say this for her: she knew how to keep punishments interesting and new. After my time in the dungeon-like cellar, I'd come to miss the coal closet.

My body was chilled to the bone. It wasn't cold enough to die. Just cold enough to wish I would.

There was no place to lie down amid the sharp, brittle pieces of coal. Every breath I took felt like it was belched from a smoking volcano.

My dress was ruined, but what of that? I wouldn't be returning to this school. Not after last night. It actually made me sad. The leaving, not the dress. How many times had I yearned to quit this dreadful place, only to realize now I would miss it! And Alice especially. Before Alice, I wasn't sure that I knew how to make friends with other girls.

And Tom. What would happen to Tom?

I wondered what kind of night he'd had. Probably shivering in a prison cell and wishing he'd never introduced himself to "Fast-bowl Franny."

I don't know how I passed the night. Dozing, twitching, shivering, nodding off, jolting awake, aching all over. It seemed to last an eternity. But eventually I could hear echoes of noise as the school, and London, woke to face a new day. Horses' hooves and wagon wheels and newspaper sellers and delivery boys. How could they go on about their cheerful business when my father was about to be sacked and ruined, and I, expelled in disgrace, and Tommy, most likely sent off to the cotton mill?

There was nothing I could do about any of it.

Time dragged on. The breakfast bell rang, and then the bell for first classes.

Mr. Treazleton had surely come and gone. My father's doom was rattling toward him over London's cobbled streets, and he didn't know it. He thought today was just another day. Poor Father.

All of it was my fault. I hung my head between my knees, grateful that no one could see me now.

Soon someone would come to shovel up coal for the day's fires. I was surprised they hadn't come already. Perhaps they still had leftover coal from yesterday, but surely a charwoman would be here before long, bucket in hand. *Would they scream at the sight of a girl locked up in the coal cellar? Or would they just laugh?*

My whole body clenched into a knot when I heard keys rattling in the lock. It would be Miss Salamanca, no doubt, fresh from a long night of sleep in which to dream up new methods of tormenting me.

But it wasn't Miss Salamanca.

It was *Alice*.

"What are you doing here?" I gasped.

She held a finger over her lips. "Quickly. Come with me."

I followed her, treading softly on the balls of my feet. We slipped up the stairs and through the kitchen. Miss Plumley stood in a starched white apron and cap, kneading dough at a table, and with her, a serving maid I hadn't seen at the school before.

I froze, and searched for a way to escape, but Miss Plumley winked at me. "Dash off with you, now, Miss Maeve!" She handed me a warm bun wrapped in an old, clean napkin. "Good luck!"

"I'll be there in two ticks," said the young woman, in a voice I knew. The servant to Mrs. Gruboil who'd fled from her abuse! The job applicant, looking for Darvill House!

"But... How..." Words failed me. "Why did she just say—"

"Come on," Alice said, practically dragging me out the door. "I'll explain everything. But come!"

She pulled me up the back stairs to the dormitory floor, and up another flight to where the servants slept, and led me to a bedroom door.

"This is Miss Plumley's room," she explained. "Why, Maeve! Have you been crying?"

In a small mirror hung on the wall, I saw little tracks of clean skin running down from my eyes across my coal-dust-covered cheeks.

She gave me a washcloth and pointed me toward a basin of water, then helped me change quickly into clean clothes.

"Now, listen carefully," she said. "Mr. Treazleton has already come and gone. You'll have to hurry after him to stop him. But don't worry; Sarah will go with you. She's the woman helping Miss Plumley in the kitchen. We have it all arranged. I've given her some money, enough to take you in a cab over to your father's bank, and you can fix everything." She buttoned the last button on my coat. "I don't know how you'll do it, but I know you'll come up with a way."

"But, Alice!" I protested. "How did you get me out? And why are Miss Plumley and...Sarah helping us? And what will happen when Miss Salamanca finds me missing?"

Alice's smile was sad. "I doubt that matters," she said. "I think your time here is up already. Pretty much. But, oh, I'll miss you terribly." She squeezed my hand. "You were the one thing that made this place bearable."

I wiped my eyes. "You too, Alice."

"Let's be friends always," she said, "no matter what happens. Let's write to each other."

I nodded. "I promise."

"Now, you'd better get going," Alice said, nudging me toward the door. "Sarah's waiting to take you downtown to the bank."

"But how…?"

Alice shook her head and smiled. "I stayed up all night trying to think what I could do to help fix things," she said. "Finally, I decided to take a chance on telling Miss Plumley. I thought maybe, now that she knows Sarah's story, she won't find ours so impossible."

I stopped in my tracks. "You told Miss Plumley? About Mermeros?"

She blushed. "Not quite. I told her that you possessed an heirloom of great value that Mrs. Gruboil had stolen from you, and that Mr. Treazleton was trying to steal from you, and that he's been threatening to have your father fired over it."

My mouth fell open. "And they *believed you*?"

Alice smiled. "People tend to believe me, Maeve. I don't have your reputation for, er, stories. Besides, Sarah could easily believe "Baroness Gabrielle" would steal from a youth. And Miss Plumley has a sister who used to be in service to the Treazletons, until they sacked her for burning some eggs." She winked. "Miss Plumley was only too eager to help you. She lent me her keys, fetched you clothes, everything."

I shook my head. "You amaze me, Alice! You've worked a miracle."
We tiptoed down the stairs. "But you'll get in a heap of trouble for
skipping class."

She shrugged. "After facing monsters in Persia and thieves in my
bedroom, I'm not too frightened of Miss Salamanca anymore."

"Bravo, Alice!" I said. "That's the fighting spirit!"

She laughed. "No, I'm still a great chicken. I didn't have an ounce
of nerve last night. I ought to have summoned Mermeros, but I just
couldn't bring myself to—"

I stopped halfway down the stairs. My heart pounded in my
chest. "You ought to have *what*?"

She clapped a hand over her forehead. "Gracious heavens. Didn't
I tell you?"

"Tell me what?"

She reached into her pocket, looking rather proud of herself,
and pulled out a shiny tin of sardines. Sultana's Exotic Imported.
It wiggled in the palm of her hand. I seized it and cradled it in my
hands like a kitten.

"But how?" I whispered. "I don't understand!"

She tried not to show it, but she was awfully pleased with herself.
"You saw me tussle with him, didn't you?"

"Yes, and I could scarcely believe my eyes."

"Well, I wasn't trying to stop him. I was trying to get your sardine tin back." All her modesty couldn't stop her from smiling. "And I did."

I hugged her tight. "You're like a fairy godmother, Alice! You've fixed everything!"

She frowned and shook her head. "No, there's more." We crept down the stairs and back toward the kitchen, keeping out of sight of any of the servants. She pulled a small object from her pocket. A heavy gold ring. For a terrible moment, it reminded me of the ring of the sorcerer-king.

"This," she said, "is what I was doing when I went after his fingers. Remember, when he hung from the windowsill?"

I laughed. "How can I forget? I thought you were trying to murder him!"

She rolled her eyes. "I got a glimpse of the ring when I lit my candle, and I thought that the ring would provide a clue to whom he was. I didn't want to let him leave without taking it." She held up the ring so I could see it more closely. From the flat golden surface of the ring, a sold letter T arose, surrounded by laurel leaves.

Alice pulled from her pocket the letter I'd received from Mr. Treazleton before Christmas. "See?" she said. "It's his own private seal. The initial and the laurel leaves are exactly the same." She looked embarrassed. "I happened upon it in your desk once. When I needed a pencil."

I took the ring and turned its heavy weight over in my hand. "I don't understand, though," I said. "Why would this man have Mr. Treazleton's ring?"

"He'd have it if he worked for him," Alice said. "My grandfather has a secretary who handles most of his correspondence. Papa trusts him completely. He has Papa's seal more of the time than Papa has it himself."

I slipped the ring into my pocket. "So the ginger-whiskered thief works for Mr. Treazleton," I said. "I suspected as much. And now we have proof." I pocketed the letter as well. "I *knew* he was following me! My family thought I was absolutely cracked, but I knew I was right."

"Mr. Treazleton's fingers are fatter," Alice said, "so this ring slipped right off Mr. Ginger Whiskers's hand."

"Did someone say my name?"

We both froze as Theresa Treazleton appeared in the stairwell. She shouldn't be here! But neither should we, so there was nothing I could say about it.

She pranced over to us with a mocking, smug expression.

"Hello there, Maeve, Alice," she purred. "Today's the day, Maeve, dear."

Alice gave her a withering look. Alice Bromley, as I live and breathe! "The day for what, Theresa?"

Theresa simpered. "The day for me to win and Maeve to lose."

She leaned closer and whispered in my ear. "It's going to be mine, you know. And do you know the first thing I'll do to you with my very first wish?"

"Theresa," Alice said sharply.

"Yes?" She actually batted her eyelashes, the faker.

"Mind your business," Alice snapped.

Theresa looked as surprised as I did.

"And you've got something on your nose."

Theresa's hand reached up and rediscovered her pimple. She gasped. Commenting on Theresa's imperfections, of course, was *not allowed*. She scowled at Alice in a most unladylike fashion and disappeared down the hall in a huff.

"Alice Bromley," I told my roommate. "You never cease to surprise me."

She took a deep, satisfied breath. "I've longed to give her a good ticking-off ever since I arrived at this school," she said, "but up until now, I hadn't the nerve."

I laughed. "Watch out, world," I said. "Alice Bromley is unleashed."

She laughed. "Oh, go on with you, Maeve. Good luck."

Sarah, the former maid to "Baroness Gabrielle," poked her head into the doorway. "Are you ready, Miss Maeve, to accompany me on a little trip downtown?"

I nodded, and took the coat and hat Alice handed me.

"One more thing," Alice whispered. "I went to the grocer's this morning."

"All by yourself? You snuck out?"

She grinned. "I'm learning bad habits from you. I thought you might need... Well, I left something for you in a coat pocket, in case you get hungry."

I gave Alice one final embrace, then followed Sarah outside.

"You'd best wait over there, miss, out of sight of the school's windows, while I hail a cab," she said. "Behind that fence ought to do the trick."

I waited behind the fence and ate the bun Miss Plumley had given me. As I chewed, I watched the grim, squat front of Mission Industrial School and Home for Working Boys reaching up into a weak tea-colored sky. My school's many chimneys puffed out smoke from its many fireplaces, but the boys' home sent only a wisp of smoke upward, no doubt from the cooking stove.

What had it been like for Tommy to stay overnight at the prison? It might've been awful. Or it might have been his first warm sleep in a long, long time.

The door opened, and a man hurried out toward the street. Again, I had to pause and take a second look to be sure my eyes were right. They were.

"Mr. Poindexter," I said as he came near. "Good morning to you."

"Ah! Miss Maeve, am I right? Tommy's young friend?"

I nodded. "What brings you here to Mission Industrial School? I saw you come a few days back, also."

His face became grave. "I received a notice from the director of the home informing me that Tom had some trouble with the police last night. Incidents of breaking and entering?" He looked at me thoughtfully. "They said something about a girl from the school being involved. Was that you?"

My mouth went dry. I nodded. "I can explain—"

"It's all right," he said. "It grieves me, because I was quite interested in taking him on as an apprentice. He's a fine young man, and conditions at this school are appalling! No boy should be here." He gazed at me intently. "But I began to have second thoughts after he told me all about your magical flight to Persia and your battle with ancient protector spirits." He studied me closely, as though my eyes might reveal some clue to a mystery. "As I said to you on another occasion, Miss Maeve, to dream is a wonderful thing, but to draw your friends into your fancies can be dangerous."

I tried to speak, but the words wouldn't come. Had I ruined Tommy's life again?

"Young Thomas was so insistent, even when I pressed him to tell the truth, that all of this had actually happened," Mr. Poindexter went on. "It suggests a mind not quite in tune with reality. He'll need some kind of help, which, a bachelor like me, a busy shop owner, is not equipped to provide." He sighed. "This unfortunate business with the police only confirmed the decision I'd already reached. I need someone upright and solid to work with me in the shop. Especially if an apprentice is to join me in my travels."

He sighed and checked his pocket watch. "And now I must be going. Opening the store won't keep."

Sarah came bustling around the corner "There you are, Miss Maeve! It's taken an age, but I finally have us a cab. Oh!" She saw Mr. Poindexter. "Pardon me, sir."

"No pardon needed," he said. "I was just leaving." He tipped his hat to me. "Good day, Miss Maeve."

I reached for the sleeve of his coat. He turned in surprise.

"Mr. Poindexter," I said, "Tommy is…" What could I say? I had to say something. "Tommy's clever, and brave, and sensible. You wouldn't go wrong with him as your apprentice."

From the side yard of the school I heard the cabbie bark out, "You coming or what? I ain't got all day, you know."

I swallowed hard.

"Mr. Poindexter," I said again, "please. You don't know how much this means to him. He'll never let you down. Any blame in this matter—the fanciful stories, the scrapes with the constables—all the blame is mine."

Mr. Poindexter rested a hand on my shoulder. "And that," he said, "must be a heavy source of regret to you indeed."

Sarah stood at my side, urging me toward the cab.

I'd failed. Again and again, I had failed.

"It was good of you to speak up for your friend, though," Mr. Poindexter said. "It says much for you, and for him." He smiled. "Good day, now. Come by the shop anytime you please."

And he was gone. Sarah bundled me into the cab, apologizing to the driver, and away we went. We headed into the heart of town, the banking district, for St. Michael's Bank and Trust. I watched out the window and silently prayed I could do a better job helping Father than I'd done helping Tom.

CHAPTER

35

The cab drew up in front of the bank, and my stomach sank into my shoes. This was the moment of truth, and I had no more of a plan than I had wings to fly.

Then again, I'd flown with a djinni once. That djinni was back in my pocket now.

Maybe more was possible than I thought.

Unless I had to give him to Mr. Treazleton to save Father.

Would I? Would I give away my last wish, and place untold power into the hands of a rich, greedy, selfish, arrogant man? Think of the harm he could do! Make himself king, even!

But what choice did I have?

Maeve Merritt does not give in to bullies. She refuses to play their games.

Was that still true? Or was that the arrogance that had gotten me into such a deep mess?

The cabbie helped Sarah out of the cab, and she haggled with him over the fare, then paid him, while I climbed out. We both gawked at the marble columns that seemed to disappear into the clouds. Guarded by men in smart uniforms, decorated with grand carved doorways and windows, the bank felt like a fortress. A fortress guarding another, protected world—a world of men in important suits, carrying important papers, wielding important fortunes, moving important goods via ships and trains around the world.

All I had to storm the fortress was a tin of sardines.

"Do you know what you plan to say, then, Miss Maeve?" Sarah asked.

"Not a bit of it," I told her. "Come on, let's go."

The guards watched us out of the corners of their eyes as we entered the bank. Without Sarah there, I'd be shooed away like a stray cat. Unchaperoned youths were about as welcome in banks as rats.

The inside of the bank was even more imposing than the outside. Chandeliers and gleaming furnishings. More columns, and granite floors. More guards and clerks, working silently by the light of flickering gas lamps in the cool dimness. The occasional clerk who puttered softly from one door to another, reverently, like a priest in an ancient temple.

"May I help you?"

A tall man in a black suit materialized at Sarah's shoulder like an apparition. Judging from his wrinkles and his gravelly voice, he was probably a hundred and two. Possibly already dead.

"I'm looking for Mr. Edgar Pinagree," I told him. "May I speak with him?"

The man's eyes widened. "The director of the entire bank? Might I ask what is the nature of your business with him, before I inquire into his availability?"

I cleared my throat and tried to sound grown-up. "It's a matter of private business involving Mr. Alfred P. Treazleton."

Again the eyes widened. They seemed to have an infinite capacity for it.

"Mr. Pinagree is meeting with Mr. Treazleton at this very moment."

"Inquire into his availability," my eye. You knew that all along.

"Then it's all the more important that I be shown in to speak with them."

Sarah nodded. "That's right. It's very, very important."

Our interrogator sniffed at our important business—our important *feminine* business, no doubt. "Your names, please?"

"Maeve?"

I looked up to see my father hurrying toward me as rapidly as a bank clerk is allowed to hurry in the financial sanctum. The sight of him gave me a little pang. He looked even more worn with worry than usual. Thinner, even, than he'd been just a short while ago at Christmas. *Poor Dad.*

He reached my side. He looked as happy to see me as he would be to greet, for example, my highly religious, scolding great-aunt.

"Maeve, what are you doing here? Why aren't you in school?"

"Pardon me," said the deep-voiced man. "You know this young person?"

I'd swear I saw my father flinch. "She's my daughter, Mr. Smithers."

"Ah." The man wrinkled his ancient nose. (*Huge* nostrils.) "She claimed to have urgent business with Mr. Pinagree and Mr. Treazleton."

His gaze moved briefly to a wood-paneled door. Father's gaze went there, too. The meeting location. I was sure of it.

My father stiffened. "Thank you, Mr. Smithers. I'll take it from here."

Father steered us toward the opposite end of the bank, to a small office, and gestured me inside. I smelled a trap. I wouldn't go in.

"Maeve," he whispered, "what is the *meaning* of this? Why aren't you in school? Who is this person accompanying you?"

Sarah curtsied. "If you please, sir, I'm Sarah Trippin, and I'm newly in service at Miss Maeve's school. I came to escort your daughter on an important errand."

"I see. Er, thank you."

Father gave up on trying to stuff me into the private closet. He pulled up a chair to see right into my eyes.

"What possible business could you have with the general manager of the bank, Maeve? And with Mr. Treazleton, a member of the board?" He blew out his breath. "Even I scarcely ever speak with Mr. Pinagree. Of late." He sighed, then locked eyes with me. "Maeve, I forbid this. Whatever you're planning, I forbid it. Go back to school right away."

I took my father's hand.

"I know you won't understand this, Daddy," I told him, "and there's nothing I can do to explain it, but I promise you, I *swear* to you, that I need to do this. It's for your good. For everyone's."

Father's mouth hung open. He'd worn this same look of bafflement over the holidays whenever Evangeline tried to explain to him why a certain kind of costly silk fabric was absolutely, positively essential to a respectable Christian wedding.

He pulled himself together and drew me closer so he could whisper into my ear, out of Sarah's hearing.

"This is hardly the place or the time for one of your schemes, Maeve," he said. "Especially now. I can't afford even the tiniest misstep with Mr. Pinagree. I'd be thrown out on my ear if my young daughter went waltzing in there, interrupting him with some cuckoo idea."

My eyes stung. "You'll be thrown out on your ear if I *don't*, Father," I told him. "Even now, we might be too late. Please don't delay me any further."

"Mr. Merritt," Sarah said. "I have strong personal reasons for believing your daughter is telling the truth."

My father wasn't impressed by the intrusion, nor swayed by the opinion of a domestic servant and a stranger. He wiped his forehead with a handkerchief, then tucked it back into his pocket. When he spoke again, his voice was angry and hard.

"Now, you listen to me, Maeve," he said. "That's enough. Whatever you're playing at, it ends now. My associates are starting to stare at me. I'm not here to hold picnics with my children during the workday. Go back to school this instant." He glanced at Sarah. "I request you to accompany my daughter safely back to school."

"Mr. Merritt?"

A clerk from a nearby office called to Father. He straightened up to answer him. He turned his back toward me.

I made a terrible decision.

I bolted and ran straight for the wood-paneled door.

aeve!" my father cried.

But I didn't stop, and he didn't catch me. Sarah stepped in front of him to block his path. Bravo, Sarah!

I burst into the office. The enormous portrait of a long-ago general manager of the bank, in a long, powdered wig, frowned down upon me, while two men seated on opposite sides of a vast desk looked up at me in astonishment: Mr. Treazleton and Mr. Pinagree. I'd only met the latter once, but I couldn't forget that shiny dome of a head, round as a cannonball and nearly as hairless, with a monocle screwed tightly into one eye. He wore a gray coat and trousers, with a gray-checkered vest buttoned tightly over his round belly. He reminded me of an angry gray sausage.

There's a fortune to be made in buttons.

"What is this?" the bank manager barked in his nasal voice. "Who are you?" He rang a tinkly bell on his desk. "*Smithers!*"

Mr. Treazleton's eyes gleamed. "This is the daughter of the very man himself," he told his comrade. "Miss Maeve Merritt. She attends my daughter's school, though not for much longer, I'll wager."

Father burst through the door and skidded into my back. "Gentlemen," he panted. "I regret this interruption. I'll show my daughter out, and you can return to your conversation."

Spooky Mr. Smithers followed Father in. I wondered where Sarah was. Not that she could offer me any protection in this den of lions.

Mr. Pinagree waved a pudgy hand. "No, Merritt, stay. You might as well sit down. Never mind, Smithers, you may go, there's a good man. Close the door behind you, that's right. Take a seat, Merritt, take a seat. This brings me no pleasure, I assure you, but it must be done, and there's no sense putting off a duty just because it's an unpleasant one."

The color drained from my father's face. He took a seat quietly, looking very small in his chair, submitting toward the Almighty Power of Pinagree.

"*Mis*-ter Merritt." Pinagree spoke like a magistrate passing judgment. "You have been with this establishment for fifteen years now. In all that time, I thought I could trust you. I *thought* you were an honest man."

"Sir," my father said quietly. "Might whatever you wish to say be better said without my daughter present?"

Mr. Pinagree shrugged. "Send her out, then, send her out. It's all the same to me. Deuced if I know what she's doing here in the first place."

"I think the girl should stay," purred Mr. Treazleton, Titan of Industry. "Life's full of hard lessons. She might as well know the truth. She'll feel the effects of it, and she had a hand in causing it."

Mr. Pinagree frowned. "How's that? How could this girl have had a hand in this matter?"

Time to make myself heard. "Because Mr. Treazleton has falsely accused my father of dishonesty to you, Mr. Pinagree."

My father's eyebrows rose, while the bank manager's cheeks flushed with indignation. "How dare you, young lady, cast an aspersion upon my esteemed colleague, Mr. Alfred Treazleton? He's a giant of commerce in this city and a member of the board of directors of this very bank!"

"I dare to say it, sir, with all respect, because it's true, and I can prove it," I said.

At this, Mr. Treazleton let out a loud, boisterous laugh. Overdoing it, if you ask me. "She can prove it!" he scoffed. "I tell you, Edgar, the tales my daughter tells about this hoyden of a girl would curl your hair." He chuckled. "Not that there's much left of it to curl."

Mr. Pinagree didn't appreciate the joke.

"Maeve," my father said quietly. "This isn't helping. Please go."

"No, Merritt," said the bank manager. "I want to hear her tale.

Ludicrous though it may be." He adjusted his monocle and peered at me. "Well, young lady? You claim to have proof of this absurd charge? Produce it."

My hands trembled as I pushed them into my pockets. This one? No, that one.

"Mr. Treazleton covets an object of mine," I told him. "He wants it so badly that he threatened to slander my father to you, and jeopardize his position with the bank, if I didn't give him the object."

"Pah!" cried Mr. Pinagree. "What could a scrawny schoolgirl possibly have that he wants?" He jerked a thumb toward my father. "I know precisely what your family's worth per year, and I assure you, anything you possess that Treazleton wants, he could buy without batting an eye."

"Not if it's magical," I cried. "Not if it's something ancient, and impossible to find in a store. Not if it's more powerful than all the world."

Mr. Pinagree's eyes narrowed. "What kind of folderol is this, Treazleton? What's she jabbering about?"

I jumped in before Mr. Treazleton could answer. I'd made my choice between arguing Mr. Treazleton's guilt, or his insanity. I decided upon insanity.

"I have a sardine can," I said sweetly, "with a djinni in it."

"A djinni," repeated Mr. Pinagree.

I tried to nudge his understanding. "Like the one in Aladdin's lamp?"

"*Whose* lamp?"

I sighed. *Bankers.* "You know the old story, from *One Thousand and One Nights*?"

"Oh. That." He sniffed. "Proceed. Oh!" He clapped his hands together. "A djinni in a sardine can? You mean, a '*sardiney djinni!*' Ho, ho!" He seemed enormously pleased with his joke. (I'd thought of it already.) Mr. Treazleton snickered, too, the faker.

My father stared at the Persian rug like a convict waiting for his execution.

"Theresa Treazleton told her father about it." I plowed onward. "He came to the school and pulled me out of classes, twice: first to try to buy it from me, and then to threaten to destroy my father's character in your eyes, sir, if I didn't give it to him. Then he said he'd steal it."

"Ha, ha, ho!" Mr. Treazleton boomed with false laughter. "Quite a tale, isn't it?"

I pulled his note from my pocket and handed it to Mr. Pinagree. "See for yourself. Do you recognize his stationery? His writing and his seal?"

Mr. Treazleton's face froze as Mr. Pinagree's eyes scanned the note. Thoughtful lines furrowed his shiny brow. He pulled another note of his own from a desk drawer and compared it to my letter.

"That's Treazleton's seal, all right," he said, scratching his bald head. "I'm no expert, but the writing looks like the same hand."

He looked quizzically at the giant of commerce. "What's this about, Treazleton? The note's rather cryptic. 'Consider my offer,' 'I'm not a man to be trifled with,' 'Don't force my hand'?" He shook his head. "What possible reason could you have for corresponding with this young girl about anything, djinni or no?"

"I'm wondering the same thing, myself," my father said. "That's rather menacing language. Especially to one so young."

Mr. Treazleton held up both hands placatingly, and laughed as though this were all just a jolly misunderstanding.

"Do you or do you not acknowledge that to be your writing and your seal?" demanded Mr. Pinagree. He shoved the two specimens across the desk.

Mr. Treazleton stopped smiling.

"Now, there, Edgar," he said. "Be careful." There was an edge to his voice. A warning reminder of who was the more powerful in London society. A warning about what a board of directors can do to a bank manager.

Mr. Pinagree was no fool. He stewed a moment, then pushed the notes away. "If you have some business with this schoolgirl, something involving your daughter and their fairy-tale games, it's hardly my affair."

I felt the floor sink underneath me. How could Mr. Pinagree be so blind, so willfully blind to the truth when it stared him in the face? He didn't want to offend the All-Powerful Alfred P. Treazleton. That would be bad for business. Bad for keeping his job.

"It *should* be your affair," I said hotly, "when his slanders and lies are the reason you're about to sack my daddy, who's never done a thing for this bank that wasn't right and proper. You've always known it to be true. Haven't you?"

Mr. Pinagree sat back a bit in his chair. "Well, I..."

"*He* threatened *me*," I insisted, "because I wouldn't be bullied into giving him the thing he wanted. It doesn't matter if it was a magical djinni, or a make-believe one, or a hot pork-pie. He did more than threaten. He's had someone following me since before Christmas. A tall, frightening man in a black coat, with ginger whiskers."

Mr. Treazleton scoffed. "That describes one quarter of all the men in London."

I wanted to sock him right in his velvet-vested gut.

"Maybe so, but the same ginger-whiskered man followed me home to Luton on the train. He burgled our house on Christmas Eve. And he broke into my dormitory room in the middle of the night last night. The police were summoned. You can verify this, if you like."

"That's true," my father said. "We did have a break-in on Christmas Eve. Only Maeve's room was entered, and nothing appears to have been stolen. We summoned the police. They filed a report. Someone had come with a ladder and forced the window."

Mr. Treazleton shrugged. "One of her hooligan friends, no doubt. I hear tell that she runs about with orphan boys from the charitable home across the street. At her age! What does *that* say about her character?"

My father blushed. If he thought I was another Deborah, flirting and chasing shamelessly after brainless young men, I would scream.

"I fail to see," said Mr. Pinagree, "how this ginger-whiskered burglar, if he even exists, has anything to do with my friend Mr. Treazleton."

His "friend," now. I'd already lost.

It's one thing to lose. Another thing to surrender.

"The ginger-whiskered man began pursuing me immediately after Mr. Treazleton threatened to steal my djinni." I stuck my hand back into my pocket. Still there. "And," I added, "last night, when the man tried again, we tussled with him and managed to get this off his finger before he got away."

I produced the ring, handing it first to my father, who passed it to Mr. Pinagree. He adjusted his monocle and peered at its gold face, and at the two pieces of mail. He reached into his desk for his own wax, which he held above a gas lamp until it swam with glistening liquid. Then he dropped a dollop of hot wax onto a piece of paper, blew on it to cool, and pressed the gold ring down into it.

"Exactly the same," my father said, peering over his shoulder. "It's the same imprint."

Mr. Pinagree examined the pair, then pressed his fingers together thoughtfully. "Using your own hand and seal to send a note like this to a schoolgirl leaves a trail that's hard to overlook, Alfred."

"The ring means that the ginger-whiskered man who broke into my room works for Mr. Treazleton," I said. "Maybe he's his private secretary."

"It *means*," said Mr. Treazleton tersely, "someone has enacted a clever forgery."

My father frowned. "A forgery," he repeated, "calculated to persuade the world that Mr. Alfred Treazleton is trying to steal a schoolgirl's sardine can, when in fact, he's not?" My father coughed significantly. "That does stretch belief."

Mr. Treazleton thumped the end of his cane on the floor. "What stretches belief," he said loudly, "is the fact that I'm sitting here, being grilled by two puny *bankers* over the ludicrous accusation that I perpetrated crime and violence to obtain an imaginary *creature* who lives in a schoolgirl's *sardine tin*. I tell you, not only am I insulted, sirs, but I stand in serious doubts with regard to your mental soundness. I shall have to notify the board at our next meeting, Edgar, of these alarming developments."

Mr. Pinagree's stout frame seemed to sag like wet, gray laundry. All his bluster died.

"Now, come, Alfred," he said soothingly. "Nobody's 'grilling' anybody, as you so quaintly put it." He forced a laugh. "I'm accusing you of nothing, naturally."

Losing and losing. Again and again. Neither truth nor logic had a candle's chance against the whirlwind of Mr. Treazleton's wealth and power.

"It's not ludicrous," I cried, "if I actually have an all-powerful djinni. And I do. Mr. Treazleton knows it, and he wants it, more than anything."

My father sighed, and shrank smaller in his suit. Mr. Pinagree took a lozenge from a desk drawer and popped it into his mouth.

Time to try my last hope: humble surrender. And a trap.

I took a step toward Mr. Treazleton. "I came here," I said meekly, though it galled me to do so, "to bring you the djinni. Mermeros."

I saw his eyebrows rise, ever so slightly.

"That's his name. He's a djinni of the sea, so he's rather like a fish himself."

Mr. Pinagree and my father begin to look slightly dizzy.

I pulled the sardine tin from my pocket and held it in my outstretched palm.

"I came here to give him to you, to stop you from slandering Father falsely to Mr. Pinagree. It appears I was too late."

Mr. Treazleton's eyes bulged at the sight of my fishy treasure. He licked his lips. If he'd been Aunt Vera's dog, he'd be slobbering. I was on a fishing expedition myself, trying to hook a shark of a business-man with an eight-ounce sardine lure.

I pulled the sardine tin back. "But since Father's certain to be sacked, now, I'd better keep this. We'll need those wishes to get by once Father loses his job."

I dropped the tin in my pocket and turned to go. My heart sank at the sight of my father's forlorn figure. "I'm sorry, Daddy," I told him. "I'm so sorry I couldn't help you. I promise, I'm telling the truth."

The doorknob was heavy in my hand. I turned it slowly.

"Wait."

All eyes turned to Alfred P. Treazleton. His face shone with perspiration. With eyes darting back and forth between Mr. Pinagree and my father, he let out a booming laugh. "Now, now, come," he said. "I may have been too soon to believe my sources, Edgar. Too hasty in coming to the conclusion that Mr. Merritt here, whom, as you say, has been so faithful to the firm, is the source of the ongoing thefts. My sources may have been mistaken. Heaven knows it can happen."

Stout Edgar Pinagree leaned back in his chair and watched Mr. Treazleton thoughtfully. "It can happen, indeed."

I took a step out through the open door.

"Naturally I only wanted to be helpful." Mr. Treazleton's words poured out in a torrent. "As your friend, I felt it my duty to pass along these reports. But perhaps I spoke too soon."

Mr. Pinagree drummed his fingertips against one another, while Mr. Treazleton kept his eyes on me, specifically on the region of my pockets.

My poor father watched them both.

"Wait, Maeve," my father called to me. "Come back."

I hovered in the doorway. One foot in, one foot out. Mr. Treazleton inched forward in his chair, all but quivering.

Father turned back to him with a look of astonishment dawning on his face. "You *want* that tin of sardines, don't you?"

"Well, I..." Mr. Treazleton attempted a friendly smile. "You must admit, the girl's boasting does give a fellow some curiosity, doesn't it?"

"None whatsoever," said Mr. Pinagree. "It's pure nonsense."

"Just as I thought," I said. "I'll be going. Excuse me, gentlemen."

"No." Mr. Treazleton blushed pink. "Ha-ha! Let's make amends. What do you say, Pinagree? Will you take Merritt, here, back into the fold? Reinstate his place in the bank?"

I held my breath.

"Well, I don't know," Mr. Pinagree said gravely. "The accusations you've brought me are of such a nature that I can't, in good conscience, overlook them. At least, not without further investigation."

"Come to think of it," Mr. Treazleton said, with all the poise of a beginning tightrope-walker, "I just remembered something. Yes, of course. How foolish of me! The thing I remembered is... Oh, well, it's complicated. But the long and short of it is that I, er, just remembered something that proves that my source was wrong. Not even trustworthy. I'll have to cut him off. No more dealings with his sort, I'll tell you!" He cleared his throat. "So I feel certain, Edgar, that you can consider those accusations to be completely false. Mr. Merritt here is a man to be trusted."

I took another step toward leaving. Mr. Pinagree watched back and forth between the other two men in the room.

"You want that tin *desperately*," he said. "Why, Alfred? Why?"

Mr. Treazleton sank back in his chair.

I reentered the room, but stayed with my back to the door and held the sardine can once more where anybody who wanted to could take it. But they'd have to come to me and get it.

Come on, Treazleton! Come on! Take it!

Nobody moved. Nobody spoke. All eyes rested upon the silvery tin in my hand.

A knock sounded at the door. I stepped out of the way as Smithers entered, followed by another man.

"A Mr. Rooch to see you, Mr. Treazleton, sir," was his announcement. "Please pardon the interruption. He said it was urgent."

Mr. Smithers bowed and left. The man strode across the room to Mr. Treazleton.

"Not now, Rooch," Treazleton said in a strangled voice. "This is not an opportune time."

The newcomer paused. "Your message said to join you here if I couldn't..."

Mr. Treazleton halted him with a look aimed straight at me. Mr. Rooch turned about and saw me. Saw my face. Saw the tin in my hand. His jaw set, and a muscle popped out in his neck.

Mr. Treazleton seemed to reach some sort of decision. He nodded to Mr. Rooch, who retreated toward the door, blocking it, and folded his arms across his chest. Only a few feet away from me. My breath caught in my throat.

It was the ginger-whiskered man. Minus the whiskers.

He glowered at me. I was glad to see that his fingers were battered and bruised. *Good job, Alice.*

But I was fairly certain that when he wasn't dangling from a windowsill for dear life, Mr. Rooch could do some damage with those hands. To Father, and to me.

Must I summon Mermeros in order to make it out of here in one piece?

Mr. Treazleton surveyed the room with a gleam in his eye. With his hired guard, or whatever he was, in the room, a new confidence seemed to fill him.

"Now, where were we?" he asked the room.

"You were about to tell us, Albert, exactly why you want that girl's sardines so badly," Mr. Pinagree said. "I confess I can't wait to learn the answer."

Mr. Treazleton's lips curled into a smile. "I'm afraid you'll have to wait, Edgar," he said. "This conversation has grown tiresome to me. Once I have the djinni, I won't need to bother with explanations." He pointed at me. "Now, little girl. Are you going to give me the sardine tin, or do I need Mr. Rooch to relieve you of it?"

My father rose to his feet. "Are you *threatening* my daughter?"

I'd never heard that tone from Dad before. I gazed at him in wonder.

This was the moment. This was the time. I sank both hands into my pockets. Mermeros's tin squiggled against my fingertips. I took a deep breath just as Rooch shifted toward me.

"I say, Treazleton!" cried Mr. Pinagree. "This is most astonishing! Explain yourself, sir."

I stepped forward, holding out my sardine tin once more. My father stood behind me with a protective hand on each of my shoulders.

"It's all right, Mr. Pinagree, Father," I said. "So long as Father won't lose his position at the bank, I'm satisfied."

"That he won't," declared Mr. Pinagree.

"Good girl, Maeve," my father said softly.

"Though I'm beginning to think," Mr. Pinagree went on, "that some alterations would be advisable in our board of directors."

I addressed Mr. Treazleton meekly, submissively. Once more, I held the tin just out of his reach. "Don't make your ginger-whiskered man take the tin," I told him. "I'll give it to you myself."

Take it, you villain. Take it now.

He lunged for the tin and snatched it from my hand, ignoring the protests of the bank men. With trembling fingers, he wrenched the key from the bottom, fitted it over the flap in the tin, and cranked open the top of the can.

Nothing happened.

He brought the tin closer to his face, peering, sniffing, tilting it this way and that. Sardine-smelling oil dripped from the tin onto his gray trousers. Silvery fish slipped out onto his waistcoat and flopped down to the Persian rug.

God bless Alice and her illegal morning trip to the local grocer's.

There was silence in the room.

Mr. Treazleton seemed to have turned an aquatic shade of green. Just like Mermeros.

Mr. Rooch wouldn't look his employer in the eye.

Mr. Pinagree slowly shook his head.

"Come along, Maeve," my father said gently. "It's time I took you back to school. With your leave, Mr. Pinagree?"

CHAPTER 37

We rode in silence back to Miss Salamanca's School for Upright Young Ladies. Sarah got out there, with my father's thanks, and returned to her post in the kitchen. Before he could usher me out of the cab, I made my request. It was time, and if I didn't do it now, I might lose my resolve and never do it.

Some things mattered more than wishes.

"Please, Dad," I begged. "I have one more stop I must make. But I can't do it alone. Will you take me? I promise to make it quick."

Ordinarily, my father would decline, citing the pressing demands of work waiting for him back at the bank. But, this time, he nodded and repeated the address I gave him to the driver. He'd said not a word the entire drive, but only watched me curiously. It was strange, in a way; comforting as toast with tea, having the father I'd always known see me as if for the first time.

Soon we arrived. Dad paid the fare, then turned to see where

The bank manager nodded absently.

"Treazleton, my good man," Mr. Pinagree began. "The rigors of business can wear anyone down. What you need, Alfred, is rest. I know a lovely place, out in the country, where they specialize..."

I never heard what they specialized in, out in the country. Just then, we passed by Mr. Rooch. Something poking from his outer pocket caught my eye. Before he could stop me, I snatched it out and held my itchy prize high.

"Here, gentlemen, are the ginger whiskers."

Pinagree and Treazleton gaped at the ratty clump of hair as though it were the much-anticipated djinni.

I dropped the ghastly thing on the floor and left with my dad.

we'd come. I gulped back the memory of meeting Mermeros's father here, right on the very pavement beneath my feet.

"The Oddity Shop," my father read aloud. "Mysteries, Marvels, and Wonders from Beyond the Seven Seas. We Buy and Sell Rare and Wondrous Things."

I nodded. "Marvelous, isn't it?"

"Maeve?"

"Yes, Daddy?"

"Please tell me you're not planning to try to sell another businessman a phony djinni in a can?"

I squeezed his hand. "Definitely not," I said. "Well, mostly definitely not."

I hurried down the steps and through the door before Father could stop me.

The bell on the door tinkled. Morris the owl hooted a hello. Father jumped.

Mr. Poindexter stood behind his counter, poking away with a brush at the grooves of some old carving.

"Miss Maeve," said the world traveler, chief buyer, and proprietor. "Twice in one day. To what do I owe the pleasure?"

My father groaned. "Twice?"

"This is my father, Mr. Poindexter," I said. "Mr. John Merritt."

"Pleased to meet you, sir," said the shop's owner.

"Likewise," my father replied. "Say, are those scarab beetles I just saw?"

Scarab beetles. What could be the secret to their appeal?

I wandered around the shop and spoke a few words to Morris. He even let me stroke his feathers, along his side. The heavenly softness of him took me by surprise. He seemed like such a large and fearsome bird, but underneath my touch, he felt as light as air. Still, he'd protected me, in a way, not long ago, though I couldn't explain how. I just knew he had.

Mr. Poindexter returned to my side after a bit, while Father pored over antiquities with a magnifying glass.

"Thank you for bringing your father here," he said. "Much obliged."

"It's not why I came," I told him. "I came to correct a misconception, and to make you an offer you can't refuse."

"Is that so?" Mr. Poindexter's muttonchop whiskers couldn't hide his wide smile. "You have my attention."

"Good." I reached into my pocket once more. Only one sardine tin there now. Only one, and I'd know it blindfolded.

"You said," I began, "that you couldn't bring on an apprentice like Tommy if he didn't understand the difference between fanciful nonsense and reality. Is that right?"

"Something to that effect," said Mr. Poindexter. "I'm not

heartless, whatever you might think. They boy needs treatment. Medicine, maybe. A proper mother's care."

I leaned closer to Mr. Poindexter. "But what if every word he said was true?"

The Oddity Shop proprietor blew out his breath, then began to chuckle. "That's rather a stretch, don't you think?"

"Not at all." I shook my head. "What if I could prove to you that it wasn't fanciful nonsense? That I really do have a djinni?"

His eyes narrowed. "Can you prove it?"

"If I could," I said, "you'd have to believe Tommy is honest and in his sound mind. Wouldn't you?"

He nodded. "I suppose I would."

"Would you bring him on as an apprentice?" I asked.

"No child should be in a place like that dismal, unhealthy orphanage," he mused. Then he stroked his whiskers. "How do you know," he asked, "that I wouldn't steal your djinni from you, if you proved to me you really had one?"

Drat! He'd dodged my question.

"I don't know you wouldn't steal it," I said. "But I don't believe you would."

He smiled.

"You said, on the day I met you, that you would pay a small fortune for a real djinni of the lamp," I said. "Is that still true?"

"Oh ho," he said. "Now we get to the 'offer I can't refuse' part of the deal."

"Is it still true?" I repeated.

He pursed his lips. "Well," he said, drawing out the syllable, "I would, but only if I knew without a doubt that I was getting a real djinni of the lamp." He chuckled. "But I can't imagine anyone ever parting with one of those, if they had it. Not for any price. Why would they?"

Why would they, indeed?

Perhaps, to make sure that Mermeros's dire prophecy never came true, that gold lust never tore their soul apart.

Or perhaps, because some dreams coming true are more important than others.

"Here's my offer, Mr. Poindexter," I said. "I'll prove to you that I have a djinni, and you'll agree that Tom's not a liar or deluded."

Mr. Poindexter nodded. "Fair enough."

I realized my father had left off looking at antiquities and now stood nearby.

"Then," I said, "I'll give you the djinni, and you'll be its new master, if you take Tommy on as an apprentice, and treat him right, and make sure he never has to live in that wretched Industrial School anymore, and that he never wastes away his life in those dangerous mills. Working dawn till dusk. Breathing all that fluff."

Mr. Poindexter shoved his thumbs into the pockets of his vest. "You'd do that?" he said. "You'd give up your djinni for your friend?"

I gulped. "I would."

Mr. Poindexter and my father exchanged a look.

"One other thing," I said. "You mustn't ever let Tommy know that I made this bargain with you."

Mr. Siegfried Poindexter nodded.

"That's my price," I told him. "Say some stranger sold it to you. I don't want him feeling like he owes me anything."

"All right, Miss Maeve," said the proprietor of the Oddity Shop. "I accept your price. But first, you must prove your djinni is real."

My hands were trembly, and my stomach weak, as I pulled the sardine tin—the real sardine tin—from my pocket for the last time. At the sight of it, my father shook his head in dismay, but I ignored him. I fitted the key to the tab and cranked it back.

Out poured the cloud of sulfurous fumes. Out slithered the serpentine form of the rascal himself, swelling and stretching his dark-green muscles underneath his scaly chest. His white eyebrows and mustaches wobbled as his own personal whirlwind raged around him.

One more wish, I thought. There's my djinni. I hold the vessel, and I'm still owed one more wish. I could claim it right now.

But that was *not* what I'd come to do.

"By jingo, would you look at that," whispered Mr. Poindexter.

"Who? Who?" called Morris.

Mermeros noted the owl's presence, and his eyes narrowed. *Interesting.* Good old Morris. He'd saved me once before. Perhaps he'd be a good-luck charm to carry me through this moment.

My father goggled at the djinni. He held my shoulders protectively, but he couldn't even find words.

Mermeros, on the other fin, had no shortage of them.

"You!" he bellowed. "Stinking, sniveling, slinking little girl-spawn! My father's ancient curse is nothing to the curse of having to cope with *you* as my master! Oh, the shame, the shame! Girls and children, playthings and nonsense! Give me a mighty man of valor, and I'll make the world his empire to command. I'll—"

"Is he always like this?" Mr. Poindexter asked.

I nodded. "Pretty much. You get used to it."

Mermeros's great green head swiveled sharply to where Mr. Poindexter stood gaping at him.

"Are *you* a mighty man of valor?"

Mr. Poindexter's tongue seemed to have gone dry. "Well, I... That is to say..."

"Quick," said Mermeros urgently, "bind the girl in chains and lock her away. Then you'll be my master!"

"See here," my father said indignantly. "Let's have no talk of chains."

"Actually," Mr. Poindexter said, "the girl has made a bargain with me, and given you to me. So I will be your master now. We don't need to lock her away."

The whirlwind halted abruptly. Mermeros sank in midair. His mighty limbs fell slack.

"She gave me away?" His voice was low, deep as the dark sea. "She valued my colossal might *so little* as to bargain with a mortal for worthless rubbish in return for *my power to command*?"

I wanted to laugh. But even this great brute, this great fishy egotist, had feelings, too, I supposed. And I'd wounded them.

"Oh, Mermeros," I teased. "It's nothing personal. You've grown on me, you know that? We could almost be pals. If I had to have a djinni, I can't think of anyone I'd rather it was than you."

Mermeros's fishy lips puckered in disgust. "'If I had to have a djinni...!' Pals! Has such idiocy ever been spoken by a mortal?"

He turned to me. In his hand, he conjured another swirling orb, white and gleaming. Me, playing cricket. A team of girls playing cricket. Teams upon teams, and leagues, stretching across all England. Across the Queen's empire! Around the world!

In his other hand, other images swelled to life. Mountains, jungles, rivers, fjords, deserts, riverboats, glaciers, forests, cities, palaces, monuments, and wonders. The whole earth unrolling before me like a tapestry, and in each scene, a young woman, dressed for travel, equipped for exploration, fearlessly striding across every magnificent mile.

Me. Just a little bit older, taller, wiser, braver. Me, someday, exploring the world.

"You have one more wish, little mistress," Mermeros said softly. Where had this polite djinni been earlier?

One more wish.

"You have one more?" Both men, Mr. Poindexter and my father, spoke at once.

I nodded.

"Use it, Maeve!" urged my father.

Morris's golden eyes blinked at me. That owl was wiser than even owls were said to be. I'd swear it.

I closed my eyes. I saw an image of my own, needing no magic to paint before my mind's eye. The wondrous, scrolling earth, once more, and Mr. Poindexter striding along those miles, with Tommy at his side. Breathing clean, healthy air, finding oddities, and seeing the world's wonders.

Summoning Mermeros to make a wish of his own. Maybe I'd be invited to join the adventure.

"Go on, make the last wish," added Mr. Poindexter. "I don't mind."

I took one last breath, and I made my firm decision. Again.

"You should mind," I told the proprietor of the Oddity Shop. "He's trying to trick me. I could use my last wish, but if I did, Mermeros would vanish, this sardine tin would be empty, and he'd reappear somewhere else, in some other vessel, at some future time. Perhaps a century or more down the road."

Mr. Poindexter looked puzzled. "But then—"

I didn't want to hear him say it. "But then, the deal we've made is worth it to me." To my great embarrassment, some little tears pricked my eyes. I clamped my eyes shut and willed them away. "I'll just have to find my own way to form a cricket league for girls. And travel the world. Nobody said you have to have magic for that."

I snatched Mermeros's tin from the floor and cranked it back shut. A howling green Mermeros disappeared into it, bawling curses at me all the way.

"*Au revoir, Mermeros,*" I whispered to him as the tin sucked him in. "*You were wrong about me. Remember that.*"

I handed the tin to Mr. Poindexter. "You promise to make Tommy your apprentice?"

Mr. Poindexter's smile was hard to read. "Actually, I don't."

I wanted to tackle him and snatch back my tin. "I trusted you!" I cried. "You promised!"

"Is this how you conduct your business, sir?" demanded my father. "Reneging on your promises?"

Mr. Poindexter held up a hand of surrender. He went behind his counter and pulled out a sheaf of long papers.

"I told you, Maeve, that when Tommy insisted he'd flown across

Europe and Asia Minor with a magical djinni, that I began to be very concerned about taking him on as an apprentice. I felt he needed help I couldn't offer him. Yes? You remember this?"

I nodded, though my fists were clenched. "You told me. So, what?"

"So," he said, pushing the papers toward me, "before I became hesitant about his, well, sanity, this is what I proposed doing with Tommy."

I turned the papers around, and my father and I studied them together.

"Application for Adoption of an Orphan," read the title across the top, in careful script. "Adoptive Father. Name, occupation, address," and so on.

My fists uncurled. I leaned against my father's side, and together we looked up at Mr. Poindexter, who blushed.

"I'm...not the marrying kind, I daresay," he said apologetically. "But I always did hope to have a son." He smiled. "Your friend Tom is a remarkable young man. He's quite won me over."

I was so happy, it made me dizzy. "Oh, he's all right, once you get to know him," I said. "Just don't leave that sardine tin lying around where he can easily find it."

CHAPTER

38

I was expelled that very day from Miss Salamanca's School for Upright Young Ladies for leaving the property without permission, skipping classes, reporting an intruder to my bedroom when there wasn't one, breaking into Darvill House, sassing Mr. Treazleton, socking Theresa Treazleton in the eye, and, I suppose, just generally being myself. I can't pretend that I was surprised.

I never breathed a word about Sarah Trippin escorting me on my illegal errand. She works in the school kitchens still, under the friendly eye of Miss Plumley, and I'll daresay the students there are eating much better and more happily than we did during the reign of La Gruboil.

Polydora wasn't available to come fetch me home from school. She had, apparently, a choir rehearsal to attend. I never knew Polly considered herself musical, but I later learned that Constable Hopewood was a noted local baritone. I could put two and two together easily enough to figure that one out.

It was Father who came and fetched me home, that same night, after work ended. Miss Salamanca had sent a telegram home, and I suppose Mother must've asked Aunt Vera to telephone the bank. We rode to St. Pancras and boarded a train.

"Tell me, Maeve," he asked me, once the conductor had punched our tickets, "how did you find your djinni?"

I glanced around me on the train, but saw no ginger-whiskered man this time, nor anyone else paying us the slightest attention. So I told him the entire story. He asked me in particular to tell him about the visions Mermeros had shown me, there in the Oddity Shop—cricket leagues and traveling the world. I did so, and braced myself for a lecture on the impropriety of either goal for a respectable young lady. None came.

"A cricket league for girls," he repeated. "A cricket league for girls…"

When we returned home, my mother assailed me in the front entryway, ready to flay me alive for being expelled from school. Father helped me off with my coat, and waited for Mother to pause for breath. When he could get a word in edgewise, he said, simply, "Maeve is better off without that school." And that was the end of that.

But I wasn't sure I was better off.

Days dragged like lead weights around my ankles. I missed Alice. I missed Tommy. I missed commotion and bustle and even the thrill of getting into trouble. It's possible, though not certain, that I even missed learning. I could only conclude that I really was a hopeless case. If I didn't become a famous world cricketer, I'd probably end up a criminal.

These and other cheery thoughts were all I had to occupy my time. That, and finishing *Nicholas Nickleby*. (Alice, by post, promised to mail me her copy of *Oliver Twist*.)

Preparations for Evangeline's wedding had reached a fever pitch, so Mother, Evangeline, and Deborah were no company at all, not that they ever had been much, to tell the truth. Polydora, bless her, was a dear as always, but her thoughts were elsewhere, probably hovering somewhere in the vicinity of the Luton police bureau. I was happy for her. But one dull day dragged on after another, and the cold and wet January made it hard for me to leave the house. I thought I might quietly disintegrate into dust, and no one would notice.

Until one Saturday afternoon.

I sat in the parlor, under Mother's orders, but buried my nose in *Oliver Twist* for my own pleasure. We heard the sound of the bell, and Jenkins's footsteps as she went to answer it. Moments later she appeared in the parlor doorway.

"A Mr. and Mrs. Bromley, madam, sir, here to see you, and their granddaughter, too, a Miss Alice."

She bowed and showed them in. Mother and Father sat up in their seats and smoothed out their clothing. Mother hid her reading glasses while Deborah stuffed her fashion magazine under a seat cushion.

Alice came in before her grandparents, and I hugged her before I remembered I ought to introduce her all around. My parents welcomed the Bromleys cordially, and soon they all sat down over cups of tea and a plate of biscuits and cheese.

"You're so kind to welcome this unexpected visit," began the genteel and fragile Mrs. Bromley.

Daddy protested that the honor was all theirs, etc. Finally, after what seemed like a prolonged competition to see who could be the politest, Mr. and Mrs. Bromley managed to state their purpose.

"We've always been supporters of Miss Salamanca's school," said Mrs. Bromley.

"Because our daughter spent happy years there before her marriage," added Mr. Bromley.

"Back when it was run by the present Miss Salamanca's aunt," Mrs. Bromley said. "And so, when our son and his wife passed, leaving Alice in our care—"

"—naturally, we thought of that dear old school, and no other, for our precious girl." Mr. Bromley beamed at Alice.

"Alice is our son's daughter," explained Mrs. Bromley. "He and his dear wife succumbed to the influenza when Alice was very young."

"I'm so sorry to hear that," murmured my mother.

"How dreadful," my father added.

"Thank you kindly." Mrs. Bromley went on. "I only mean to say, that is, I mean, our daughter, Alice's aunt, is alive and well, but Alice's parents are not. Which is why we're her guardians."

"I see," Daddy said.

"Crystal clear," added Mother.

The elder Bromleys exchanged a look, then nodded to each other.

"But we have come to the conclusion—" Mrs. Bromley began.

Mr. Bromley chimed in. "...that tradition alone should not enslave the young."

"And so," went on Mrs. Bromley, "we have decided that for Alice's good she should leave the school. She hasn't been happy there."

Mr. Bromley nodded. "Quite right. Aside from her friendship with your charming Maeve, of course."

"Our charming Maeve," repeated my mother, as waking slowly from an odd dream.

Mrs. Bromley took up the baton. "Alice will leave the school and be privately instructed at home, with excellent tutors."

Mother smiled on cue. "How very suitable."

Not to my mind, it wasn't. The thought of being taught alone at home was only slightly less boring than sitting home alone with nothing to do. I looked at Alice to sympathize, but she was too busy grinning to notice.

"Of course, we wouldn't wish our dear granddaughter to be lonely," said Mr. Bromley.

"Certainly not," said Mother.

Mr. Bromley nodded. "When we heard from Alice that your family had also removed your daughter from the school..." She paused.

"We did indeed," my father said.

I coughed.

"We thought," Mrs. Bromley said hopefully, "seeing how beautifully the girls get along with one another..."

I took a deep breath, and held it. *Could it be?*

"We wondered," Mr. Bromley went on, "whether you might consider allowing Maeve to join us at our home and be educated with Alice?"

Mother and Father looked at each other. Mother's mouth hung open.

"We realize it's a great deal to ask, parting you from your darling girl," Mrs. Bromley said apologetically. "We can arrange any visits you wish."

"Oh, no," my mother said quickly, "it's not that—"

Dad put a hand on Mother's. "We *would* miss her."

"Please don't give a moment's thought to any expense, my dear lady," urged Mr. Bromley. "You'd be doing us the utmost courtesy to allow us the pleasure of sharing our home with your daughter."

Mother gulped. "No expense?"

"No expense will be spared in ensuring these girls receive the finest education to be had in London." Mr. Bromley answered the question my mother had never thought to ask.

Mrs. Bromley watched the stunned looks on my parents' faces. "I hope you don't mind our coming here to propose this idea. I'm sure you'll need time to think it over?" She rose.

My mother rose, too. "My dear Mrs. Bromley, it's an offer too generous to refuse!"

Father rose also. "We should consult with Maeve, shouldn't we?" He turned to me. "What do you think, Maeve?"

Alice's hopeful face made me want to laugh. *How could she even think I wouldn't jump at this chance?*

"Thank you, Father, Mother," I said, and curtsied, in a rare moment of remembering the proper thing to do. "Mr. and Mrs. Bromley, I don't know how to thank you for this offer. I think I would enjoy staying with you very much, and studying with Alice and her tutors."

Alice clapped her hands. Mr. Bromley hoisted himself off his chair, beaming like a lamp, and shook hands with my father. My mother was all in a flutter, and could barely answer Mrs. Bromley's questions about my care and keeping.

It was soon settled that I would return to the Bromleys' home in four days' time. Before they left, Alice came and spoke with me privately.

"I've told my grandparents about what you did for Tommy," she said. "Of course, I had to fudge a bit around the djinni. But they know you got into trouble with the school for sticking up for him. They think it's simply wonderful of you."

I shrugged. I didn't want to be praised, after all the trouble I'd caused. All the ways my friends could've been hurt even worse. The Persia trip. The Darvill House robbery, and Tommy's run-in with the police. The malice of the sorcerer king. I hugged my arms tightly around my ribs. We were all lucky to be alive. I was grateful to be rid of Mermeros and Family for good.

"One thing puzzles me, though," Alice said. "Why did you bargain with Mr. Poindexter for the djinni, instead of just giving him to Tommy?"

That had been my original plan, to be sure. I tried to think how to put into words how I felt.

"With Mermeros," I said slowly, "Tommy could've wished himself out of the orphanage, away from the mills, and even into a life of wealth," I told her. "But I doubt there's anything Mermeros could've done to give Tommy a family."

Alice squeezed my hand.

"My grandparents have promised we can go visit the Oddity Shop often."

I gave her a hug. "It's just the place for the three of us oddities."

"Oh, Maeve," Alice whispered. "Just think what fun we'll have!"

I smiled. "I already am."

Acknowledgments

The idea for a story about a feisty boarding-school girl who finds a djinni in a sardine can was first born on a red-eye flight. So I suppose I should first thank JetBlue Airlines for their unlimited snack policy. I must also thank my father-in-law, John Seney, for presenting to me, at my wedding shower, a gift-wrapped tower of sardine tins, after learning that his son's fiancé actually ate them. I did eat them, though not, I hasten to add, at the shower, nor at the wedding.

My agent, Alyssa Eisner Henkin, has kept long-suffering faith with this project, and with me. My editors, Heather Alexander at Audible, and Molly Cusick at Sourcebooks, have showered Maeve and me with constant support and encouragement. I thank them both for helping her to sparkle, and for inviting her to pursue additional adventures. Many thanks also to the entire team at Sourcebooks for bringing *Wishes and Wellingtons* so joyfully into print for young readers, including Heather Moore, Michael Leali, Lizzie Lewandowski, Jackie Douglass, Ashlyn Keil, Valerie Pierce, and

Margaret Coffee. Thanks also to Danielle McNaughton, Brittany Vibbert, Jordan Kost, and Chloe Bristol for their artistry in making the book such a visual treat.

Jayne Entwistle, actress *par excellence*, brought Maeve and Company to life with her brilliant audiobook performance. Through our collaborations, she has become a dear friend. Hers has become the voice I hear as I write.

My husband, Phil Berry, who has given me a highly amusing father-in-law, four entertaining sons, and twenty-five hilarious years, is the reason I first began to write stories, and the reason I write them still. If a djinni granted me three wishes, I'd wish for him three times.

About the Author

Julie Berry is the author of the *New York Times* bestseller *Lovely War*, the Printz Honor and *Los Angeles Times* Book Prize shortlisted novel *The Passion of Dolssa*, and many other acclaimed young adult and middle-grade novels, as well as picture books. She holds a BS from Rensselaer in communication and an MFA from Vermont College. She lives in Southern California with her family.